RED LINES

James Bultema

P.D. Publishing

Also By James Bultema

Fiction

Sea of Red

Attack From Within

Invaders of the Heartland - (New Series, Coming in 2025. A Police Action Thriller)

Non-Fiction

Guardians of Angels: A History of the Los Angeles Police Department 1869-2019

The Protectors: A Photographic History of Police Departments in the United States

Unsolved Cold-Case Homicides of Law Enforcement Officers

Gangsters and Cops: Prohibition, Corruption, and LAPD's Scandalous Coming of Age

Documentary Video

Behind the Badge: An Insider's History of the Los Angeles Police Department

Website: https://www.jamesbultema.com
P.D. Publishing – Scottsdale, Arizona
This book was edited by Karen Stoff, www.vocostoff.com, and Jennifer Duty, Jen4editing@yahoo.com
Cover design by Momir Borocki - Proi! book covers
Author photograph by Carole W. Bultema

Dedicated to my girls, Carole, Sarah, Jennie, Lula, and Maisy, with all the love you could ever imagine

<u>**Glossary**</u>

ACO	Air Control Officer
ACS	Aegis Combat System
Actual	Aircraft call sign refers to the commanding officer. Also called "ONE"
AESA	Active Electronically Scanned Array
AI	Artificial Intelligence
AMRAAM	Advanced Medium-Range Air-to-Air Missile
AO	Area of Operations
ATGM	Anti-Tank Guided Missile
ATR	Automatic Target Recognition – mines
BATARG	*Bataan* Amphibious Ready Group
BDA	Battle Damage Assessment
BWA	Buoyant Wire Antenna – submarine communications
C2	Command and Control
CAG	Carrier Air Wing Commander
CAP	Combat Air Patrol
CENTCOM	United States Central Command
CICO	Combat Information Center Officer
CIWS	Close-in Weapon System
CSG	Carrier Strike Group
FITREP	Navy fitness report
HMDS	Helmet-Mounted Display System
HUD	Heads-Up Display
IAEA	International Atomic Energy Agency

IFF	Identification Friend or Foe
IRGC	Islamic Revolutionary Guard Corps
ISR	Intelligence, Surveillance and Reconnaissance
LPI	Low Probability of Intercept
MADL	Multifunction Advanced Data Link (used by the F-35)
MANPADS	Man-Portable Air-Defense Systems
MCM	Mine Countermeasures Mission
MEU	Marine Expeditionary Unit
MEUSOC	Marine Expeditionary Unit (Special Operations Capable)
MLO	Mobile Laid Offensive mine
MOIS	Iranian Ministry of Intelligence
MOS	Military Operational Specialty
MRAP	Mine-Resistant Ambush Protected
ODA	Operational Detachment Alpha (Green Berets)
PMO	Paramilitary Operations Officers – CIA
ROE	Rules of Engagement
RWR	Radar Warning Receiver (in aircraft)
SAR	Search and Rescue
SAS	Synthetic Aperture Sonar
SBIRS	Space-Based Infrared System
SDB	Small-Diameter Bomb
SOAR	Special Operations Aviation Regiment
SOCCENT	Special Operations Command Center Component of CENTCOM
TACON	Tactical Control

TLAM	Tomahawk Land Attack Missile
Toophan	Iranian wire-guided anti-tank missile
UAS	Unmanned Aircraft System
UUV	Unmanned Underwater Vehicle
VLS	Vertical Launching System
WEPS	Weapons Officer

Principal Characters

United States Government

Mark Taylor	President of the United States
Elena Ramirez	Director of National Intelligence
General Harrington	Chairman, Joint Chiefs of Staff
George Mitchell	Secretary of Defense
Roland Stinson	Secretary of the Treasury
Brad Kelly	Secretary of State
Dan Steele	Central Intelligence Agency

United States Military

Albert Richards	Seaman, USS *Ford* Culinary Specialist
Andy Boykin	Staff Sergeant, Green Berets
Anika Jones	Commander, USS *Truxtun* captain
Anne Hawthorne	Lieutenant, MH-60 Seahawk helicopter pilot
Brett Jansen	Lieutenant, USS *Chief* XO
Dakota "Cowboy" Remy	Lieutenant Colonel, B-2 pilot
Damien Wagner	Commander, USS *Reagan*, E-2 squadron CO
Dick "Mad Dog" Johnson	Captain, USS *Ford* CAG
Gail Osborne	Lieutenant, E-2 Hawkeye pilot
Harley "Snake Eyes" Jennings	Gunnery Sergeant, Marines, former FBI agent
Jessie "Swagger" Hampton	Lieutenant Commander, F-35 pilot
John "Snake" Harrison	Captain, F-22 pilot
Jose Alvarez	Petty Officer Third Class, USS *Chief* machine gunner
Marquis Holloway	Rear Admiral, TF-70 CO

Mateo Navarro   Commander, USS *Georgia* CO
Otis Albright   Captain, USS *Ford* CO
Ozzie Sullivan   Captain, 26th MEUSOC CO
Pavati Talas   Lieutenant, USS *Ford* Cryptologic
                        Warfare Officer
Roger Ashburger   Captain, Green Berets team leader
Ross Carter   Lieutenant Commander, SEAL
                        platoon leader
Russ "Bulldog" Lockwood
                        Lieutenant, F-35 pilot
Sarah "Danger" Freeman
                        Lieutenant Commander, E-2
                        Hawkeye pilot
Thomas Worthington   Brigadier General, Al Udeid Air
                        Base CO

Islamic Republic of Iran
Aisha Bilal   Agent, Ministry of Intelligence
Akbar Hashemi Rafsanjani
                        Black market billionaire
Amir Massad   Supreme Leader
Amir Nasserian   General, IRGC Aerospace Force
Arash Zamani   Major, Su-35 pilot
Arman Shirvani   General and lead scientist, Natanz
                        Enrichment Complex
Farhad Daryani   Major, IRGC, nuclear bomb convoy
                        leader
General Jarari   IRGC Aerospace Force, commander
Navid Shadmani   Major, IRGC, Ahvaz Oil Field
Reza Mahdavi   Captain, *Tareq-901* submarine CO
Samir Makhlouf   Council of Guardians member

Islamic Republic of Iran - Courtesy of Central Intelligence Agency Maps

Chapter 1

The White House
Washington, DC

As the bright lights came up on President Mark Taylor sitting behind the Resolute Desk in the Oval Office, he knew this would be one of the most important speeches of his nearly eight years in office. He and the nation were devastated, and it was time to explain to the American people who were responsible for destroying Independence Hall.

The director held up his fingers while saying, "And four—three—two—" Going silent, he used one finger for the last count and then pointed at the president of the United States to begin.

My fellow Americans,

Tonight, I address you with a heavy heart and an unwavering spirit. Yesterday our nation was the target of a cowardly and heinous act of terrorism. The historic Independence Hall in Philadelphia, a symbol of our democracy and the birthplace of our nation's founding principles, was attacked and destroyed. This act of terror has claimed countless innocent lives, inflicted severe injuries on many, and profoundly shaken the very foundation of our great nation.

This attack was not just on a building. It was an assault on the ideals of freedom, justice, and the rule of law that define us as Americans. It was an attack on our history, our values, and our way of life. It was an attempt to break our spirit and sow fear among us.

To the families and loved ones of the victims, our hearts are with you in this time of profound grief. The entire nation mourns with you, and we vow to honor the memory of those you lost by ensuring that justice is served. We are committed to supporting you through this unimaginable tragedy.

He felt his emotions getting the better of him, so he paused, looked down, and took a sip of water. He looked back up at the nation.

We ask ourselves who could have committed such a cowardly act, to kill Americans as we celebrated our national birthday—Independence Day. I will tell you exactly who.

He let those words echo across the nation as he stared through the camera lens into the eyes of every American.

We now have irrefutable evidence that agents of the Iranian regime orchestrated this attack. This hostile act will not go unanswered. Let me be clear. Those responsible for this atrocity will be held accountable. Our nation has faced adversity before, and each time we have emerged stronger, more united, and more determined to defend our freedoms.

To you, the Iranian regime, I say this. Your unprovoked act of terror will not intimidate us. The United States will respond with the full force of our capabilities. We will dismantle the networks that support terrorism and will hold accountable those who threaten our security. Your attempts to undermine our freedom and destabilize our nation will fail.

To the international community: We call upon you to stand with us in this time of crisis. Terrorism is a global threat that requires a unified response. Together, we must work to prevent such acts of violence and ensure that those who support and carry out terrorism face the full weight of international justice.

The lights dimmed, but the spirit of the leader of the free world did not.

Chapter 2

ROY'S BAR
Dearborn, Michigan

Joe Cartwright had been a law-abiding citizen his entire life, although he didn't think he could say the same thing for the two buddies he was hanging with tonight. But he thought, "Screw it, who cared?"

The one thing the three men all shared was that they were military combat veterans who had served in the Middle East. For the past three hours, they had been pounding down beers, and their only topic of conversation had been about how Iranian-backed Hezbollah had had the balls to destroy Independence Hall and everything it represented. The fact that it had been an American terrorist who had pulled the trigger and that he'd had help from a local Lebanese gang just pissed them off even more.

Along with the entire world, the three men had watched the horrific news reports for the past five days. Even tonight at the bar, they saw the pictures of the Ohio couple and their baby posing happily in front of the Hall, dressed in matching Fourth of July outfits and unaware that they would be blown to pieces just minutes later. On TV, there was the continuous graphic video of dead Americans sprawled all over the courtyard, despite the network's attempts to blur out the charred bodies. There were photographs of the 128 dead, and that number was increasing daily. Those portraits brought it home that they weren't just numbers; they'd had lives, loved ones, and futures that were taken away in a split second by some radicalized US citizen of Lebanese descent.

"Bro," Joe said, "are we going to do something about those assholes or what?"

"Fuckin' A," Adam replied. "We sit here drinking all night, complaining about them SOBs, but the only thing we do is give it lip service. We don't do shit."

"Right on," said Stan the Man. "I say it's time to get even, and we do it tonight, in fact, right fucking now. You with us, Joe?"

"Hell yeah," Joe said. "And we've got all the shit we need in my truck. I've got an idea. You two get in the bed of my truck, and we'll do a drive-by on those Lebanese pricks at Tip a Few. Time to teach them to never again fuck with the US of A."

The three raised their longneck beers in the air and smacked them together, splashing beer all over.

As planned, Cartwright drove Adam and Stan the Man to the Tip a Few bar. It was late as they approached, and only a few vehicles were parked in the lot. At the last minute, Cartwright changed tactics and stopped the truck at the back of the bar. Adam jumped out and ran to the front while the other two grabbed their own Molotov cocktails with long, gasoline-soaked wicks dangling in the wind. Everyone had lighters.

As soon as they got in position, all three lit the fuses and threw the bottles as hard as possible at the decrepit building. Adam threw his right through the front window and watched a massive explosion erupt inside the bar. Two guys sitting at a table immediately went up in flames. "Fuck you, ragheads!" he screamed as loud as he could.

Just as Adam threw his bottle, Cartwright and Stan the Man nailed the back of the building with their projectiles, which exploded precisely on the back door. The flaming gasoline splashed onto the door and the rotting wall, allowing the fire to spread quickly.

Within seconds, the three commandos were back in the truck, heading down the alley out of sight. They hollered and smacked their hands in high fives to celebrate their success. Inside the bar, it was a different story.

Two Warren Bros gang members who happened to be sitting near the front window were smothered with gasoline that instantly set them both on fire. The two men tried to run out the front door, but the quickly spreading flames blocked it. Completely engulfed in fire, they both fell to the floor, unable to even try and find another exit.

Five other patrons and the owner headed for the back door. As they opened it, the flames jumped at the oxygen flowing through the open door, blowing them all backward. Seeing the front burning, they headed to the only side window, but the fire was too intense and robbed the air of oxygen. All six fell to the floor and burned like six individual bonfires. By the time the Dearborn Fire Department arrived, the building was fully involved, and nothing they did made a dent as the flames jumped hundreds of yards into the air. It was seen from miles away.

Chapter 3

NATANZ ENRICHMENT COMPLEX
Isfahan Province, Iran

You don't know what pressure is until you have Iran's Supreme Leader Amir Massad on your ass, thought General Arman Shirvani. Bombing the United States of America wouldn't have been high on his list, but orders were orders, and Shirvani loved what was being planned.

With a PhD in nuclear engineering from Iran's famed Amirkabir University of Technology, the man from humble beginnings was at the right place at the right time. A combat veteran with a superior intellect, sixty-three-year-old Shirvani was now staring retirement in the face. But retirement wouldn't happen until he completed the most important assignment of his life—creating Iran's first nuclear bomb. Just the thought of his mission sent chills down his spine.

The man with a full head of dark hair but a completely white beard oversaw scientists and support personnel, few of whom knew exactly what was happening. The key to their collective success, and for that matter, the success of his country, was to keep the project a state secret, with no hint of what they were doing leaking out.

But it had.

Just last week, one of the scientists involved with the project was rushed away from a crowded bar by MOIS, the fearsome enforcers of the Ministry of Intelligence, when he bragged to one of their undercover agents about a top-secret project he was working on that would make him famous. The scientist was now restricted to home and work. He would have ended up in a work camp, but his knowledge was indispensable. Shirvani ensured word got around to lessen the chance of a repeat.

While the world had been distracted with wars in Ukraine and Israel, Shirvani had overseen the enrichment of twenty kilograms of UF6 uranium hexafluoride to the magic number of 90 percent U-235. Iran would soon become a member of the nuclear club as the tenth country to have a weapon of mass destruction, joining the US, Russia, France, China, the United Kingdom, Pakistan, India, Israel, and North Korea—even though no congratulatory letters would come in. The Doomsday Clock had taken a tick toward midnight.

Chapter 4

SITUATION ROOM, THE WHITE HOUSE
Washington, DC

It had been a week since the destruction of Independence Hall, and the world was waiting to see how the US would retaliate. Many Americans didn't want to wait. Violence in the US against Muslims, or anyone who even resembled someone from the Middle East, was ongoing. Mosques, businesses, and schools were being attacked, and some were even torched. It was time to make some decisions that would direct the nation's anger away from American Muslims and toward Iran, the country behind the terrorist attack. That job fell to the man at the top.

The Situation Room was packed with members of the National Security Council— the elites of their professions. Sitting around the sizable table were the Vice President, the Secretary of State, the Secretary of the Treasury, the Secretary of Defense, the Secretary of Energy, the Attorney General, the Secretary of Homeland Security, the representative of the United States of America to the United Nations, the administrator of the US Agency for International Development, the president's chief of staff, the president's assistant for national security affairs, and the chairman of the Joint Chiefs of Staff. All eyes were directed squarely at the president, who was not seated at the table. He refused to sit down on this day and wasted no time emphasizing why the NSC was gathered.

"These attacks on our country must stop. We must punish—no, destroy—those responsible. We must send a message to the world that if you target the US, we will target you, and we won't miss. We have proof that this American Hezbollah terrorist received most of his training in Iran. They've been sponsoring proxy militant groups and terrorist organizations in the Middle East for too long. Attacks on our bases, the loss of American lives, and the attacks on international shipping all must stop. Now is the time to act and prevent further attacks on the US.

"Listen, I understand that this isn't a 9/11 when almost three thousand people lost their lives on American soil. We all remember that day as the deadliest foreign attack in our nation's history. But even though the assault on Independence Hall wasn't on the same scale, it was still a direct attack on our home, our birthplace, our enduring symbol of democracy, and an international symbol of standing against tyranny. If America won't stand up for freedom, few will. So it's time to take that stand." The president struck his fist into his palm. Those closest to him couldn't help but notice tears welling up in his eyes. After taking a second to collect himself, he continued.

"We've been discussing how to respond to this attack for a week. For years, our country has used economic sanctions, diplomatic measures, and legal action, but nothing has stopped Iran from disrupting the Middle East—and now our own country. It's time to narrow our options, starting with our military possibilities. George, tell me what you've got." The president took a seat.

Following his boss's example, the secretary of defense stood up. Although it remained unspoken, the significance of civilian control over the military was clear to everyone in the room. US law stipulated that the SecDef could not have served in the military within the previous seven years or, if a former general, within the last ten years. George Mitchell, a Harvard graduate who had never served in the military, possessed a keen understanding of how to effectively deploy the 1.4 million people in the country's all-volunteer force.

"Thank you, Mr. President. If I may, I agree with you completely. These attacks on our country and around the world must stop. The DOD has been working nonstop to compile some recommendations for today's discussions. But first, some background." SecDef picked up his notes.

"In 2002, the Pentagon was tasked with setting up a very sophisticated wargame to test a future enemy, one equipped with advanced technology and tactics. The congressionally-mandated exercise pitted a US blue team against an Iranian red team. At the time, $250 million was allocated for the project, which used live exercises and computer simulations. As it progressed, upwards of 13,500 service members ran the exercise using seventeen simulation locations. Within days, the red team sank nineteen of the blue team's ships and rendered the carrier battle group ineffective. While the rules used remain in question, the wargame's outcome emphasized the detriment of group thinking and the power of asymmetric warfare. In the end, the US blue team suffered a dismal defeat." He paused to let his points sink in before continuing.

"Our ultimate conclusion was that US advanced technology and sophisticated weaponry didn't guarantee a win. Innovative warfare combined with adaptability can be just as lethal. Iran has proved that, just like Ukraine has proved it by holding off Russia for years."

"Point well taken, George," said the president, "but what about with today's military forces?"

"Let me start by saying a US-Iran war has the potential to be one of the deadliest conflicts in all of history. There would be thousands to hundreds of thousands killed, and the scale would dwarf the early 2000s war in Iraq.

"Consequently, I believe it's imperative to use our overwhelming air and naval power to beat the Iranians into submission. First, we would have to eliminate their will to fight. Our military would have to bomb their navy, take out their parked aircraft, take over their oil fields, and destroy their nuclear facilities. We would need to launch cyberattacks on the entire nation and their military infrastructure. Our goal would be to degrade Iran's conventional forces within the first few days and end it all within two weeks. We don't want a full-scale ground war. The cost of lives lost would be prohibitive."

"Mr. President," said Elena Ramirez, the director of national intelligence and the president's most-trusted associate, who had been with Taylor since he first ran for office in Pennsylvania. "A word of caution here. Tehran knows it can't match our firepower. But it can spread chaos in the Middle East and around the world in the hope that the US public would quickly become war-weary. The Iranians can escalate the situation in a lot of different ways. Their vast network of proxies and elite units could be called upon to kill American troops, diplomats, and citizens who are in Iraq, our numerous bases in the Middle East, Africa, and places beyond."

After taking a breath and quickly scanning the room to ensure she had everyone's attention, the DNI continued. "Years of intelligence collection indicate that Iran would encourage and bribe terrorist organizations such as Hezbollah, Hamas, and the Houthi rebels to strike Saudi Arabia, the United Arab Emirates, other Gulf nations, and the United States. Currently, the US has twenty-five hundred troops in Iraq, another nine hundred in Syria, and several hundred in Jordan. Every one of those bases is a potential target.

"This chaos in the Middle East and the world would extend into the cyber realm. Recall what they did to fifty American banks back in 2011 by using malicious computer code to institute denial of service. They disabled bank websites and prevented customers from accessing their online accounts. The list of targets is a who's who of banking, including JPMorganChase and Bank of America. In addition, we know they have the capability to shut down our oil and gas sector, not to mention the electric power grid.

"We envision their use of fast-attack boats in the Strait of Hormuz to place bombs on oil tankers, and their use of drone swarms to sink naval and civilian ships, possibly blocking the Strait of Hormuz. This war would be a nasty, brutal fight that we would have no guarantee of winning. Iran's strategy will be to wear down Americans until they lose their willingness to fight, which we believe would happen soon, notwithstanding what happened in Philadelphia. As we have learned over the years, the American public has a short, selective memory.

"Lastly, a campaign that relies on air and naval power alone to beat Iran into capitulation will face significant challenges. Recall that Iran has a stockpile of cruise missiles with a 600-mile range. They also have advanced long- and short-range air defense systems and have over three thousand ballistic missiles. As the war in Ukraine demonstrated, Iran has the most capable unmanned aerial vehicles of anyone. Essentially, history has shown us that any combined operation involving just air and naval power has limits and is rarely successful."

"General Harrington," said the president, "please inform us of what a ground invasion might look like."

"For one," said the chairman of the Joint Chiefs of Staff, "this would be no Iraq. Iran is much larger, with eighty-three million people across 617,000 square miles. Iraq has only thirty million people and 170,000 square miles of territory. During the conflict with Iraq, we deployed a high of 180,000 troops. For Iran, our projections are for as many as 600,000." A few folks in the room gasped, but the CJCS continued.

"On the ground, we would face the fourteenth-rated global military power. The human and materiel costs would be enormous. Getting our troops into the country would be difficult. Iran has a significant water border and will use their anti-ship and anti-aircraft missiles to cover its 1,500-mile southern coastline. In littoral waters, our Navy would face thousands of mines, and our forces would be challenged because of our lack of minesweepers.

"Another possibility we have examined is an attack on Iran's oil production, which we know is the core of their economy. Most of their oil fields are located outside the protection of their mountain ranges and, as such, are much more accessible. But within their mountainous terrain, they have a high-ground advantage. Our forces would need to pressure their military to remove their terrain advantage as they repositioned to coastal and desert plains to defend their oil and shipping resources. There, the advantage belongs to our forces.

"In this scenario, we would capture or destroy vital oil resources to cut off money to support Iran's war effort. With no money, the mood in their country would turn against the regime, and changes that might benefit the US would come into play. We must also consider where to stage from to get a significant number of troops into Iran."

"Sir, if I may," interrupted the second-term secretary of state, Brad Kelly. "I would like to comment on this."

"Go ahead, Brad," said Taylor.

"Thank you, Mr. President. As most of you know, we have strong allies in the Middle East. Qatar is where we have our largest military base, and we've had diplomatic relations with Jordan since 1949. We have Kuwait, who we've considered a major non-NATO ally since 2004, and of course there's Saudi Arabia, which has been there for the US for over seven decades. As in the Iraq war, these nations will most likely give us staging access and whatever else we need."

"And," interrupted SecDef, "we have the *Bataan* Amphibious Ready Group with the 26th Marine

Expeditionary Unit, Special Operations Capable, on the way to the Arabian Sea from Darwin, Australia. We tasked them less than twenty-four hours after the bombing to end their multi-national exercise and head to the Middle East as a show of force in the Mediterranean Sea." Looking around the room and hearing no objection, he continued.

"In addition, on orders from the president, we can soon have the *Ford, Reagan,* and *Nimitz* Carrier Strike Groups combining to become Task Force 70. That's 240 combat aircraft and hundreds of Tomahawk missiles added to the arsenal of US Central Command. No one wanted war in the Middle East, but Iran's sponsorship of terrorists plus Hezbollah's blatant attack on US soil changed the equation. Additionally, we have two *Ohio*-class and two *Virginia*-class submarines on station in the area. Mr. President, we in the DOD stand by for your orders."

"Thank you," said the president. "Roland, would you address the sanctions in place and what can be done to further our efforts in asset control?"

"Thank you," said Roland Stinson, the new treasury secretary. "According to the Office of Foreign Assets Control, Tehran currently exports approximately 1.4 million barrels of crude oil daily. With tens of billions of additional dollars to spend, Iran has directed more funding to Hamas and Hezbollah. We've seen what these terrorist organizations can accomplish with additional funding, such as the attacks on Independence Hall, on Israel, and on our bases in the Middle East. We must develop additional sanctions targeting foreign banks that facilitate financial transactions for Iran. The US should communicate our actions to Tehran's trade partners, such as Turkey, United Arab Emirates, Iraq, and finally, China, which imports 72 percent of its oil from Iran. Besides the military option we're considering, sanctions are all-encompassing and effective with no loss of US lives."

The meeting continued for another two hours, working on different details and possibilities. Whenever you put US troops in harm's way, decisions became much more difficult. But all agreed: The time to respond to such a blatant attack on US soil must come now, and we must send a message to the world to never again attack America.

Chapter 5

USS GEORGIA

Arabian Sea

To Commander Mateo Navarro, it was like the story his father—a retired Albuquerque, New Mexico, police officer—loved to tell about that day in the barrio when he received a robbery-in-progress call and looked up to see the bank two blocks away. His dad would always say that it didn't get better than that. And today, Navarro had just received a secure message from US Central Command while his submarine was located right off the coast of Iran in the Arabian Sea—the latest hot spot in the world.

"XO," Navarro said, "I want all non-essential officers in the wardroom in ten minutes."

"Aye, sir, wardroom in ten."

As he waited in the wardroom for the last of his officers to arrive, Navarro reflected on his days growing up in Albuquerque. In high school, he had to break away from his quiet, reflective demeanor to learn how to fight against the bullies who detested his heritage as a Mexican American. Muscular and standing just over six feet tall, he could handle almost any confrontation.

For as long as he could remember, he'd had a strong sense of duty and a yearning to serve his country. He had chosen the Navy for its programs, where he could combine his technical skills with his leadership ability. His unwavering dedication to his crew and to the mission earned him the respect of those under his command.

After the last officer entered the room, Navarro stood to address ten of the fourteen men and women who led the boat. Teamwork was essential, followed by open communication when allowed. Now was that time.

"As we discussed several days ago, the attack on Independence Hall will not go unanswered. I just received classified comms from CENTCOM about our role in that response. The specifics are need-to-know, but understanding our role will be critical to the success of the overall mission. What happens in the next few days, weeks, and possibly months will depend on how each of you performs your duties and gets the most out of the crew. We have a full combat load of 154 Tomahawks, and you can bet we'll be using most of them." As the captain looked around the room and made eye contact with each officer, he felt confident of what may lie ahead.

Chapter 6

AHVAZ OIL FIELD
Khuzestan Province, Iran

Major Navid Shadmani's friends in his Islamic Revolutionary Guard Corps brigade headquarters liked to make fun of him for what they said was a do-nothing job at the Ahvaz oil field near the border with Iraq. But he didn't see it that way, especially now that it had been a week since the daring attack in the US. Everyone was speculating how the infidels of America would respond. Shadmani thought it was simple—they would attempt to take the valuable oil fields to cut off the money that funded his country. Duh. The sprawling Ahvaz oil complex, the largest in Iran, produced almost a million barrels of oil daily.

Today, his small IRGC security force was out in the desert preparing to do some rare anti-tank guided missile live-fire exercises. What made today exceptional was that they were using his country's latest version of the Toophan, a wire-guided anti-tank missile reverse-engineered off an American BGM-71 TOW missile. His men had two targets, each a deuce-and-a-half truck. Although his team had two Pirooz anti-tank missile carriers, they used a Ranger. This light attack vehicle resembled a side-by-side all-terrain vehicle equipped with a portable tripod and two ATGMs. They were responding to a simulated armor attack.

"51, this is 50," said Shadmani. "Enemy armor spotted 800 meters out. Stop and deploy your ATGM."

"51 copy, positioning now."

Efficiently, the Ranger halted next to a level spot on the desert floor. Two soldiers quickly set up the large tripod and spread the three legs wide to gain maximum stability. The loader put the wire-guided missile into the receiving end of the launcher. Using the optical sights, the shooter aimed at the truck on the right, taking his time with the most critical aspect of his job. He had spent hours training to maintain a visual line of sight to the target to prepare to guide the missile manually using the inputs to his weapon. When he was satisfied, he fired.

As the missile tore through the air and roared toward the target, the shooter maintained visual on the target and made one slight adjustment to the course. The high-explosive, anti-tank warhead, designed to penetrate armor and inflict maximum damage, slammed into the target, blowing the truck into a burning heap of metal and debris.

"51, this is 50. Great shot, well done."

Shadmani thought, My friends may joke about my assignment, but with Allah's blessing, my troops and my every move will stop the Americans dead in their tracks.

Chapter 7

HOUSE OF LEADERSHIP
Tehran, Iran

The House of Leadership, a testament to the grandiosity of Iran's leaders, was a sight to behold. Its halls were adorned with Persian carpets and intricately designed tapestries, their purpose not only to beautify but also to reduce the sounds of the voices of the country's most influential figures to a mere murmur. The majority of those present were draped in traditional robes and turbans, embodying the spiritual and political amalgamation of the Islamic Republic of Iran.

Samir Makhlouf settled in his seat just two chairs away from the most powerful man in Iran, Supreme Leader Ayatollah Amir Massad. Makhlouf had earned his position, in part, because of his successful leadership of the terrorist group that had destroyed Independence Hall. It had been an attack from within that the bureaucrats in America, even with knowledge of some aspects of his plan, couldn't stop. He praised Allah for blessing him with such a mission and its success.

Makhlouf was one of the twelve influential Council of Guardians members who oversaw all aspects of Parliament and had the final say about who was qualified to run for public office. As the others whispered to each other, Makhlouf knew his perspective was the reason for this crucial meeting.

When the supreme leader entered the room, the buzz hushed. In synchronized reverence, every cleric rose, a gesture of respect for the leader's vital position. As Massad took his seat, the clerics bowed their heads slightly and placed their right hands over their hearts in a traditional sign of respect. The men uttered, "Salam, Ayatollah," then everyone silently watched their supreme leader, a figure of immense standing.

Sitting at the head of the table, Massad nodded slightly and raised his hand in a modest wave to acknowledge their deference. While the supreme leader began a prayer, Makhlouf couldn't believe how such simple gestures made him feel honored to be an essential part of the Islamic Republic.

With the prayer over, Massad said, "After numerous meetings with everyone in this room, and with the help of Allah, I have reached a decision." He paused and noted that he had everyone's complete attention before he continued.

"Based on the best intelligence we have, the United States will attack us in three to four days. As in Iraq and other unjust wars, the US will use their shock and awe method, an overwhelming initial display of force to paralyze their enemy. But it has been brought to my attention that we could take the initiative away from the Americans by striking them first with missile attacks on US bases and naval ships." He noted momentary looks of disbelief on many faces, and he pitied them for not thinking that Iran could take on the might of the infidels.

"Additionally," Massad continued, "we have all our Shia allies, including Hezbollah, Hamas, the Houthis, and Iraqi militias, who could launch coordinated attacks on US positions using missiles, drones, and guerilla tactics. At the same time, we could disrupt global shipping by using our stockpile of naval mines, anti-ship missiles, and small boat swarms to sink vessels.

"We could also use our cyber warfare prowess to target US military networks and critical infrastructure, and protect ourselves from them doing the same.

"By taking the initiative away from the US, we could—with Allah's blessing—become the dominant power in the Persian Gulf region and significantly expand our influence over Iraq, the Gulf's Arab states, and the vital Strait of Hormuz.

"Additionally, the US public's demand to seek revenge for our victory at Independence Hall will sour quickly after their soldiers come home in body bags. Their weak-stomached people will riot in the streets and demand a ceasefire and complete withdrawal of US forces from the Middle East. Again, we will rule our part of the world for many years to come." Standing and raising his arms to the sky, Massad said, "I ask you—are you with me?"

The entire room of clerics jumped to their feet, pumping their arms and fists to the heavens. "Yes," they cried, and many added, "Praise be to our great leader and to Allah."

No one jumped higher or shouted louder than Samir Makhlouf, the brains behind the strategic plan.

Chapter 8

USS Chief

Near the coast of Iran, Arabian Sea

Lieutenant Brett Jansen was on the Navy's promotional fast track. His courage and performance in the Chinese war, as well as feedback from his previous COs who wrote his FITREPs, helped him land a respected assignment as the XO on a minesweeper, the USS *Chief*.

This came only six years after graduating from the Naval Academy. Early on, he gained valuable experience from his two years as a weapons officer aboard the USS *Mustin*, an Arleigh Burke-class guided-missile destroyer, and he was initiated by fire during the war with China. Listed in his FITREPs were repeated references to his reputation as a leader who inspired and motivated his subordinates, had strong integrity, displayed continual professionalism, and used clear decision-making skills. He even received a commendation from his CO for stopping a sailor from launching an unauthorized missile at a Chinese fighter jet before the start of the war.

Even though he was the ship's XO, he might as well have been the captain. In his first meeting with his commanding officer, the CO had done a lot of talking about how worthless it was to command such an old bucket and how he should have been given command of an Arleigh Burke-class destroyer. Even getting orders to clear mines for what was obviously going to clear the way for some type of response by the US didn't bring the captain out of his quarters. He scheduled Jansen for the watches when mine-clearing was happening and handed over his other watches to the officer of the deck after about a half hour.

As the new XO of the thirty-three-year-old ship, Jansen was learning about it firsthand. The experience wasn't how he envisioned being second-in-command of a US warship. Ever since he was a kid growing up in Grand Haven, Michigan, he had envisioned himself on the bridge of a guided-missile destroyer, confidently giving orders to his crew. Well, that wouldn't happen for a few years, so he was determined to make the best of this opportunity given to him as the XO of the *Chief.*

The *Chief* had been ailing and had endured almost two years of constant repairs and maintenance. The Navy had finally upgraded the ship's navigation system, which had been running on Windows 2000. Even the useless sonar, designed to detect mines but instead flagged everything from discarded dishwashers to crab traps, had finally been modernized. But getting parts was still challenging. Companies that used to make spare parts for minesweepers had either gone out of business or moved on to more lucrative manufacturing enterprises. To Jansen and the crew, the *Chief* seemed like the ship the Navy forgot about. When scarce money could be spent on the latest and most modern weapons, fighters, and submarines, who cared about minesweepers? Besides, the Navy was planning to retire the Avenger-class minesweepers sooner rather than later, as the new class of minesweepers, the Freedom and Independence classes of littoral combat ships, were coming online. Jansen knew that he would be the last XO of the *Chief*. And he promised himself to make its last cruise an honorable one for the old, neglected tub and its crew.

When Jansen arrived in Sasebo, Japan, to become the XO, the *Chief* was about to deploy to the Persian Gulf. After nearly two years in dry dock, the investment made in updating the ship was about to pay off in the aftermath of the attack on Independence Hall. There were thousands of mines to clear, and Jansen was pumped and ready to help lead the crew in that mission.

Chapter 9

*USS F*ORD

Persian Gulf

Captain Dick "Mad Dog" Johnson, who was the USS *Ford*'s carrier air wing commander and affectionately called the CAG, found himself daydreaming while he waited for the wardroom meeting to begin. It was his way of managing the stresses of command. Today, his thoughts were on the ship he considered his home away from home. He lived on a floating city with forty-five hundred neighbors sharing the same digs—a twenty-story aircraft carrier. They formed a tight-knit community—eating, working, and commuting together. The floating city was like any other, complete with police, firefighters, electricians, and high-tech jobs. Still, it had unique personnel who performed round-the-clock choreography to launch aircraft from the four-and-a-half-acre deck of the flattop. Mad Dog had to admit that living on the *Ford* had its moments, but he deeply cherished everyone in his city.

As he scanned the wardroom, he took note of some of his neighbors. They were waiting for the floating city's mayor, known in the Navy as the commanding officer. The XO, who was like a deputy mayor, sat next to the empty seat at the head of the table. The others in the room were the equivalent of city staff and were the department heads from all over the ship: operations, engineering, weapons, maintenance, supply, and a host of others. Today was a crucial meeting because the city was going to war.

The XO loudly said, "Ten hut." Mad Dog and the others in the room immediately came to life, and twenty officers jumped to their feet in unison.

Walking quickly, the CO said in a conversational tone, "As you were." There was some shuffling as everyone retook their seats.

Captain Otis C. Albright, the CO of the *Ford*, sat down and said, "As you know, we're sailing at top speed and will continue to do so until our friends get to the northern sector of the Arabian Sea. We'll team up with the *Nimitz* and *Reagan* CSGs to form Task Force 70." He'd cut right to the chase. That was who he was, a no-bullshit sort of guy. You didn't casually discuss the weather with him and never wasted his time with meaningless jabber. And he respected everyone else's time, so he pressed ahead.

"All CSGs should be on station within two days. The *Ford* will stay in the Persian Gulf, the *Reagan* will take up position in the northern Arabian Sea, and the *Nimitz* will come from the Med to the western Arabian Sea. I expect the *Reagan* will go into the Gulf and the *Nimitz* will reposition. Additionally, we have the 26th Marine Expeditionary Unit aboard the three-ship *Bataan* Amphibious Ready Group approaching the northern Arabian Sea. The BATARG has 2,500 special-operations-capable Marines ready to kick ass. As you know, when the president puts this many ships in one specific area of the world, it sends a strong message to our adversaries. This will be the largest concentration of US sea power since the war with China. As we await our specific orders, we'll prepare for what we all know will be a shooting conflict. You don't attack our homeland and expect no retribution—there will be, and we will deliver it.

"Now, XO will give you a refresher on what to expect from Iran and its allies and what will be threats to TF-70 and our aircraft."

"Thank you, sir," said a young-looking second-in-command. "Just for the record, understand that the briefing you're receiving today is repeated on every ship in the task force and beyond. As you all should know, Iran's missile arsenal is the largest and most diverse in the Middle East. Throw in their burgeoning land-attack cruise missile force and their three thousand ballistic missiles, and we face a formidable enemy. Over the past two years, Iran has made substantial improvements to the precision and accuracy of its missiles. Ladies and gentlemen, this makes them a very potent conventional threat."

After letting his words float in the air for a second, the XO continued, "But that's not all. Many of their missiles are inherently capable of carrying nuclear payloads despite Iran's continued denials of owning weapons of mass destruction. You might ask yourself if they'll use them, and my answer is yes, they will"—a few jaws dropped—"considering their ballistic missile attack on Iraqi bases in 2020. Iran has also transferred missiles to Yemen's Houthi rebels, who have since struck civilian targets in Saudi Arabia and the United Arab Emirates. And we saw what they accomplished with the sinking of one of our destroyers during the recent Israeli-Hamas war. Never take any of our enemies for granted. They want to destroy us as badly as we want to take them out. We must be at the top of our game, and you must instill in our crew the same attitude." The XO took a seat.

"Thank you, XO," said the captain. "The CAG will brief us about what to expect in the air."

Mad Dog stood up and worked his way to the front. He took a moment before speaking, not hiding his uncompromising expression. "Listen, as I've always preached, we all function as one team on the *Ford*. I don't care what your job is—I want us all working as one team. Let your subordinates know how important this is to all of us. Teamwork equates to success, and what we could be facing makes success critical.

"Here's some background on what to anticipate from Iran. Since Russia invaded Ukraine, Iran has become a significant weapon supplier to Russia, including drones, tank rounds, and millions of artillery shells. Why do I mention this? Because of what Iran is getting in return. They're getting unprecedented defense cooperation, which includes Russian missiles, electronics, and air defense batteries. In addition, Tehran has been purchasing Russian fighter jets, specifically Sukhoi Su-35s, and the Russians have been training Iranian pilots to fly them.

"The point here is that what used to be an outdated Air Force with F-4 Phantoms and F-14 Tomcats is now a much more capable force with the addition of those Flanker-E aircraft, which aren't quite fifth-generation but close enough to put my aircrews through their paces. Once we're within range of Iran's defensive weapons, we could be greeted with a barrage of missiles fired from ground-based launchers, commercial ships, and aircraft. Also, our task force can expect swarms of explosive-laden speedboats and killer drones to harass us. If anyone in this room thinks Iran will be an easy mark, think again. We all must be at the top of our game and get the same from those under our command. Thank you."

Mad Dog took his seat. There was a collective stillness in the room as everyone realized this impending clash with Iran would not be a walk in the park.

"Thank you, CAG," said the CO. "To close things out, the task force commander has decided to stray from convention and use the *Ford* as his flagship. He wants to be in the Gulf instead of heading toward it, and it's a good operations security measure, so ready the flag bridge and expect him to fly in soon. As we await our final orders, stay vigilant and prepare for war." The officers nodded, each with a serious, determined expression.

Chapter 10

Arabian Sea

There is a saying in the military—hurry up and wait. Harley Jennings had known it all too well before retiring after twenty years in the Corps. As one of the lead FBI agents working the terrorist attack on the US electrical grid, which had turned out to be a cover operation for the Hezbollah attack on Independence Hall, Jennings hadn't been happy. In fact, he'd been pissed off. He'd let his country down by failing to prevent the attack, despite killing the two Lebanese gang members responsible for the cover operation.

A single man with no one to answer to, he decided to offer his services to fight the bastards from Iran who had sponsored all that bullshit. The retired gunnery sergeant with a military nickname of "Snake Eyes" had gone through legal channels to volunteer for service using 10 USC §688. Basically, if he wanted back in the Corps, he had to have a critical-skill MOS the Marines needed, and then by God, the Commandant would make room for him.

Since Jennings had experience with the Naval Strike Missile Defense System, which the Marine Corps was still adjusting to after its conversion to littoral regiments, the Corps wanted him back. After all, his exploits on Woody Island during the war with China had earned him several commendations. So just two weeks after the rocket attack on Independence Hall, Harley had his gunny stripes on again and had been flown out to join his new unit, the 26th MEUSOC, which the BATARG was navigating into position near Iran. He had taken a two-day crash course to get up to speed on the new refinements to his weapons system.

It hadn't taken him long to return to the mindset of being in a forward-deployed, self-sustaining air-ground task force designed to provide a rapid response capability in differing operational environments. The MEU had three components: command, ground combat, and aviation, and his unit would support them all by delivering long-range strike capabilities and enhanced fire support with lethal precision against targets at extended ranges.

On his third day aboard the *Bataan*, Jennings stood in front of his unit alongside his commanding officer, Captain Ozzie Sullivan, in the designated spot for his unit on the ship's deck. It was their time slot for PT, and it was invigorating to be on the deck of a naval warship cruising into battle to perform precisely what he was trained to do.

The *Bataan* was a *Wasp*-class amphibious assault ship that resembled an aircraft carrier. It was the MEU commander's flagship. The USS *Carter Hall was* accompanied, carrying amphibious assault vehicles, landing craft, and the transport dock USS *Mesa Verde*. The three BATARG ships were under the command of Task Force 70 and headed towards the Persian Gulf.

Under the bright sun and with the wind blowing through Jennings's hair, everything was just right. Even the burpees added to the moment. As Jennings performed them flawlessly, he was ready to bring it to a country that had dared to destroy a symbol of American freedom. It was payback time.

Chapter 11

USS FORD

Arabian Sea

Nineteen-year-old Culinary Specialist Seaman Albert Richards had been told he would be working his next shift—and all shifts until further notice—in the admiral's mess for a task force commander who was coming aboard soon. He had no idea who the person was or what his job would entail, but it sounded a heck of a lot better than what he'd been doing. He was tired of cleaning up after his shipmates. They were messy and seldom ate everything on their plates, which went against everything he'd been taught growing up in Provo, Utah.

In his loving home, you helped prepare the meal with whoever oversaw the cooking that day. You set the table, ate everything on your plate, and when you were finished—careful never to say done—you did the dishes, not in a dishwasher, but by hand with one of your siblings. When everything was put away, you did your homework.

If there was any time before lights out, he used that time to go on his favorite app, the popular TopVid. He loved to post videos, and he was good at it. He had a large following because his posts were creative and super funny.

His specialty was behind-the-scenes videos, which he personalized with his likable personality. More importantly, he always made them enjoyable by encouraging engagement with his viewers. One of his best pieces of work was a school play where he put together some hilarious outtakes with just the right music added. The expressions of the student actors sold the show. It was a huge hit.

After graduation, Richards enlisted in the Navy because he thought traveling the world and making videos would be fun. His job classification was culinary specialist, and his first tour of duty was aboard the USS *Ford.* By then, the Navy had outlawed sailors' use of Chinese-owned software because it could be used for phishing and location tracking. Specifically, he had been taught that TopVid harvested extensive amounts of sensitive data from a user's search and browsing history, keystroke patterns, and biometrics, including face prints and voice prints. He had also been told that the dangers of all these were amplified in a military context. But even though the Navy said it couldn't be installed on any of its computers, there was no restriction for personal use by the sailors. The trouble with that was there was no personal Wi-Fi for the crew when out to sea.

The teenager didn't believe the negative bullcrap about TopVid and continued using it. The previous month, the *Ford* had visited Bahrain, where he let fly with some behind-the-scenes videos. He couldn't believe how many likes he was still getting. But there was one he kept playing back in his head as if it had just happened.

He had been getting some great videos of a nightclub bartender flipping glasses like a circus performer when he heard a girl's voice say, "I bet you're Albert."

As he turned his attention away from his phone, he couldn't believe who was speaking to him—one of the most beautiful women he had ever seen, with long black hair, and eyes that penetrated his soul. He was enchanted by her olive-toned complexion.

"I'm sorry if I startled you," she said, "but I just had to say hi. I follow all your posts on TopVid, and I love them."

Albert looked around. At five-six with close-cropped brown hair, he wasn't a looker and couldn't believe this woman was talking to him.

His hand went to his scraggly mustache, and he tugged on it before answering, "Hello . . . I mean hi. Thanks for that. I love doing these videos." As he stared at the beautiful Middle Eastern woman with expressive eyes and a body to kill for, he was immediately at a loss for additional words.

"I'm sorry," she said. "I didn't mean to interrupt your creative expressions. I just wanted to meet the person behind all those cool videos. I'll get going." She turned and walked toward a table.

"Wait," said Albert, who had decided there was no way he would blow this opportunity.

She stopped and turned with such confidence and poise it took him a moment to collect his words.

"May I join you?" he said. "I'm with a bunch of drunk guys who are getting too rowdy for my taste."

She eyed him again, and a smile formed on her full lips. "Sure, I'm there." She pointed to a small table in a corner. "My girlfriend just took off with a guy, so I'm alone."

"Great, I mean, yes, that would be nice. By the way, I'm Albert Richards." He awkwardly stuck his hand out. As she took it, chills rushed through his body, and he couldn't believe how soft her skin was. He felt possessed. They took a seat at her empty table.

"I'm Aisha Bilal." When she said that, he swore she squeezed his hand a little tighter. "So, Albert, what brings you here making videos?"

Staring at Aisha, his butt almost missed his seat when he sat, and his chair wobbled. Shit, he thought to himself, get it together before this goddess figures out I'm not the best-looking guy in the nightclub.

As they talked and drank for hours, Albert thought Aisha seemed to like him. Before he reported back to the *Ford*, they agreed to have dinner together the following night.

At the Monsoon restaurant in Manama, Bahrain, they sat together at a table overlooking a sparkling pool with large figurines spewing water. Albert pinched his leg to make sure he wasn't dreaming. But it was real—she liked him. He could tell by the way they were holding hands under the table. Once, she even rubbed her foot against his calf.

"Albert, tonight feels bittersweet. This may be the last time I see you before you set sail around the world. My heart tells me there's something special between us."

"Aisha, even though we've only known each other for two days, I feel connected too. I've been thinking—I have leave in a few months, and I would love to spend it here in Bahrain with you. I mean that. Can you promise to text and email me every day until then? Maybe even send some pictures?"

"Of course, I will, and I would love to spend time with you online."

"There is a problem, though." He grabbed nervously at his mustache. "We have no internet while deployed."

"What? We can't talk online? Doesn't the ship have all those connections?" Aisha's frustration was evident.

"Yes, of course, but the ship's computers and Wi-Fi are for official business only. No personal stuff," Albert said.

Aisha looked hurt and sad, which nearly melted Albert's heart. He knew he had to fix this quickly.

"Let me see what I can do," he said. "I have a buddy who's a computer whiz. He once told me he knew how to get into the ship's computers without the cyber people knowing it. He talks with his girlfriend back in the States all the time. I'll give him a shoutout."

"That would be amazing," said Aisha. "Never being able to talk would be hard. I gave you all my contact information last night, so please try."

"Oh, I promise I'll make this work."

The couple left the restaurant, and Aisha invited Albert to her apartment, where the two lovebirds discovered each other. "I love you" passed their lips as they said goodbye the following day. As he was leaving, Aisha handed him a stapled bag and told him to open it later. She said it contained a special surprise for him.

Albert was cool with anything she said or suggested. He was determined not to lose this new woman in his life. Whatever it took, he would make it happen. Whistling as he walked down the sidewalk, he'd never felt so emboldened.

Chapter 12

AL-TANF GARRISON
Southeastern Syria

No one in the 5th Special Forces Group's Operational Detachment Alpha could believe a homegrown Hezbollah terrorist could have destroyed Independence Hall. It was devastating news to the twelve Green Berets fighting an undeclared war in Syria. Captain Roger Ashburger was over-the-top pissed off about the whole mess. As team leader, he had just been told by his commanding officer that his A-Team was to prepare for a new operation. They would be flown out of Syria with a ticket to Al Udeid Air Base in Qatar. He was unsure what followed next but knew it would include Iran.

As he waited for his troops to show up at their small team room, which served as a command post and sometimes bar, his mind drifted back to his family in Golden, Colorado. His father was a Colorado School of Mines professor, and he had always hoped his only son would follow in his footsteps. "No thanks, Dad," was Ashburger's usual comment when his dad pressed him on it, because he wanted to fight for his country like Uncle Bill had done as a career Green Beret officer. He loved all his uncle's war stories and always imagined himself leading troops into battle. It just seemed right for him.

Ashburger excelled in the Army ROTC program at Colorado State University, where he met the love of his life. As fate would have it, she ended up teaching at his dad's university. Even after all these years, his dad still didn't support his decision, but so be it.

As the eleven men filed into the room, everyone found a place to sit, including one on a cooler and another on a pallet of ammo. Ashburger gave them a chance to stop bullshitting about why they were meeting, then he spoke.

"Here's what's going on. CENTCOM is moving assets to Al Udeid Air Base in Qatar. We'll be part of that deployment. I need you to gather all your gear for tomorrow's departure at 0500 hours ." Some in the room grumbled.

"Captain," said his comms sergeant, Staff Sergeant Andy Boykin, "I thought we were rotating out of this shithole in three weeks. What the fuck, over."

"I hear you, Boykin, but that was before Hezbollah decided to take out Independence Hall. We all understand there's a price for that, so we'll be part of the payback. And let me tell you, I can't wait to deliver it." This earned an oorah that echoed around the small room. The men were ready for whatever they were dealt. They were, after all, Green Berets.

Chapter 13

USS Reagan
Arabian Sea

Lieutenant Commander Sarah "Danger" Freeman, who was keeping her maiden name for the time being, was pondering the recent changes to her life as she was in the wardroom aboard the *Reagan* getting her breakfast. She was now a married woman. That took some adjusting, mainly when she referred to Jessie, an F-35 pilot on the *Ford*, as her husband. In addition, she was recovering both physically and mentally from the beating she took while a captive of a Lebanese gang when she was on leave in Michigan. That was bad enough, but she would never forget the firefight with terrorists the night the lights went out in the midsection of the US.

Flying her E-2D Hawkeye off the *Reagan* was exciting enough, but when people were trying to kill you with high-powered rifles, that was chilling. But she had survived, just as she had during the war with China a few years ago. Now it looked like she would be fighting a new war, this time with Iran. It was a good thing she embraced change.

Being a woman in the Navy was pretty even sailing most of the time. She was accepted as one of the best in her profession. She likened flying a Hawkeye to playing quarterback on a football team, something she had never done, but basically the same position, serving as an airborne early warning, command, and control platform to those in the thick of a fight. Perhaps it was her use of that analogy without having ever played football which pissed off her boss, Commander Damien Wagner, but she was sure it had nothing to do with that and everything to do with the fact that she was a female pilot. Serving as his executive officer, she was second in command and deserved more than his continual berating, which usually happened in private but was done openly at times. Sarah gave her squadron commander the benefit of the doubt since he had just transferred onto the *Reagan* and probably was trying to put his stamp on things. But she didn't like the way he was going about it.

It was 0500 when Sarah sat across from Wagner at the mess table. She had a plate of French toast with eggs over easy, her go-to breakfast.

"Lieutenant Commander," Wagner said, "would you be so kind as to freshen my coffee?" His tone dared her to say no. She didn't.

She kept her cool since she knew exactly what he was doing, so she said calmly, but loudly enough that others nearby could hear, "Sir, do you ask your male subordinates to get you your coffee?" She looked him dead in the eyes because he was nothing compared to the assholes who had kidnapped and beaten her less than a month ago. His eyes grew wide, and then he grabbed his cup and lifted it, nodding his head at the culinary specialist, the steward of the officers' mess. The young woman quickly refilled his cup and placed it on the table before him. Sarah knew he was enjoying the compensatory power trip.

The CO sipped his coffee and gently set the cup down in the exact spot he had lifted it from. "Freeman, I have you going out this morning so you can provide leadership to crew members with zero combat experience. See what you think of this crew and report the details in writing when you return. Do you have any questions?"

Looking up from her empty plate, Sarah said, "No, Sir, no questions." With that, she got up and headed to the ready room, leaving her boss to stare after her. As she went, her thoughts turned to her husband and how much she missed him. Be safe, Jessie, she thought, we'll both get through this.

Chapter 14

USS CHIEF, ROYAL SAUDI NAVY SHIP AL KHARJ, AND UNITED ARAB EMIRATES SHIP MUBARRAZ
Gulf of Oman

With a conflict with Iran imminent, Lieutenant Brett Jansen was busy clearing mines for an ingress waterway for TF-70. Jansen was the XO for his crew of ninety-four and the mission commander of two allied ships. Jansen had taken command of the *Chief* when his CO reported to him that he was confined to his room with a painful abdominal issue. Jansen was too busy to worry about that now; there were other pressing issues.

This was Jansen's first command, and he was feeling the pressure. He was concerned that none of the ships had any real firepower, should it be needed. All that could be scraped up for protection was the outdated UAE fast-attack ship *Mubarraz*, which was equipped with outdated missiles and large secondary guns. TF-70, comprised of the *Ford, Nimitz,* and *Reagan* CSGs, was in the area but not close enough to render immediate aid.

Working with Saudi Arabia's minesweeper *Al Kharj*, another timeworn ship built in the 1990s, they had just finished demolishing twenty-four floating contact mines using deck weapons. Their UUV, an unmanned underwater vehicle, found and eliminated two mine-like objects.

"Mine 2, Mine 1," said Jansen, "prepare for a return run using sonar to detect MLOs on the seabed. Break. Mine 3, remain in cleared area and cover our six." Turning to his operations officer, standing beside him, Jansen said, "Ops, I want lookouts and radar operators to be alert to any activity in our zone. No exceptions, got it?"

"Yes, Sir. On it."

In years past, classifying and analyzing mines was time-consuming. Jansen appreciated that his newly upgraded sonar had AI to better detect, classify, and target mines and mine-like objects. The AI was replacing sailors since it was programmed to rapidly analyze texture-based features, patterns, and variations of mines and MLOs. It also looked at geometrical features, such as length and dimensions, and even used color variances to locate the underwater killers.

As the trio of ships maneuvered back through their sector, an excited voice said over the radio, "Mine 1, Mine 3. Radar indicates twenty contacts approaching from the coast. They are fast-attack craft and are just now splitting into two groups. Distance 2.1 nautical miles. Speed 45 knots. Unknown flag."

"Mine 1, roger," said Jansen.

Using his ship's internal comms, Jansen ordered, "General quarters. General quarters. All hands, man your battle stations. Speedboat attack imminent aft. Bearing zero-six-five."

Now comes the tricky part, Jansen thought.

His rules of engagement weren't specific to this situation, in which his ship hadn't been fired upon but was in danger of taking fire. Not firing at the threats now could put his command at serious risk. Seconds ticked by as he followed the intent of the ROE. Since he was off the coast of Iran, he had to assume the threats were Iranian—vessels from the nation that had blown up Independence Hall.

He had to act now.

"Mine 3 and Mine 2, use defensive fire to warn the incoming threats. If there is no immediate response—commence firing on targets."

"Mine 3, roger."

"Mine 2, roger."

"Comms," said Jansen, "contact TF-70 and get us some help."

At the aft of the ship, Petty Officer Third Class Jose Alvarez arrived at his assigned battle station. Breathing hard, he chambered a round into his Browning M2 .50-caliber machine gun mounted on a stabilized platform. He wished his hands were equally stabilized since his right hand was shaking all around the trigger guard of the powerful weapon. He was experienced, having fired thousands of rounds with the M2, but he'd never shot at a living person. He tried to calm down but wasn't sure if he was winning.

He yelled, "Morris you got any targets?"

Petty Officer Second Class John Morris, his team leader and assistant gunner, blurted out, "Not yet."

Just then, they heard a heavy gun firing several rounds. Alvarez couldn't believe it; his hand went rock steady, his finger resting on the trigger. Shit, yes, he thought, I can do this.

ROYAL SAUDI NAVY AL KHARJ (MINE 2)
Gulf of Oman

"Bridge, Weapons. We have target acquisition. Ready to fire the 20."

The captain, Ahmed Abdullah Al-Fahad, didn't hesitate to give the command to his gunnery team. "Weapons, permission to fire. Close into leading target." He knew he would not hesitate to activate the close-in weapons system if necessary.

"Weapons, roger." Two reports echoed as the 20mm gun hurled projectiles toward the incoming speedboats.

The spotters reported, "Sir, no deviation. Targets continuing on a course to intercept."

"Weapons, Bridge. Fire for effect. Break. CIWS, prepare for encounter. Break. Attention all personnel. This is the captain. Enemy fast-attack craft are approaching both our starboard and port. Distance 1.5 nautical miles, speed 50 knots. Prepare to engage vessels."

The sound of the 20mm took over as it pumped out round after round.

USS Chief (Mine 1)
Gulf of Oman

Things were happening quickly. On the bridge of the *Chief*, Jansen had an idea. "Helm, make new course one-one-five degrees, flank speed." Helm repeated the order and steered the ship to the new heading.

Since he knew exactly what area was cleared of mines, Jansen would put the minesweeper on the western edge of the cleared zone so that floating mines would impede the approach of the fast-attack craft. He ordered the *Mubarraz* to do the same on the eastern edge of the minefield. As the ship adjusted course, Jansen heard his M50s open up.

On the deck, the gunnery team leader screamed, "Targets incoming, port side. You are locked and loaded."

"Firing," shouted Alvarez, pulling the trigger on his M2. The enemy boats were near his weapon's maximum range of nearly one mile, so Alvarez let loose with a short burst of belt-fed ammo. "Adjusting aim."

"You need to lead them more," said Morris. "The rounds are hitting behind the lead boats."

Not saying a word but doing as instructed, Alvarez watched as the lead boat seemed to drive right into his line of fire. A massive fireball blew debris high into the air. Those topside on the *Chief* couldn't help but let out a cheer as pieces of the speedboat cartwheeled across the sea. But there was little time for celebration because a shitload of other boats were closing fast.

After pumping out five hundred rounds a minute, Alvarez yelled, "Reloading." Morris helped him put the next ammo belt in. It seemed like an eternity before the gun was hammering rounds at the fast-closing boats.

Alvarez saw a red stream of tracers heading his way. He didn't flinch as incoming rounds ripped into the *Chief*. As he aimed at his next target, he couldn't help but notice several other boats getting blown from the water. He realized the *Al Kharj* had used its 20mm rounds to slow the enemy's advance. Suddenly, the entire sea seemed to be boiling over as vast spouts of water and exploding boats lit the sea. It sounded like an out-of-control chainsaw. Then he saw a jet flying over the water, just feet from the tops of the swells.

Persian Gulf, southern sector

Lieutenant Commander Jessie "Swagger" Hampton had a way of stealing the show. As one of the Navy's top fighter pilots, he made a point to prove it. Even when he was walking, his swagger was so pronounced that he could be spotted from a mile away. Since marrying the love of his life, Sarah, a Naval aviator herself, he hadn't slowed down.

As the flight lead of two Lockheed Martin F-35C Lightning II aircraft from Carrier Air Wing 8 off the USS *Ford*, he was again at the right place at the right time—and it wasn't by chance. Knowing that an American minesweeper was working with other allied ships in the waters near Iran, he'd made a tactical decision to overstretch his assigned CAP sector. With him was his wingman, Lieutenant Russ "Bulldog" Lockwood.

They hadn't been on station for ten minutes when they received an emergency broadcast from the USS *Chief*. Going to afterburners, the two fighters were on scene within minutes. Hostile fast-attack craft were attacking in two formations.

Using his stealth Multifunction Advanced Data Link comms, Jesse said to his wingman, "Two, you take the attacking boats on the port side—low altitude. I've got starboard. Confirm guns."

"Two's in, port side, guns."

Both Lightning IIs used the Northrop Grumman AN/APG-81 active electronically-scanned array radar system to adjust to the uneven air just above the sea surface as they approached their targets. To complement the AESA radar picture when they arrived within gun range, the pilots got a visual of several speedboats attempting to maneuver off their course. Both aircraft were equipped with a General Dynamics GAU-22/A, a four-barrel 25mm Gatling gun capable of firing three thousand rounds a minute. As the pilots entered the kill zone with their weapons set to strafing mode, they fired. The explosive armor-piercing shells immediately began shredding the boats into burning hulks resembling anything but speedboats. There were several secondary explosions, indicating several of the boats were laden with high explosives and had planned to ram the ships in suicide attacks. One of the boats managed to evade the fire from the F-35s but turned sharply into a surface mine, blowing the craft upwards in a spectacular tower of water.

The F-35s made a perfect combat turn and headed back the way they came, dumping rounds into anything that looked like it might have survived. Nothing was moving.

Jessie said, "Bulldog, let's do a flyby and give a wave to our friends—who now know we just saved their bacon."

Bulldog answered quickly, "Roger that, Swagger. My pleasure."

This time, the fighters went vertical, made a formation high-altitude turn, and approached the ships at fifty feet, waving their wings as they thundered off out of sight.

"Mine 1, Jedi 11. Call us anytime."

USS CHIEF
Gulf of Oman

"Jedi 11, Mine 1," said Jansen. "Thanks for the assist. Be safe."

On the deck, Alvarez and his team leader, Morris, almost tripped over the pile of brass shell casings surrounding them as they gave each other a buddy hug and thanked the heavens for the F-35s.

All the men and women on board the three ships were thankful to be alive, but they fully understood that this was only the beginning.

Chapter 15

NATANZ ENRICHMENT COMPLEX
Isfahan Province, Iran

General Shirvani was used to visitors. The heavily fortified, top-secret Natanz Enrichment Complex, which was built inside a mountain bordering a desert, was a frequent destination for international inspectors whose visits were meant to ensure his country wasn't producing nuclear bombs. The latest visit by members of the Department of Safeguards from the International Atomic Energy Agency carefully noted all the current readings and measurements from Iran's nuclear program. The IAEA visitors wrote it all in clinical language, which even the general found confusing. It was like attorneys who wrote contracts so only other attorneys could interpret them—otherwise known as job security.

Shirvani had to remind some newly minted inspectors that Iran had not enriched uranium under the 2015 nuclear accords, nor would they. He inwardly chuckled before he told the inspectors that he was currently overseeing the processing of a "type" of highly enriched uranium, something that wasn't weapons-grade but was meant for peaceful uses.

Then he smiled.

He hated politics but had to secretly thank President Mark Taylor, who had ordered his country to withdraw from the nuclear pact. Since then, restraints had slipped away, leaving Iran more room to maneuver in the direction of the Supreme Leader's vision—a nuclear bomb.

All the journalists and naysayers said it would take Iran at least two years or more to develop a nuclear warhead that could be mounted on a missile. Two years had passed, and guess what had happened.

The key to developing the bomb in secret had been to collect all the needed ingredients but to make no apparent move to build one. In this way, the inspectors couldn't get a whiff of what was up. To accomplish this, Shirvani needed at least one billionaire who understood Iran's cause and shared the conviction of not only reducing the influence of the US in the Middle East but also increasing Iran's power projection into all its neighboring states. The goal was to be the single power moving the Islamic revolution forward.

Now, all the pieces were coming together thanks to Iran's geography, fossil fuel reserves, military capabilities, and budding regional influence. A nuclear entrepreneur could secretly take Iran to the next step, a nuclear bomb, and with it the threat of using it. Fortunately, the Supreme Leader knew just the man to help, Akbar Hashemi Rafsanjani, a black-market billionaire who made money by trading and selling almost anything, including top-tiered weapons. He wasn't picky. You paid his asking price, and he ensured you got what you wished for, like a genie that appeared from a magic lamp and granted the owner three wishes, except Rafsanjani didn't care how many wishes you used.

The Supreme Leader had a wish—nuclear bombs—and he was willing to pay whatever was necessary for them. Rafsanjani was intent on delivering them so he could add more zeros to his total wealth. So everyone was happy.

Chapter 16

KC-135R Stratotanker
Skies over Saudi Arabia

After thumbing a ride from the Air Force in a KC-135 Stratotanker, the men of Captain Roger Ashburger's ODA were flying to Al Udeid Air Base in the small country of Qatar, which they would call home until they forward deployed. Eleven of the twelve Green Berets grabbed some shuteye as the plane droned on with put-you-to-sleep white noise. The exception was Team Leader 18A, Captain Roger Ashburger. He was checking his downloaded notes on Qatar.

Compared to the country's futuristic-looking city of Doha, Al Udeid looked like an afterthought. Positioned in the desert, away from civilization, it would never make the poster for a chamber of commerce. But it did serve its intended purpose. It had been a US base since 1996, could house over 10,000 troops, and was a crucial forward hub for CENTCOM. Situated on a peninsula in the Persian Gulf, the base provided proximity to various conflict zones and enabled rapid deployment to areas of need. Ashburger had a good idea of where they would be sent, but he didn't know the exact mission yet.

Staff Sergeant Boykin came over and sat beside him.

"What's up, Andy?" Ashburger said.

"Not much. I saw you were awake and wanted to ask if you've heard anything about our next mission."

Ashburger repositioned himself in the plane's uncomfortable seat and put his notes in his pocket. "I'll brief our team shortly on what I know. But just as a heads-up, the mission will involve a ride on two Black Hawks. I was told to be prepared for insertion into Iran and that we should refresh our fast-roping skills. So that's what we'll be doing tomorrow, and you should get some sleep. We're still an hour out."

Pulling his hat over his eyes, Ashburger practiced what he preached. He knew there would be little time for sleep in the coming days.

Chapter 17

TF-70 FLAGSHIP USS FORD
Persian Gulf

Rear Admiral Marquis Holloway had fought against the odds his entire life. Growing up in a tough area of Hampton, Virginia, Holloway was the first African American man to reach the rank of admiral in the United States Navy who had not attended the Naval Academy. Instead, he had done it the only way he could, by attending Hampton University, one of the nation's historically African American colleges or universities, and by joining ROTC.

With his trademark thin mustache, the man of average appearance was anything but ordinary as a person. His motto in life was to overcome the odds by outworking everyone else. If you told him he didn't have a chance to overcome an obstacle, then he would rewrite the book. Sitting aboard his flagship, the USS *Ford*, was just another example.

He alone was responsible for TF-70's three aircraft carriers with a force of more than eighteen thousand personnel. The 180 aircraft on the carriers were numerically larger than most countries' air forces, including Iran's. Throw in a score of escort cruisers, submarines, and destroyers, and he had the command of a lifetime.

When asked what one of his driving forces in life was, he would always answer the same: Samuel L. Gravely. It wasn't a household name to most. In Holloway's senior year at Hampton University in 1995, Gravely was a guest speaker addressing the students of the ROTC program. Gravely talked about his life and his fight up the chain of command during the Navy's period of racial segregation before October 1944. After that month, commanders were finally allowed to assign Black sailors to positions as they saw fit, an outcome of a racially motivated trial following the disaster at Port Chicago, California, in which fifty Black enlisted sailors were convicted of mutiny for peacefully refusing to return to dangerous work conditions tolerated and encouraged by white officers. But even after President Truman's 1948 order to desegregate the military, racism didn't disappear. But neither did Holloway. Whenever he was down, he would recall Gravely's accomplishments and know he would be alright.

A loud knock at Holloway's door startled him from his thoughts. "Yes, come in." His chief of staff entered.

"Admiral, as you requested, the two pilots involved in protecting the minesweeper are in the ready room for a debrief."

"Good. Are the CO and CAG present?" His chief of staff nodded. "Let me reiterate: I'm just observing. They will do the questioning."

"Yes, Sir. They understand."

"Good, let's go."

Arriving in the ready room, Holloway told everyone to keep it low-key. The two pilots casually sat in the front row seats while the four senior officers sat up front. As Holloway scanned the setup, he wished he only had two officers up front, but it was too late now.

After exchanging greetings, the CAG, Captain Mad Dog Johnson, got things going. "As you both know, I'm a man who likes to cut to the chase, as does the admiral,"—Holloway nodded—"so, Hampton, you were the flight leader, and it appears you strayed from your assigned CAP sector. Care to inform us why?"

Looking first at the admiral, then at the CAG, Jessie replied, "Sir, I made the tactical decision to push our sector parameters closer to where the three-nation joint minesweeping operations were taking place. In our morning brief, they mentioned that the ships would be without support, so a warning bell went off in my head. I ensured the rest of the CAP could cover their sectors, and I knew they could respond to any eventuality in our sector."

"I see," said Mad Dog. "So you thought a do-it-yourself approach trumped the decisions of people like me who spent considerable time reviewing the threats and carefully making those sector assignments." Shaking his head, he said, "Interesting."

"No, Sir, in no way did I think that for a moment," Jessie said. "I learned much about mission strategies during the China War, so I'm continually considering different eventualities. I thought through my assignment and fine-tuned it to cover the possibility that Iran might attack those ships, just as they did, Sir."

"Commander," said the admiral, despite his desire to keep out of the review, "if every one of our pilots adjusted their orders according to their perceived interpretation of operations, I ask you, what kind of Navy would we have? If you believe hitting a home run when you were given a take sign is cool, I know of a desk chair in Washington that would fit your ass nicely. You left part of our airspace exposed."

Jessie took a second and, looking the admiral straight in the eyes, said with as much conviction as he felt, "Sir, if the batter sees a pitch he's supposed to take sailing toward his wheelhouse, then his instincts take over, and he smashes it for a home run—that's a win. I adjusted my sector because I felt, in my best judgment, that it was the right thing to do. As everyone here knows, we saved three ships today from certain disaster. Hundreds of lives were saved by the tactical decision I alone made. I appreciate your observation, Sir, but I seriously believe your pilots need to be given some leeway. We're fighters."

Mad Dog glanced at the admiral, took his lead, and said, "Listen, what you did out there today made me damn proud of your actions, and I thank the heavens for the outcome. But this is the United States Navy, and we have a way of doing things. Understand?"

Both pilots blurted out, "Yes, Sir."

Everyone in the room understood what had to be said for the record. But they also realized a war was coming and knew the Navy needed fighters like these two pilots.

Chapter 18

Undisclosed location, West Coast of Yemen
Houthi Missile Launching Site

Amir Ahmed Al-Saud was cursing to himself again, as the Houthi rebels under his command had seen many times before: You can't quite make it out but you can see the commander's lips moving with little sounds escaping, but you can't be sure what he is saying. Al-Saud had been mumbling, "These men are going to cut my life short." Then, in his command voice, "How many times have I demonstrated that you must stabilize the launcher to get proper alignment for firing?"

As soon as the words were out of his mouth, three mujahid ran around like they were in some slapstick comedy, positioning the launcher for the Scud D ballistic missile they were about to launch. This was a big deal to Al-Saud, as they seldom were given this type of powerful missile with a range of over 500 kilometers. His Iranian brothers were constantly feeding him coordinates for their target, the *Ever Heart*, a massive 1,312-foot container ship operated by Evergreen of Taiwan and flying a Panamanian flag.

With the missile and warhead loaded into the launcher, he ordered the liquid fueling to begin. As he closely observed his crew's actions, he was happy that this process was done with precision—something he was not used to.

With the ballistic missile loaded with fuel, Al-Saud input the final target coordinates. The crew moved back to the control vehicle, which contained all the electronics and was where he was preparing for the launch sequence. He silently prayed for Allah to guide the missile to his target as he ordered the two-minute countdown.

Chapter 19

NORTHROP GRUMMAN E-2D ADVANCED HAWKEYE
Arabian Sea

This was different, thought Sarah as she observed a novice Hawkeye crew from the *Reagan*. She was too used to being the pilot, not an observer. However, her CO assigned her to check on this inexperienced crew and provide them with leadership to level their learning curve while operating in an area that would soon be a combat zone.

The pilot was Lieutenant Gail Osborne. Sarah knew that only 10 percent of Navy pilots were women and thought it was cool that two of them were in the same aircraft. In the little time she had known Gail, Sarah saw much of herself in this pilot. Gail seemed comfortable and friendly with her crew, but she ensured that friendliness didn't cross the line to fraternization and disruption of good order and discipline.

Cruising at 25,000 feet, the radar operator caught something on the space-based infrared system and interrupted the crew's soft chatter. "SBIRS alert. Missile launch detected, bearing two-three-one, range 125 miles."

"Roger," replied the air control officer. "AIS indicates the vessel *Ever Heart* in closest proximity, a Panama-flagged civilian cargo ship."

Gail said to her copilot, "Eyes open." She turned the aircraft toward the *Ever Heart*.

On a discreet channel, the E-2's combat information center officer told *Reagan*'s CIC, "Gipper, Hawker 31, probable Houthi missile inbound to merchant *Ever Heart* in the Gulf of Oman."

"Hawker 31, Gipper. ROE is weapons-free to defend commercial traffic." The Hawker 31 repeated the ROE to the air control officer seated next to him.

Quickly scanning for the nearest fighters, the ACO saw a flight of two Boeing F/A-18E Super Hornets. He toggled onto the CAP net. "Bonzo 11, Hawker 31. Vector to the intercept coordinates sent over data link."

The RO said to the Hawkeye back-end crew, "Missile ID is Scud-B, based on velocity and trajectory."

The ACO called on Guard frequency, saying, "*Ever Heart*, this is United States Navy aircraft callsign Hawker 31. Inbound missile. Take immediate evasive action. Help is on the way."

Chapter 20

Ever Heart
Gulf of Aden

Standing on the deck of his massive command, the *Ever Heart*, one of the largest container ships in the world, Dwi Wahyu slowly put the photo into the breast pocket of his neatly pressed uniform. It didn't matter if it was stored away because the image taken just a few months ago was burnt into his brain—he and his wife, Ratna, held hands while standing on a beach in his home country of Indonesia. The love of his life and the mother of their two children had just been diagnosed with stage four breast cancer—no warning, no symptoms, no nothing.

He cursed out loud as he flashed back to their recent goodbyes.

"I won't go," said Dwi.

"You must, my love. This is your first command of such a mighty ship, something you have waited for your entire career."

"Like that's important anymore," said Dwi. "Nothing comes before you and the family. Nothing."

"I will be fine, Dwi. Even though my chemotherapy will start while you're gone, my sister will stay with me to help. You know I'll be fine."

The memory faded as the strong wind in his face reminded him of his duty.

His ship was making 15 knots and would need another course correction in five minutes. But his wife was correct in her assessment. This was by far the largest ship he had ever commanded. It was the assignment of a lifetime.

He reminded himself that he needed to give his full attention to his crew of twenty-eight and the exacting navigation through these contentious waters. With a war brewing between the US and Iran, he knew this would be the last trip of its kind for a while. His bosses back in Taiwan understood the risk but had felt confident in their decision to make this passage since there had been no problems with the Houthis in Yemen for nearly two months. It was a roll of the dice, but with so much money riding on the outcome, Dwi had been ordered to proceed with his valuable cargo.

Dwi turned and headed for the bridge. When he took the first step up the ladder, the Scud's guidance system made its final adjustments as it closed in on its target.

Just as Dwi reached the top step, he heard a Navy aircraft sending a warning over the radio—it was the last thing he ever heard.

The two-thousand-pound warhead struck the mid-section of the *Ever Heart* at a speed of 4,000 miles per hour. Penetrating several layers of cargo containers, the missile released so much energy that the explosion's shockwave ripped apart the massive ship's hull. Thousands of fragments flew in every direction. The blast tore through the windows of the bridge, instantly killing everyone inside. Below deck, water-tight compartments caved in like an accordion playing the death song of the *Ever Heart*.

E-2D Advanced Hawkeye
Arabian Sea

"Bonzo 11 on station in two mikes," the F-18 lead said.

The RO said on comms, "Disregard, Bonzo 11, missile impact on the *Ever Heart*."

A collective gasp went over the E-2's crew radio as the pilot and copilot saw a faint fireball on the distant horizon."Bonzo 11, ACO. Report any signs of survivors."

No one on the E-2 spoke. There was nothing else to say.

Chapter 21

SITUATION ROOM, THE WHITE HOUSE
Washington, DC

President Mark Taylor was a patient man. Even his daughter Jennie would agree, which said something about the family's free spirit. But she and others knew that his patience had limits. Right now, his NSC was treading on thin ice.

"Listen," said the president, "before any of us leave this room today, we'll have a consensus on our approach against the country that blew our symbol of democracy from the face of the Earth. There will be no maybes, nor BS, but a solid policy we agree on. I'll start by laying out my interpretation of where we stand.

"Since 1979, Iran's leaders have believed that we want regime change and to control their country. But this has not been the case in our current policy. Over the years, we've given them less attention than other areas like Taiwan and Ukraine. As a result, they now believe that we're too weak to stop their power moves in the Middle East. Accordingly, Iran is now a significant threat to stability and peace in the area because of their state-sponsored funding of Hezbollah, their support of the Hamas-led attack on Israel, and their support of the Houthi rebels' attacks on shipping and our

Navy. If we don't change our approach to Iran now, regional stability will only continue to fragment.

"Without question, we do need a change of leadership in Iran. Supreme Leader Massad must go. His control of Iran and his position as head of state gives him control of the armed forces, the judiciary, and all key government posts. It's a stacked deck."

While the president spoke, he had the complete attention of everyone in the room. He'd made some solid points and continued, "We need to develop a new policy to support the Iranian people who desire change to their government. We must support the anti-regime Iranians, including dissidents in exile and women's rights activists, and empower them to lead a revolt and reclaim Iran. The key to this strategy is to remain on the sidelines, allowing the anti-regime Iranians to choose their leader for a future beyond the Islamic Republic.

"We can accomplish this by driving the current regime out. As we've discussed, we do that by destroying their military infrastructure and taking over their oil fields to cut the flow of money financing their war machine. We should also degrade Iran's conventional forces within the first few days and end it all within two weeks. This would open the path for Massad's overthrow by anti-regime Iranians, and then we could help install a new ruling party, a democratic one."

As the president surveyed the room, he saw many in his NSC nodding their heads in agreement—as it should be, he thought. They had gone over this strategy many times. Now he just needed a formal consensus.

After another hour, everyone agreed with the plan. Military operations would begin in one week, allowing more time to move assets into the region. A new era was about to take place in Iran. With the Iranian regime and its proxies disarmed and removed, the future would include a secure Middle East. Despite the inevitable fog of war putting a few kinks into the plan, those on the NSC hoped that US military superiority would provide that ray of sunshine to burn off the mist and make for a cloudless future.

Chapter 22

*USS F*ord

Arabian Sea

Alone time on a carrier was as rare as not finding a plate loaded with leftover food. Seaman Albert Richards needed some time to himself. For the first time in his young life, he had a girlfriend he could brag about. He had only been gone from her and out to sea for a short time, but every waking moment his thoughts were almost entirely on his girl, and the leave he would take in eighty-three days when the *Reagan* made another port visit to Bahrain.

Alone time was important for many reasons, but for the lovesick sailor, it all had to do with Aisha. Before he left her, she had given him a sealed bag and had told him not to open it until he was aboard the ship. Now, as he hit the sack, he opened the bag. Inside, he found a thumb drive and a computer accessory.

With shaking hands, he inserted the drive into his laptop and put in his earbuds. The first thing he saw was a video selfie of Aisha as she slowly panned down her nude body, giving him closeups of all the right spots. He couldn't believe what he was seeing. "Holy shit," he murmured.

The video went black for ten seconds and then cut to Aisha dressed in a perfect blue pantsuit. "Hi, my love. I just wanted to give you a peek at what you're missing while you're away playing soldier. I bet you're missing me now." Richards felt sweat forming on his forehead and swore he was having one of those hot flashes his mom always complained about.

Aisha said, "We need to get you hooked up to the internet so we can share photos and other things." She flashed him the sexiest smile he had ever seen. "I have so much I want to say to you. I can't believe how our love was truly at first sight. This is so exciting, because I've never met anyone like you. I miss you terribly."

She looked so hot that it was hard for him to concentrate as she went on about the other item in the bag. "Now pay attention, my love. For this to work for us, you must set everything as I tell you. What you will be using is common here in Bahrain. It's called a Raspberry Pi. I know, strange, right? The software to make it operate is already installed. You mentioned that your ship has internal Wi-Fi to order food, so identify that network's name and the password you use to get into it."

Noticing one of his shipmates approaching, Richards paused the video on his computer. Once his fellow sailor passed, he hit play again.

Aisha continued, "I made sure to include some instructions for you to set up the Raspberry Pi, so please take a look at them. I know this must be a pain, but we can talk whenever we want once it's done. After you set up the Raspberry Pi to Wi-Fi, you need to configure a VPN client for it. It's in the instructions too. This will encrypt what we do and make it difficult for anyone to trace. Remember to use a strong password to prevent anyone else from gaining access to our conversations and other things.

"Next, set up remote access so you can control it from your laptop nearby. It would be best to hide it somewhere near where you sleep. You mentioned all your stuff was kept in a locker. That would be perfect. You can hide the device anywhere, say a boot or something like that. Make sure no one sees it. Next, test it, and if it doesn't work, just go through the instructions and my video again. But I'm sure you will do it perfectly the first time. I love you, Albert, and I can't wait to hear from you. Bye." The screen went black.

Richards fell asleep, dreaming of the video he had just watched. He knew he would get the Raspberry Pi set up no matter what. He missed Aisha so much.

Chapter 23

NATANZ ENRICHMENT COMPLEX
Isfahan Province, Iran

They were getting close. General Shirvani now had enough enriched uranium that he was seven days into the ten-day process of making a weapons-grade nuclear device. It's incredible, he thought, what rich friends can get done.

He didn't know how much Rafsanjani had been paid to get him the necessary enriched uranium, but the black-market billionaire had sure delivered. Unfortunately, it was only enough uranium for one bomb, but for now, that would have to do. The second bomb would take another month or so to make—the third less than that.

Shirvani clearly understood the critical importance of delivering the nuclear bomb on time. With a possible war against the US on the horizon, his country would need leverage against any possibility. A nuclear bomb provided that and more.

The world had no proof of what he was doing deep in the bowels of the Zagros Mountains, nor would they get any. He felt confident in that. He and his staff were working nearly one hundred meters underground, which was no random number. Iranian intelligence knew that US bunker-buster bombs, like the GBU-57 Massive Ordnance Penetrator, could only penetrate around sixty meters before detonation. And he knew any US aircraft and missiles would have to evade the Russian-made S-300 surface-to-air missiles scattered around the mountain. Along with protection from their Revolutionary Guard, he was in one of the most protected sites in the world.

The one thought keeping him from a restful sleep was how to get the nuclear warhead onto his chosen means of delivery, the road-mobile and accurate Ghadr-110 ballistic missile. With a range of nearly two thousand kilometers, it was just the right size to strike the Americans or Israel, praise Allah.

Chapter 24

USS Reagan
Arabian Sea

Hearing a knock at the stateroom door, Sarah Freeman wondered what was up. She was on her own time—if that even existed aboard a ship of war.

"Yes?" she said.

"Ma'am, Commander Wagner requests you report to the wardroom."

"When?"

"Now, Lieutenant Commander."

"Tell him I will be there as soon as I can."

"Yes, Ma'am." Sarah heard the sailor walk away.

Shit, what is with this guy? she asked herself. He could have set up an appointment through email or told her himself when their paths crossed, which was often the case. That was normal behavior. But there was nothing normal about him, she thought as she threw on her uniform.

When she entered the wardroom, she saw Wagner sitting at the end of a long table with a few papers scattered about. There was no one else present. She walked over and took a seat as he kept his head down, looking at his papers. After a moment, he finally acknowledged there was a human sitting across from him. Sarah refused to say a word. He'd called her for this meeting, so she would let him begin the conversation.

He did.

"Lieutenant Commander, is it not customary when called before your *superior* to stand at attention and present yourself?" She noted how he'd emphasized *superior*.

"Sir, you looked busy, and I didn't want to interrupt." She kept her tone even and her expression neutral.

"Don't let it happen again, understand?"

"Yes, Sir. Do you want me to re-enter properly, Sir?"

"Don't be a smartass, Freeman."

"Sir, it was an honest question."

"If we're done with your bullshit, I would like to go over a few things. Why didn't you file a report on our new E-2 crew after your flight?"

"Sir, I was in the process of doing just that, but with this war brewing, I have, as you know, been very busy flying sector patrols. I didn't know there was a deadline, but I'm working on it now, Sir. I could have it to you by the end of the day."

"Listen, Freeman, when I give you an assignment, it's due promptly. You're late. Make sure I have it within the next two hours."

Sarah replied, "Yes, Sir, it won't happen again." The words came out of her mouth, but in her heart, she wondered what was with this dude. She was a combat veteran with accolades and medals to prove it, and all he wanted from her was paperwork—with a war brewing, for crying out loud.

"That's all, Freeman. Get to work on my report."

Sarah jumped up from her seat and headed to the door.

"Wait a minute, Lieutenant Commander. Aren't you forgetting something?"

Sarah turned and gave him a what-the-fuck look.

"Is it not a rule in the United States Navy that when in a formal meeting with a superior officer, you stand at attention and salute when entering and upon completion of the meeting? For Christ's sake, Freeman, we just went over this. Do you have a problem we need to address?"

Knowing it was technically wrong to report out when she hadn't formally reported in, Sarah still walked back to her CO, snapped to attention, and threw a brisk salute. "Sir, request permission to leave."

"Get out of here, Freeman," he said as he returned her salute with a wimpy one.

Gladly, she thought.

Chapter 25

*USS C*HIEF *AND USS C*ANBERRA
Gulf of Oman

After swiftly patching some machine-gun holes on his ship, Lieutenant Brett Jansen had the USS *Chief* and his team back on station, thirteen miles off the coast of Iran, performing its mine countermeasures mission of locating and neutralizing mines. His MCM team was working in tandem with that of the USS *Canberra*, a much newer ship categorized as a littoral combat ship. The *Independence*-class LCS was outfitted with a special minesweeping package and had enough defensive firepower to handle almost any enemy encounter.

Jansen grimaced as he compared his decades-old wood-constructed warship to the latest minesweeping technology. This new version was the exact type of ship that sentenced his ride to the boneyard after his tour in the Middle East concluded. The *Canberra* had the latest technology and specialized equipment for mine countermeasures operations. Made of aluminum and steel, the LCS had sharply angled specialized hulls, sonar systems, remotely operated vehicles, and other tools specifically designed to detect and neutralize mines in littoral waters. It even had its own air force with two Sikorsky MH-60R Seahawk helicopters.

For added security after what had happened to the *Ever Heart*, TF-70 had assigned the Arleigh Burke-class guided-missile destroyer USS *Rafael Peralta*, call sign RP-1, near his area of operation as an umbrella of protection for any incoming missiles. Life was good, thought Jansen, because his near sinking a few days ago while acting CO of his first ship had given him a glimpse of his abilities as commander of a naval vessel. He liked how it had gone, giving him much-needed confidence. Today, he had tactical command lead for the entire operation with TACON over *Canberra* and its helos.

He keyed his secure VHF radio. "*Canberra*, MCM *Chief*. We are heading back on sector two-niner-three and employing sonar sweep. Say your route."

"MCM *Chief*, *Canberra*. We are doing the same in adjoining sector two-niner-four. Will keep you advised."

"MCM *Chief*, Romeo 11," came a call from an airborne helo. "We're working out front and will keep you informed."

"Romeo 11, roger that," replied Jansen. He switched to internal comms. "Sonar, bring me up to date."

"Sonar here, sir. SAS is running now. We are gathering raw ping data along our current trajectory." There was a pause, and Jansen knew his sonar technician would run the synthetic aperture sonar's raw data through automated target recognition. "Captain, ATR has identified the mine as a Manta."

"Roger that, Sonar," said Jansen. Even though he knew it was being done, he felt more comfortable by ordering it anyway: "Mark the coordinates as we finish our run."

"Yes, Sir."

Jansen liked the job Sonar was doing. The most popular mine in Iran's arsenal and the most widely used mine across the globe, the Italian-made MN103 Manta, was challenging to detect. Unlike its predecessor, which was round with ugly spikes protruding from it, this mine was either cylindrical or spherical with a smooth outer casing and miniature protruding antennas designed to detect the magnetic or acoustic signatures of passing ships or submarines. Once identified, the victim would have problems surviving the blast, and Jansen was not about to let that happen. His Dutch trait of quality over quantity had made him move slowly through the search area to reduce the chances of missing a mine.

Jansen immediately notified fleet HQ and *Canberra*. While clearing their sectors, the two ships had identified five mines.

"Romeo 11, MCM *Chief.* I sent you coordinates for five mines. We're continuing to our next sector. Commence neutralizing mines."

"MCM *Chief*, Romeo 11. Commencing now. We will hit the furthest mine first and work toward your direction." Jansen was getting into a command groove and liked it.

Chapter 26

Sikorsky MH-60R Seahawk
Gulf of Oman

Lieutenant Anne Hawthorne loved this part of her job. She openly admitted that she enjoyed blowing things up—submarines, mines, whatever—the entire experience was so invigorating. She guessed it started when she was the local self-described tomboy growing up in Houlton, Maine, a town of six thousand and an easy 5K run to the Canadian border. While some youngsters blew things up on July 4th, she carefully guarded her stockpile of M-80s and other assorted fireworks so they could be used year-round.

As an only child, the blond with short, curly hair and piercing blue eyes loved to play with the boys. She never gave it much thought; it was more fun than hanging with some of her girlfriends, who preferred playing dress-up with their dolls. No, she chose to demolish things.

While attending the University of Maine's ROTC program, she wanted to fly helicopters—not fighters or any other aircraft, but helicopters. She didn't know why; she just wanted to do it.

Now a six-year veteran helo pilot from *Canberra,* she was flying an MH-60R Seahawk and getting ready to do her thing—blowing up mines.

"L-T," came the calm voice of her sensor operator, Petty Officer Third Class Sean Warner, the Tactical Helicopter Aircrewman. "The launch and handling system is ready."

"Roger, SO. Launch when ready," said Hawthorne.

As the SO lowered the LHS, Hawthorne kept the aircraft stable. After the LHS entered the sea, Warner observed his sonar screen and guided the highly maneuverable vehicle toward target alpha. At the same time, Hawthorne banked her Seahawk away from the area.

"Target acquired," said Warner. "Ready to fire."

"Fire," came the instant reply from Hawthorne.

Immediately, an armor-piercing warhead left the LHS, and seconds later, a colossal explosion forced the sea upward in a vast, foamy, and watery display of US naval firepower.

Just as the water was falling back to the sea, the proverbial shit hit the fan with one radio call on the operational net. "MCM *Chief,* RP-1. Six incoming missiles identified as Iranian Nasr-1 anti-ship cruise missiles."

Chapter 27

EMBASSY OF SWITZERLAND

Tehran, Iran

Seated in an office in the corner of the Embassy of Switzerland building, smack in the middle of Tehran, dual US and Switzerland citizen Dallas Steele was holding down the fort. He was thinking he should count his blessings that this job had been open when his Swiss wife had been assigned to her post in the embassy. Then the phone rang. "Shit, howdy, something to do this week," the big man muttered. He picked up the receiver and said as nicely as possible, "Foreign Interests Section, how may I help you?"

There was a moment of silence.

"Listen carefully," said a man with an accent. "I will only say this once."

Steele pushed the phone tighter against his ear.

"They will be moving a nuke from Natanz any day."

There was a click, then a dial tone.

Steele sat frozen for a moment, carefully playing back the message in his head to ensure he got it right. Shit, he thought. Moving a nuke, that's what the man had said. His exact words were that they would be moving a nuke from Natanz any day—hot damn.

Steele was on the move. He wound through the embassy until he got to the interior room set aside for secure communications with the US. He made the required calls and gave the appropriate passwords to indicate who to talk to and how fast. Within fifteen minutes, he had a secure line with Chargé d'Affaires William Aldridge.

"What the hell are you doing, Dallas?"

"Sorry, Bill, but this is big. I just hung up with a male, most likely Iranian, who told me in accented English that the Iranians will be moving a nuke from the Natanz Enrichment Complex any day."

"What?" is all Aldridge could manage to say. "Are you sure you got this right?"

Steele took a moment to control his emotions. "Yes, Bill. His exact words were, 'Listen carefully. I will only say this once. They will be moving a nuke from Natanz any day.' Then the dude hung up."

"One more time, Dallas. Are you absolutely sure that was the exact conversation?"

Again, Steele reined in his emotions before saying, "Yes, Bill, that's it exactly."

"Okay, get back to the office and see if the man calls back. I'll run this up the chain and have one of our Swiss friends come get you if I need to talk to you on a secure line again." Aldridge hung up.

Back in DC, Aldridge immediately picked up the secure telephone line to his Department of State contact, James Pembroke, the Assistant Secretary for Near Eastern Affairs.

"Pembroke here, the line is secure. Is that you, Bill?"

"It is, and I have some urgent intelligence—it's big."

"Go ahead, Bill."

"Less than a half hour ago, Dallas Steele, a CIA operative in Iran, got a call from someone he said sounded like an Iranian. Here is precisely what he said." Aldridge repeated the one-sided conversation.

"Holy shit, that is big," said Pembroke. "What's your take on this?"

"It sounds legit. I'm also considering how and why this might be a setup, but I need more time. I wanted you to know so you can take it from here."

"Nice job, Bill. I'll be in touch. Keep me posted on any developments." The line went silent.

In his office, Pembroke pressed the secure hotline button for his boss, Sam Quinlan, the Under Secretary for Political Affairs. On the first ring, he got an answer: "Secretary's office, who's calling, please?"

"This is James Pembroke. I have an urgent situation for Quinlan."

"I'm sorry, sir, but the secretary is out of the office. Stand by, and I will attempt to get him on the line."

Pembroke was put on hold. At least they didn't play any damn elevator music, he thought. His right leg was nervously bouncing. He made it stop when he heard Quinlan's familiar voice.

"James, Mary said this was an urgent situation. I confirm the line shows secure. Tell me what you have."

After also confirming the line showed secure on his end, Pembroke repeated what Aldridge had told him and the caller's exact words.

"Got it, James. Let me talk with Brad and brief the president on what we have. I want you to brainstorm with your people and put together a brief on your interpretation of the intelligence."

"Yes, sir, I'm on it now." He heard a click, and the phone's digital screen showed no connection.

After he talked to his people and his bosses, Quinlan and the rest of the State Department's higher officials thought this bit of information changed everything, and by everything, that meant the entire world order. Iran in possession of a nuclear bomb—Quinlan shook his head. He didn't want to believe it, but did.

Chapter 28

THE WHITE HOUSE
Washington, DC

Sitting in the Oval Office, the president discerned that whatever this emergency was, it must be critical because his secretary had canceled two afternoon appointments so the Secretary of State could talk with him. With a war with Iran imminent, Taylor had no free time. Sipping on an iced tea with his feet momentarily propped on the Resolute Desk, the president was grabbing a moment of solitude and rest, that is until his secretary announced he had visitors.

"Give me a moment, then send them in."

After slipping his shoes back on, he grabbed his iced tea and sat in a leather chair by the fireplace, at the head of two white couches.

Just as he did so, SecState Brad Kelly, SecDef George Mitchell, and Chief of Staff Logan Wright entered the room and approached the two couches. When they sat down, the Seymour tall case clock rang its loud bell four times to tell those who were always in a hurry that it was 4 p.m. The president checked his watch to see how the two-hundred-year-old clock was doing. It was perfect, as always.

"What emergency do we have now, gentlemen?" said the leader of the free world, in a tone that announced this wasn't his first rodeo.

"Mr. President," said SecState, "approximately two hours ago, we received intelligence that Iran has a nuclear weapon and is getting ready to move it." Kelly gave him all the information he had and how it was received.

As everyone in the room fully understood, the president was skeptical of uncorroborated intelligence. "What's your take? It could be a crank call to make us respond in a way we wouldn't have done before the call. It could even be an Israeli who wants us to do their dirty work for them. Have we thought of these scenarios?"

"Sir," said Kelly, "the CIA agent who is a plant in the Swiss Embassy took the call. He's a paramilitary operations officer, has an immaculate record as a PMO, and is a man, I'm told, who can be trusted with his judgment in a situation like this. He recognized the caller's accent as Iranian. And he felt like the concise, one-way conversation was legit."

The SecState paused to gauge the president's reaction, and the president said, "Go on, Brad."

"In the short time we've had to run the info by our intelligence, the initial response is that we must follow up on this. The balance of power in the Middle East and the world could be altered forever if we do nothing and they have nukes. Iran with a nuclear weapon is an alarming thought."

Looking at his SecDef, the president said, "George?"

"Sir, we have assets that could monitor the area around the Natanz Enrichment Complex. Additionally, we can redirect some of our satellites to monitor the area and provide real-time intelligence. I recommend we proceed immediately on this."

"Mr. President, if I may," said Taylor's chief of staff and closest friend for most of his adult life. "We can't gamble on this and be wrong. If they do have a nuclear warhead ready to go, they have to bring it to the surface, and that's when we strike. I also believe we need to level the complex and make constructing more nuclear bombs impossible for the foreseeable future."

"Okay," said the president, "I want you to develop a plan to monitor the Natanz complex and prevent anything that looks like it could be a nuke from being taken out. Whatever you need, I will make it happen. Any questions?" No one said anything. "Okay, let's do this."

Chapter 29

TRANSIENT BILLETING
Al Udeid Air Base, Qatar

Stuck at Al Udeid Air Base, the eleven special forces men in Captain Roger Ashburger's ODA felt like bastard children. They hadn't received a peep about their specific duties even though they had been doing nothing but fast-roping from Black Hawk helicopters. They were all antsy.

An hour after returning to their quarters, while the helicopter pilots refueled their aircraft and their stomachs, an out-of-breath airman came by and told Captain Ashburger he was wanted at SOCCENT headquarters ASAP.

Ashburger and his second in command, Chief Warrant Officer 2 Dwight Riley, hauled it to HQ. Looking like they had just played a game of grab-ass in the dirt, they entered the spit-and-polish Special Operations Command Central's forward HQ building. Both men sported beards that looked like they hadn't been trimmed in months. But if one looked into their eyes, one would see nothing but confidence and determination that they were the best—for any assignment.

The two Green Berets were escorted into the commander's office and told to take a seat. They exchanged a WTF look before sitting down. Not long after their butts hit the chairs, a man entered from a side door. Seeing a star on his uniform, both operators jumped up from their seats and stood at attention.

"As you were," said Brigadier General Thomas Worthington. "I'll cut right to the chase since I'm as busy as a one-legged man in a butt-kicking contest. Get my drift?"

"Yes, Sir," they replied in unison.

"What I'm about to tell you has come from the highest levels in our government and must be treated as such. It's need-to-know and, of course, top secret."

Ashburger and Riley nodded their heads, both wondering what was about to go down.

The general continued, "We have solid intel that Iran is now in possession of a nuclear warhead stored at the Natanz Enrichment Complex in central Iran and that the nuke will be moved shortly. Your assignment is to team up with a CIA PMO who is currently in Tehran, to get to the Natanz complex and to stop the nuclear warhead from getting installed onto a delivery system. We don't know what kind of system will be used, but we do know that the warhead has to come up from underground to be installed on the delivery system, and that's where your team comes in."

The two operators glanced at each other while the general briefly paused.

"As we're talking," Worthington said, "my planners are working up a plan to get everyone in safely. I need your team to be ready to move in twelve hours. All future communication between us will be through secure comms. I know you have questions, but get moving, and we'll handle them as they arise. Let's make sure those SOBs don't join the nuke club."

The general turned and went back through the same door. Ashburger and Riley quickly and silently left the office, contemplating the complexity and importance of their assigned mission. They knew their success would have a direct impact not only on the upcoming conflict but also on the world's future. Once outside the SOCCENT HQ building, they sprinted back to their team.

Chapter 30

SU-35 FLANKER-E FLIGHT
Southwestern Iran

Flying toward the Arabian Sea, Major Arash Zamani recalled how he had always fought hard to get ahead. A poor boy from the farmlands near the Caspian Sea, he was now at the pinnacle of his career. As an Iranian fighter pilot, he had been flying antiquated jets that were mostly in museums in other countries around the world and definitely not flying missions. But thanks to the war in Ukraine, Russia needed drones, missiles, and other assorted weapons, and Iran supplied them with what they needed, even constructing a factory in Russia's Tatarstan region to build the highly effective Shahed-136 drone. As the war ground on, Iran sent more and more weapons. Russia was appreciative, and even though they had earmarked twenty-four Su-35 Flanker-Es for Egypt, Russia sold them to Iran instead. The General of the Air Force then selected forty Mikoyan MiG-29 Fulcrum pilots and sent them to Russia for Su-35 training. Zamani was one of those pilots. Upon their return, they and the valuable aircraft had been sequestered underground at Eagle 44 base, away from the spying eyes of Iran's numerous enemies.

During the Russian training, Major Zamani had learned everything there was to know about the Su-35, starting with its thrust-vectoring engines that provided excellent maneuverability and the ability to gain superiority over air targets. It could carry a wide assortment of Russian missiles and had an Irbis-E passive electronically scanned array radar. The PESA could track multiple targets at once.

But the Flanker-E wasn't just an air-to-air fighter that could use a range of air-to-ground missiles and guided bombs. Zamani was now the pilot of a state-of-the-art fourth-generation frontline fighter with advanced avionics and an electro-optical targeting system. He knew rumors were circulating around the world that Iran had Su-35s, but no proof had surfaced to back those rumors up. Operational missions and training were carefully conducted at night to keep it that way.

In the last few days, orders had come for increased preparation as war with the US seemed inevitable after the attack on Independence Hall. Major Zamani had put together a mission to attack America's F-18s that were flying patrol close to Iran's coastline.

Flying over southwestern Iran on that precise mission, Zamani, with a call sign Simorgh 15, was the lead of a flight of two Su-35s, and his wingman had the call sign Simorgh 16. He had chosen "Simorgh" because, throughout his life, he respected the mythical bird from Persian mythology. It represented traits important to him: wisdom, strength, and protection. Every day he flew the Su-35, he rapidly became more efficient and effective in using all the aircraft's tools. He was now ready to bring the battle to his enemy.

His fighter's PESA, which could detect and track aerial targets up to 400 kilometers away, didn't let him down. He got a warning that an American E-2 Hawkeye was within range.

E-2D ADVANCED HAWKEYE
Arabian Sea

Sitting in the left seat of her E-2D while flying at 25,000 feet, Lieutenant Commander Sarah "Danger" Freeman was happy to be doing her thing for the US Navy—my gosh, how she loved to fly. The only thing she loved more was her fighter-pilot husband. She supposed a lot of love was going on in her life. But her happy thoughts quickly vanished when her radio operator called out.

"Danger, I have two Su-35s in Iranian airspace. IFF identifies them as hostile."

"Get the word out, RO."

The RO identified the closest friendlies, a flight of two F/A-18Es. "Bonzo 11, Hawker 11. We have two bandits, Su-35s, 300 miles at your two o'clock, heading southwest, 30,000 feet at 500. They are in Iranian airspace."

Efficiently, Freeman turned the aircraft to optimize both the radar and her positioning in relation to the bandits.

"Hawker 11, Bonzo 11. Advise on bandit radar type." The F-18 flight leader understood that the Su-35 could be using either its search, tracking, or, most importantly, its targeting radar. The two Super Hornets didn't have the bandits on their radar yet. How the RO answered was critical to what happened next. The answer came quickly.

"Bonzo 11, search only." The RO knew he had made a mistake by not including that info in his first transmission. Still learning. Freeman noted the RO's error and would talk to the young man when they were back on the *Reagan.*

F-18 flight lead Captain Alan "Roughhouse" Northcutt switched to intercoms. "Bonzo 12, CS now."

Reacting to the combat spread call, both fighters immediately increased their lateral separation to one mile. They offset their altitudes slightly, allowing each the ability to maneuver freely so one missile couldn't take them both out. This also maximized their radar coverage by extending and overlapping the radar fields in their designated sectors.

Major Zamani knew his PESA radar, in a head-on aspect, would detect something more than just one American E-2 within the range of 400 kilometers. Just then, ground control lit up their radios.

"Simorgh 15, Radar Station Alpha. We have two bandits at your five o'clock, 50 miles from your position, bearing two-one-five. Contacts are American F-18s outside our airspace."

The Iranian command center quickly jumped in, "Radar Station Alpha, CC. Confirm the identification of the contacts as F-18 Hornets. Prepare to track and monitor their movements closely. Alert all relevant air defense units."

The Alpha radio operator's voice broke with a slight tremor, "Confirmed, Command. Contacts are positively identified as F-18s. Tracking and monitoring have been initiated. Air defense units are alerted."

Zamani toggled his radio. "CC, Simorgh 15. We have visual on two American F-18s, bearing two-three-zero, altitude 20,000 feet. No targeting radar. Request ROE."

"Simorgh 15, this is CC. Maintain current course and altitude. Do not engage unless the F-18s turn on their targeting radar. Report any changes in their movements immediately."

Zamani answered right back, "Copy, CC. They are maintaining course and altitude and using search-only radar." Using his intercoms, Zamani told his wingman it was time to head home.

After the two Iranian pilots turned their jets inland, the F-18s turned back toward the *Reagan*. Both sets of fighter pilots knew there would be a lot to talk about, especially the F-18 pilots. Now they knew that Iran possessed at least two Su-35s, aircraft that were a serious threat to all American aircraft. US tactics were about to be altered.

Chapter 31

USS FORD

Arabian Sea

After getting everything set up as instructed by the most attractive woman he'd ever met, Seaman Albert Richards tested his personal Wi-Fi system on his laptop. The pimple-faced culinary specialist saw Google come up, and as he always did when he tested for the internet, he typed "cat" in the search engine. It wasn't because he loved cats—he didn't—but because it was something he always did. Immediately, pictures of cats dotted his screen. Perfect.

With the closest sailor sleeping three bunks away, Richards put in his earbuds and pulled up his favorite video-calling app. Within seconds, Aisha appeared wearing see-through pajamas. His jaw dropped just as Aisha's voice came online.

"My, don't we look surprised," she said with a sexy smile. "I'm so happy to see everything worked. Were there any problems?"

Stumbling over his words, he whispered, "Uh, yes, I mean no, everything went as you said it would. I have to be quiet so as not to wake anyone up."

"Sure, honey, I get it. Tell me about your day." That began what would be a thirty-minute chat. Albert hung on her every word as he stared at her perfectly formed breasts. What he didn't know about those stunning boobs was that the owner was an Iranian MOIS agent who specialized in intelligence gathering, specifically the honey trap. The highly trained spy skillfully leveraged her charm and charisma to win over her targets quickly. She effortlessly made her marks feel at ease, allowing her to gather the desired intelligence smoothly, often obtaining crucial information during intimate moments.

How she got where she was as a twenty-three-year-old operator was anything but conventional. Her mom was a whore who brought home different men for a week or two before moving on to the next sucker. Some of the assholes raped Aisha while her mom barely put up a fuss, especially when she was drunk—which was often. Consequently, Aisha learned how to fight back from a street friend who claimed to have once been a mixed martial arts champion.

After running away from home and hustling on the streets of Tehran, she was surviving, but nothing more. MOIS agents were working those same streets, but for different reasons. During some of their operations, she would catch their watchful eyes. They saw potential in the blossoming young beauty when others saw failure. Aisha didn't give a fuck what anyone thought. She was surviving day to day.

Picked up one day by MOIS, Aisha fought back and was surprised when a couple of them kicked her ass good. No one had ever done that to her. But she began to hear promises of protection and finding purpose in her life by serving a cause greater than herself. She listened, and it wasn't long before she was hired and started her long, intense training to become a MOIS operator. She loved it from the beginning, and they loved her. Starting operations when she was nineteen, she began proving herself in mission after mission.

Needing more intelligence on the infidels who threatened their country, MOIS assigned her to work the bar in Bahrain, which American sailors always frequented when making port calls. It was there that she hustled Albert Richards of the United States Navy, who served aboard one of the foremost ships in the world, the USS *Ford* aircraft carrier.

Chapter 32

USS FORD
Arabian Sea

The vast expanse of the Arabian Sea shimmered in the moonlight as the aircraft carrier USS *Ford* sliced through calm waters. If only the ship's Combat Information Center had windows, then Lieutenant Pavati Talas would have been able to see the picture-perfect sight. However, located within *Ford*'s massive superstructure, the cryptologic warfare officer from the Hopi tribe was working the CIC's midwatch as the electronic warfare officer. She was too busy to look outside anyway as she watched multiple monitors, each displaying data streams and complex graphs. Inside the cold, dark room, the servers' constant hum, the technicians' soft voices, and innumerable keyboard clicks were almost mesmerizing. This was her world, and she loved every moment of being in it.

Talas was a ROTC graduate of Northern Arizona University in Flagstaff, Arizona. Coming from a landlocked state, she had been asked hundreds of times why she chose the US Navy. To her, it was simple: because she could. The five-foot-two woman with long black hair and penetrating golden-brown eyes loved challenging herself by doing things she had never done before. Besides, the idea of getting off the rez and sailing around the world appealed to her.

She had another reason. Her great-grandfather was a code talker during World War II. As Talas grew up in the high desert, she was told how he and other members of the Hopi tribe played a crucial role by using their indigenous language to create virtually indecipherable messages broadcast over radio waves. She loved those stories and was proud of him, so Talas had decided on the Navy and to become a modern version of a code talker by majoring in cybersecurity. She was a natural.

Over the years, Talas had become practiced at sensing anomalies in the digital realm. But the Navy still had its old way of doing things. Many times in her early career, she'd had to fight the ingrained "range of rings" mindset, which had dominated virtually every daily operational intelligence brief given to Navy commanders since before anyone could remember. Every intel officer was required to memorize the ranges of adversary sensors and weapons and the endurance and speeds of enemy naval platforms. Consequently, even the most junior officer could readily draw circles of death on a chart to create a picture of overlapping rings. The doctrine was simple: Inside a circle was danger, and outside a circle was safety. However, cyber warfare threats operate irrespective of geography and increase in risk over time. They were still not being taken as seriously as they should by most commanders, logisticians, and operational planners because cyber threats weren't kinetic. Leaders didn't get it that the circle of death for a cyber threat was the entire globe. Only the forward-thinking commanders adjusted their mindset regarding the range of rings appropriately.

Even though command's interest in cyber warfare had developed slowly, she never let her guard down, constantly scanning her systems during every watch. Most in her unit didn't have the motivation and would quickly move on, but Talas thought it essential and stuck with it. She was pure concentration.

Just then, something caught her eye. She had seen it earlier—now, it was back. SYN scans tapped the network like faint knocks at the door—subtle, probing. She sensed it immediately, recognizing the pattern. The Iranians were in a reconnaissance phase, testing for vulnerabilities and checking if the *Ford* had any open ports as part of a broader TCP scan. The ship's advanced defense systems detected the faint, suspicious signal. It was barely more than a digital whisper amid the routine cyber traffic, but it didn't belong.

"Chief, are you seeing this?" she asked her cryptologic technician, her voice low and concerned.

"Seeing what, Ma'am?" Chief Petty Officer Carlos Sanchez said while glancing at the screens.

"Run a deep packet inspection on this data stream," Talas ordered, pointing to a specific segment on her middle screen. "I need to know if we're dealing with a false positive or something more malicious.

A few others in the CIC with less work going on drifted over to see what the excitement was.

An experienced technician, Sanchez began typing furiously, each keystroke echoing through the room.

Moments later, Sanchez looked up, his expression serious. "Ma'am, it's confirmed. We've got a potential intrusion attempt occurring. The signature matches known Iranian cyber tactics. I believe this is the start of a coordinated cyberattack."

Talas's mind was racing. She knew the implications of a successful cyberattack on the *Ford* could be devastating, potentially crippling the carrier's operational capabilities and leaving it vulnerable. She had to act quickly.

"Mustang, Guardian," Talas called to the CIC's senior watch officer, "we have an ongoing credible Iranian cyberattack. Suggest GQ immediately."

The tactical action officer knew Talas, her duties, and his procedures. He was a good leader, so he didn't hesitate. Using the 1MC public address circuit, he said, "This is the TAO. General Quarters. General Quarters. All hands man your battle stations. Set material condition Zebra throughout the ship. This is not a drill. Captain to CIC."

Throughout the ship, alarms blared and echoed through the corridors, causing sailors to jump from their racks or wherever they were and to proceed to their assigned battle stations on the double.

Within seconds, Captain Otis Albright was on the line with the TAO, who patched Talas into the call. "Lieutenant, what do you have," said the ship's captain, calmly but authoritatively.

"Sir, we've detected a cyber intrusion attempt originating from Iran," Talas said. "It appears to be targeting our navigation and weapons systems. We're moving to full cyber defense protocols."

"Understood. Do whatever it takes to secure our systems. Keep me updated." The captain hung up.

Turning to her growing team, Talas ordered, "Activate the cyber defense response team. Isolate critical systems and initiate countermeasures. I want a full diagnostic sweep of all networks."

As she spoke, the CIC buzzed with heightened activity as additional sailors took their seats or stood near their assigned workstations. Elsewhere, most sailors donned personal protective equipment appropriate to their assigned battle station. The most powerful and technologically advanced ship in the world was preparing for battle and survival should a concentrated kinetic attack commence while the crew was distracted by the ongoing cyberattack.

Inside the CIC, every workstation was staffed. As Talas gave orders, they were instantly inputted. The firewall was reinforced, encryption protocols were updated, and decoy systems were deployed to confuse the incoming malware intruders.

As the minutes ticked by, the extent of the cyberattack was narrowed down. Talas saw the Iranian hackers attempting to breach the *Ford*'s navigational controls and disrupt communication links with the fleet. She used protocols developed and tested for just such an attack.

"Chief," said Talas, "deploy the intrusion detection algorithms. Let's track their digital footprint and counteract their moves."

Like playing some crazed video game, but all very real, Talas monitored her screens and the digital battle unfolding before her. She watched as the intruders' red lines attempted to penetrate deeper into the ship's network. They, in turn, were being fought with blue lines representing the ship's defenses that blocked their every move.

Sanchez briefly looked up from his screen. "We're holding them off, Ma'am. These hackers are persistent, but our countermeasures are effective. They're attempting to exploit a vulnerability that existed in the previous version of our software modules. Our updated version has already closed that gap and is performing flawlessly.."

Talas didn't smile or show emotion as she focused on staying one step ahead of the Iranians. An idea came to her. "Chief, ensure that the older vulnerability is patched across all systems, even if it's no longer active. Then, deploy our honeypot. I want to lure them into a controlled environment where we can monitor their techniques and gather intel.

As the team worked tirelessly, the electronic battle began to turn in favor of the *Ford*. The honeypot tripwires successfully diverted the intruders from the real network, allowing Talas's team to analyze their methods and further fortify the ship's defenses.

After an intense hour, the intrusion attempts started to wane. The Iranian hackers, perhaps realizing they were getting their butts kicked, began pulling back.

Talas reasoned that this skirmish had meaning even though no missiles flew and no shots were fired. Perhaps it had just been a test so the enemy could gauge their capabilities to counter a much larger attack. Or maybe it was the modern start of the shooting war Talas knew would be coming.

Chapter 33

EMBASSY OF SWITZERLAND

Tehran, Iran

Things were moving at hypersonic speed in the office of the Foreign Interests Section at the Embassy of Switzerland. With the possibility of Iran moving a nuclear warhead from its home at the Natanz Enrichment Complex to an undisclosed missile launching site, there was much to do. Still, the site's location was anybody's guess. To CIA agent Dallas Steele, the where didn't matter much because he had to stop it before it left Natanz.

Steele had heard rumblings that the call could have been from an Israeli wanting the US to do their dirty work by giving a false lead, which was possible. But what if the call was legit? There was no way anyone could write this one off and go about their business. No, he and everyone in the loop had reacted exactly as they should have.

Through established channels, Steele had been told to contact an A-Team posthaste to work out an ops plan with contingencies, and lots of them. Nothing was going to be left to chance. Using secure comms, he was on the line with Captain Roger Ashburger, whom Steele knew from operations in Syria. There were no pleasantries since both men knew the critical nature of the mission and understood they had little time to make it work.

Steele briefed Ashburger on their current situation. "Until we have eyes-on, I've ordered satellite coverage for both real-time feed and periodic high-resolution imagery."

"Sounds good," said Ashburger. "How soon until we get feet on the ground?"

"That's a sticking point," said Steele. "From what I've been briefed, we have forty-eight hours until shit happens, and I'm told that one of the initial targets will be Natanz. Assets will use some of the big boys in our arsenal, and all indications put us on hold until the dust settles. Let's both get our rides set up for the drop point. I'm guaranteed that some aerial assets will stay on station until we arrive. This mission has the highest priority from upstairs, so we can have whatever we need. I'll be in touch, and let's hope the initial bombing gets us some results. Either way, it doesn't matter because we'll be on site soon. Later." Steele hung up. Boy, how he hated waiting, but that was the play for now.

NORTHROP GRUMMAN B-2 SPIRIT
Over the Indian Ocean

When you flew a B-2, you had lots of time to daydream since most flights lasted over twenty hours. Today was no exception. Lieutenant Colonel Dakota "Cowboy" Remy was one of only seventy-two people in the United States Air Force still flying the B-2. When he considered there were over 320,000 active-duty members, that number of pilots was as small as a flea on a horse's ass, the cowboy from Texas thought.

He knew the lights were beginning to flicker on his career. He was a veteran of everything related to his darling, as he affectionately called his aircraft. The B-2 had been around for thirty-six years, and he'd been flying it for half of those years. Hell, he'd even flown his darling on numerous missions in the Chinese War five years back.

Like the B-2 he flew, he was becoming outdated. By choice, he was the oldest mission commander in the USAF since he hated anything like a desk. He'd tried it back at the Operations Group in the 131st Bomb Wing of the Missouri Air National Guard, but he'd take a cockpit seat that made his ass go numb over a cushioned executive chair behind a cherry wood desk any day. He just wasn't meant to fly a desk.

"Cowboy," said his young copilot, Captain George Gold, an Air Force Academy grad and a proven city slicker, "we're 200 miles out from Diego Garcia."

"George, I can still read my gauges, but thank you."

"Sir, you told me to notify you when we were 200 miles out because you wanted to take us in."

"Damn, that's right. My bad. Thanks, George."

No longer lost in his thoughts, Cowboy returned to the reality of leading a flight of six B-2s over the Indian Ocean. They were going to the place he flew out of when bombing the shit out of China. Now it seemed his target would be Iran. It was fine with him because he loved dropping bombs on the enemies of his country, though of late, it seemed like a line was forming to see who would be next. He guessed that the bullies always came calling when you were the big kid on the block.

Fine, you assholes, he thought. Bring it on, because this old man is more than ready.

"I got the aircraft, George."

Chapter 35

TOWER 22

Rukban, Jordan

Situated near the demilitarized zone between Jordan and Syria and along a brown sandy berm, Tower 22 marked the DMZ's southern edge. One positive about being isolated in open terrain was that it provided a great field of fire.

Tower 22 was home to 350 Army and Air Force personnel. Established in 2015 to fight ISIS, its mission had transformed so it was now more of an intelligence base specializing in drone operations. Its secondary mission was to strike Iran-backed militia groups in the region, of which there were many.

Private Adam Dankworth, from the Bronx in New York, couldn't care less about the hellhole called Tower 22. There was no official draft in the US, but Dankworth would disagree. After numerous bullshit misdemeanor arrests, a prick of a judge had suggested to Dankworth that perhaps he should look at joining the Army because doing so would provide much better scenery than the jail cell he was quickly heading for. And fuckin' A, that sure as hell made sense. He only hoped the Army would take him.

The key to his getting into the Army, he quickly discovered, was getting a waiver because of his three bullshit arrests, even though they were non-drug. Then the brass would make a call, possibly allowing them to boss him around for the next eight years. Let me see, he thought, prison guards versus Army sergeants, and the choice was easy.

He didn't get far with the bureaucratic BS throughout the enlistment process. Then he struck on the idea of asking the judge who started everything to write a letter. It took two days of sitting outside the judge's office, with security watching his every move, before he got in—accompanied by a marshal wearing a gun.

"So, Mr. Dankworth," said the judge, "what brings you back to see me? I hope it isn't another arrest."

"Fuck no—I mean, no, Your Honor. I took your advice, and I'm trying to join the Army. It seems they don't care much for pricks like me who've been arrested. I told them they were all bullshit arrests…"

"What?" said the judge. "Bullshit? If they were bullshit, you wouldn't have come before me. Listen, I managed to see you all three times you were arrested, and for whatever reason, I see some good in you. You just need to get out of the Bronx. Tell you what—I'll write a letter right now that you can take to the Army. If that doesn't work, let me know.

Somehow, kid, I like you and hope this works out for you. Now, let me get back to work."

To the surprise of Dankworth, the letter worked so well that he found himself in this shithole right out of combat infantry school. No matter, he kept telling himself. It was a hell of a lot better than a ten-by-ten jail cell.

"Okay, mount up," shouted Staff Sergeant Roland Jackson. "Another beautiful day awaits us."

With his locked and loaded M4 carbine, Dankworth got in the back seat of one of two Oshkosh M-ATV mine-resistant ambush-protected all-terrain tactical vehicles. He rode in the MRAP with three other squad members, and Private John "Smitty" Smith was up on the 7.62mm M240 general-purpose machine gun. In an earlier brief, Dankworth was told that today's mission was a security patrol to ensure they had no unwanted company near their exposed base. With shit ramping up after the destruction of Independence Hall, he knew things were getting serious.

As they departed the base, the first light of dawn was beginning to peek over the horizon to cast an orange glow on the desert. Dankworth had to admit it was the prettiest time of day. As they bounced along, Dankworth watched as Jackson, sitting in the front passenger seat, seemed to have his head on swivel as he scanned the area for threats. Dankworth thought that made sense and did the same from his post in the back seat.

After ten minutes, the radio crackled to life. "Alpha Squad, Base Command. Be advised, UAS shows no unusual activity in your AO."

"Copy that," answered Jackson, thankful they had an unmanned aircraft system supporting them.

Soon, the village of Rukban came into view, a village of winding, narrow streets and simple houses made from mud bricks. As they approached, the streets where children usually played were empty. It was early, but even the shops along the main drag were closed.

Pulling into the village center, the two large MRAPs came to a stop. Everyone quickly dismounted, forming a defensive perimeter around the vehicles. All eyes were looking outward. Things didn't seem normal.

Dankworth saw movement at his ten o'clock. "Sarge, movement at my ten."

"Got it," replied Jackson. "Dankworth, come with me." As the two men moved cautiously and tried not to look too threatening, they approached a lone male. Jackson recognized him as the lead village elder, a respected man who could be trusted. All three men placed their hands over their hearts in a respectful greeting.

"As-Salamu Alaikum," the elder said quietly.

"And peace be upon you," said Jackson, extending his hand, which the elder took. Dankworth was getting used to these unhurried greetings. It wasn't like the Bronx, that was for sure. There, "Fuck you—what do you want?" was the standard greeting.

After a moment, the elder said, "Welcome back to our village. How is your family?"

"Thank you. My family is well. I hope your family is in good health, too. We are here on routine patrol to ensure the safety of your village, but we have noticed the streets are very empty. Do you know why?"

The elder thought for a minute, as if deciding whether to share any information, but spoke anyway. "Things have been peaceful, but I must tell you, many strangers have been seen passing through at night. Many carried their weapons in the open." As if anticipating the next question from the Army man, the elder added, "They were traveling southeast." He nodded his head in that direction.

"Thank you, sir, for sharing that information," said Jackson. "How many were there?"

"I saw about twenty-five, but we could hear others outside our village. I heard some engines as they passed."

"Again, thank you. We will monitor the area to ensure your village is safe."

Upon their return to Tower 22, Jackson reported his intel to the base commander, who increased drone surveillance around the base. The immediate results were negative, but the commander knew that could change very quickly. He had just received notice from headquarters that in twenty-four hours, the US would be initiating hostilities against Iran—it seemed there was little time to prepare for war.

Chapter 36

USS Ford

Arabian Sea

Mesmerized by the love of his life, who unbeknownst to him was an Iranian MOIS agent, Seaman Albert Richards had turned his computer into a gateway providing valuable information to the enemy. The thumb drive Aisha had given him was loaded with malware. Topping the list was the Iranian version of Pegasus, set on AutoRun to enable the execution of a malware installer. It was initially designed for cell phones, but Bilal had given her "boyfriend" a version to run on his laptop. After Richards inserted the thumb drive, the exfiltration of location data surreptitiously kicked in every time he connected to the *Ford*'s Wi-Fi.

The program found nearby Wi-Fi networks and, using triangulation, could determine the computer's location and, thus, the *Ford*'s. It used IP geolocation and scanned emails, messages, and anything else that might contain location details or operational information about the ship.

Using encrypted channels to avoid detection, the spyware was set up to periodically send collected data to remote servers controlled by Iran. This was done using obfuscation techniques to appear as legitimate network activity. Little did Richards know, he was risking the lives of five thousand souls to have a relationship with someone he thought was the love of his young life.

Survival for aircraft carriers had much to do with their location. A carrier's mobility and speed made tracking its movement difficult for adversaries. The *Ford* was constantly changing locations, at a speed of 30 knots to evade tracking efforts. In addition, the carrier had the protection of the whole CSG to help conceal its movement and location. The *Ford* also used EMCON. Emissions control severely limited electromagnetic emissions like radar and communications to avoid detection or triangulation of their location. If an enemy fired a missile at the carrier, the *Ford* would be nowhere near where it had been when the missile initially targeted the area. So, an enemy would need constant updates for its missiles to have any chance of destroying the massive carrier—like updates from a transmitter hidden in a locker.

Iran had thought of this and had installed user activity triggers in the malware. It was designed to send data such as *Ford*'s location when specific user actions were performed, like Richards going online to visit with Aisha, which was scheduled to happen shortly.

Chapter 37

USS *Ford*
Arabian Sea

Rear Admiral Marquis Holloway had fought steep odds before, his life defined by beating the probabilities that he would fail. Today was another of those days. He was standing at the head of the table in the flag plot, the dark room dimly lit by the glow of multiple screens displaying tactical maps and intelligence reports.

Surrounding him were *Ford*'s captain and CAG, Mad Dog Johnson; pilots from the 160th Special Operations Aviation Regiment; and SEAL Team 10 platoon leader Lieutenant Commander Ross Carter, a veteran of the raid on Woody Island during the Chinese War.

The admiral got it started. "Some successes are hard-won. But through diligent planning and execution, achieving our goals comes to fruition." After taking a moment to make eye contact with those present, Holloway continued, "We're here today to finalize the operation to take Ahvaz Oil Field from the Iranians. Your input is crucial to ensure we execute the plan flawlessly."

As the meeting progressed, participants received updates, discussed potential challenges, and coordinated their efforts to ensure a unified approach. Mad Dog rubbed his stubble as he considered the tough job his close air support pilots would face to support the SOAR's insertion of the SEALs. He wasn't alone. Carter was thinking the same thing.

"Okay," said Holloway, "if there's no more input, let's get ready. Operation Black Gold commences at 0200 hours. Make it clean and quick, and we'll take control of Iran's largest and most productive oil field." Oooahs went up around the room. They were ready.

Chapter 38

AHVAZ OIL FIELD
Khuzestan Province, Iran

IRGC Major Navid Shadmani had received notice twenty-four hours ago that Iran would commence a war with the American infidels using a surprise attack. He felt that was a brilliant tactic. Why wait to be on the receiving end of an attack when you could deliver the first punch? His troops were trained and ready for an assault he was convinced would be coming, perhaps even before his country fired the first ballistic missile. He had heard that the Boy Scouts in America said to be prepared. That was his motto too. He had inspected the perimeter and felt confident that the mix of walls, barbed wire, and mines would slow any advancing force.

On high alert, he stationed his troops in strategic positions twenty-four hours a day. The major now took his position inside the headquarters to monitor the elaborate system of surveillance cameras, motion detectors, and heat sensors. In the building next to him was a rapid response team equipped with his best firearms, vehicles, and communication gear.

Shadmani had also reminded local civilian authorities of their emergency response commitment. It didn't equate to much, but everybody would count if the field was attacked. The major never left anything to chance.

Chapter 39

USS *Ford*
Persian Gulf

If déjà vu was a thing, Lieutenant Commander Ross Carter had it big time. Standing on his designated spot on the flight deck of the *Ford*, he was next to two Sikorsky MH-60K Black Hawk helicopters operated by members of the 160th SOAR, which was precisely what he had done five years ago when preparing to infiltrate Woody Island with the fifteen other SEALs that made up his platoon. Then, he had been on the USS *New Orleans*—a much smaller vessel, but to him, a flight deck was a flight deck. Most of the faces in his platoon had changed since then, and instead of being one of the boys, he was now the guy making the calls. He thrived in the role. There was something about training as a SEAL that fortified you with confidence you would succeed simply because you knew you had out-trained your enemy.

SEAL Team 10 had worked with the Night Stalkers of the SOAR many times. The all-volunteer aviation regiment was well known amongst the military for handling high-risk missions such as the raid on Osama Bin Laden, Woody Island, and scores of other top-secret missions. They were renowned for their proficiency in flying under cover of darkness to conduct insertion, extraction, and resupply missions for all special operators, not just SEALs.

The pilots started the engines. Carter signaled his team to mount up into the two specially outfitted Black Hawks. Fighting the instinct to duck as they approached the helicopters, the sixteen men of the platoon broke into two landing squads, boarded the helos, and got as comfortable as they could for their two-hundred-mile journey.

Most operators were armed with the brand new SIG Sauer M5 Modular Assault Carbine, a versatile assault rifle good for both close-quarters engagements and long ranges. Two had the Knights Armament MK 11 MOD 0 and Naval Surface Warfare Center MK 13 Mod 7 rifles used for precision shooting and sniper fire. All had the SIG Sauer P226 MK25 pistol on their hip or chest. There were also a couple of guys with the newly fielded SIG Sauer M250 Squad Automatic Weapon for suppressive fire.

Flying in combat formation, just above the swells of the Persian Gulf waters to avoid radar and visual observation, the two helicopters were cruising at 174 mph. The formation allowed them to overlap fields of fire and ensure that if one helo was engaged, the other could immediately respond.

While the highly trained Night Stalker pilots were doing their thing, so was Carter. He went over the details of the mission plan one last time. From satellite surveillance, he knew they would face the best Iran had to offer with the

Islamic Revolutionary Guards Corps. These military professionals would be heavily armed and supported by armor. His platoon's objective was to neutralize all threats and secure the oil field.

"Ten minutes out," the pilot said, his voice crackling in Carter's headset.

"Listen up," Carter yelled over the helicopter's sounds to his men. "We go in fast and hard. The primary objective is to secure the control center and eliminate all hostiles. Questions?" Nobody moved. "Okay, lock and load." Carter and his men efficiently checked their weapons and gear, a ritual as old as warfare. They were ready.

F-35 LIGHTNING II FLIGHT
Skies over Ahvaz Oil Field, Khuzestan Province, Iran

As the Black Hawks approached the landing zone, the desert night was pierced by the roar of powerful jet engines. High above the Ahvaz Oil Field, a pair of F-35s soared through the sky. Lieutenant Commander Jessie Hampton and his wingman, Russ Lockwood, were on high alert and ready to intercept any nosey Iranian aircraft. Their low-probability-of-intercept radars were set to spread-spectrum mode, and the LPIs meticulously scanned for threats from both the ground and the air.

Two EA-18G Growlers flying with their electronic warfare systems activated also supported the mission. The Growlers initiated a blanket of electronic jamming aimed at disrupting enemy radar and communications. With the enemy's electronic eyes and ears effectively shut down, the Growlers launched a volley of AGM-88 high-speed anti-radiation missiles. The HARMs targeted and neutralized surface-to-air missile sites. Explosions lit up the desert. But although the protective SAM sites were being obliterated, Iranian ground forces were still intact.

AHVAZ OIL FIELD PERIMETER
Khuzestan Province, Iran

Watching his monitors in the HQ building, IRGC Major Shadmani felt a touch of pride because he had predicted that the Americans would attempt to take his oil field, and the screens proved he had been right. The speed at which it happened made him take a step back. But even as the first moments of battle quickly unfolded around him, he was prepared for what he knew was coming next—troop-carrying helicopters.

"Team 1 and Team 2," Shadmani called on the radio. "Prepare for incoming helicopters."

"HQ, we are positioned and armed. Waiting for a target."

"Mobile 1, state your location," said Shadmani to the modified infantry fighting vehicle crew.

"HQ, sector Alpha as you directed. Standing by."

The Mobile 1 vehicle was configured with two Toophans, and the crew was ready to fire the wire-guided anti-tank missiles. Shadmani' didn't expect tanks; what mattered was that the crews were trained to use wire-guided warheads that could be controlled until impact to target low-flying and hovering helicopters.

Teams armed with man-portable air defense systems with infrared-guided missiles supported his flanks. These MANPADs were the Chinese QW-1 Vanguard and the reverse-engineered Iranian version, the Misagh-3.

Shadmani liked his odds as he returned to watching his monitors to see the helicopters enter his trap.

SIKORSKY MH-60K BLACK HAWKS
Ahvaz Oil Field, Khuzestan Province, Iran

As the Night Stalkers approached the landing zone, they used electronic countermeasures to jam enemy radar. The pilots also augmented the ECM by using varied flight paths into the LZ. To limit time on site, the SEALs were prepared to fast-rope down from the helicopters. Both helos were close enough to the ground at the LZ to minimize exposure and dust.

"Go, go, go," yelled Carter. Quickly, the ropes were thrown out of each Black Hawk, and sixteen gloved men slid down. As the SEALs' feet hit the ground, each scanned the surrounding area for any immediate threats as they spread out from under the rotors to quickly set up a defensive perimeter.

The first SEAL down saw two bright flashes and keyed his radio: "Two incoming missiles." Everyone scattered from the probable impact zone.

Inside the helicopters, radar warning systems alerted the crews to the missiles. Acting instinctively per their training, both pilots fired chaff and flares. Stalker 12's pilot forced his Black Hawk to the ground in a controlled crash. Stalker 11's pilot went full power and made an immediate hard right. ECM jamming from the Growlers caused one missile to fly over the blades of Stalker 12. At almost the same instant, while turning, Stalker 11 was struck by the remaining upgraded Misagh-3 missile. It struck just below the rotor, and the Black Hawk erupted in a massive fireball. Debris rained down toward the LZ. A part of the rotor struck one operator in the head, killing him instantly. The others had just barely cleared the kill zone.

Overhead, the F-35s' infrared search and track radars picked up the signatures from both missile launch sites. Immediately, the IRST data was pushed to an airborne C2 asset and confirmed missile launch coordinates were sent to the F-35s.

"Jedi 12," said Jesse, using a helmet-mounted display system. "I have visual confirmation of Target Alpha. You take Bravo." Jessie's HMDS showed him the precise location of the infrared signature detected by the AN/AAQ-37 Electro-Optical Distributed Aperture System. When the DAS combined with the Distributed Infrared System, they provided him with an augmented reality overlay for a real-world view of what was happening on the battlefield.

"Two has Bravo," Lockwood responded.

Both stealth fighters positioned themselves to deliver their ordnance. Jessie used his helmet controls to lock on Target Alpha. He selected a Paveway II Plus laser-guided bomb. By looking at his target, Jesse locked the laser onto the site from which a soldier had fired and guided his missile.

At Target Alpha, several Iranian soldiers moved to take cover. Jessie watched them as they ran. In flight, the bomb guidance fins adjusted minutely, steering it toward the laser dot painted on the Iranian soldier's firing position. The bomb's onboard guidance system made a final adjustment as the soldiers continued to run. The man with the shoulder-mounted launcher threw it to the ground, running faster. Just as the launcher hit the ground, a bright flash lit up the sky, momentarily turning night into day. For those on the ground, a powerful shockwave from the 500-pound warhead rippled through the area, killing and wounding several Iranian troops.

Jessie monitored it all on his HMDS and confirmed the strike's success. The data was also sent to all others involved with the strike. Jessie's HMDS highlighted enemy positions and displayed the safest egress route, and he navigated away from possible additional threats. Looking over his shoulder, he saw a bright flash off to his left as his wingman's missile struck Target Bravo, the second Iranian missile team. Payback.

Chapter 40

BATTLE FOR AHVAZ OIL FIELD
Khuzestan Province, Iran

"Command, Alpha 1. Confirm one down and Stalker 11 down. Continuing to target," said team leader Ross Carter on the command net.

After SEAL Alpha Squad quickly loaded the body of their brother onto Stalker 12, the helo took off from where it had landed to avoid a missile. Bravo Squad leader Lieutenant Roscoe Harris knew there couldn't be any survivors in the other Black Hawk, but he sent two from his eight-man squad to check the charred helicopter anyway. No one left behind was more than just a slogan.

"Bravo 1, Bravo 5. No signs of life at Stalker 11. No bodies. It's pretty ugly."

"Copy, Bravo 5. Form up on us, five zero meters, your six."

"Bravo 1, Alpha 1," said Carter, who had led his seven men seventy-five meters to the east, "employ EMCON." Emission control of all electromagnetic emissions, including radio and radar, was critical to keeping a low profile as the squads moved to take over Iran's largest oil field. Carter thought it essential to remind everyone to use their secure encrypted communication system.

"Bravo 1, wilco," replied Harris.

Carter led his squad cautiously off the beaten path, all using their night vision goggles to navigate toward the heart of the oil field and Iran's headquarters.

As they tactically moved along, one of Carter's men whispered, "Ross, any news on our boys from Stalker 11?"

Carter bit his lower lip, drawing blood as he fought back his strong feelings over the loss of the Black Hawk crew. "Roberts, concentrate on the mission. Both pilots are dead. We can grieve later. Now move out."

Not unlike his American counterpart, Major Shadmani had his own casualties and problems. He also didn't dwell on what might have been; he was in the present. His IRGC men were ready for the enemy. Inside his HQ, he studied the feed from his single UA, which provided him with real-time intelligence. Fortunately, he had one of Iran's more sophisticated drones outfitted with infrared and night vision capabilities.

"Teams 1 and 2," Shadmani radioed, "we have eight enemy moving toward HQ in 1's sector 4-alpha. Two, you have seven in your sector 2-bravo. Mobile 1, stand by for any breaches."

Using cover provided by a slight indentation in the desert floor, Team Leader 1 was looking over sector 4-alpha using his night vision goggles. As he eyed the area, he adjusted his Iranian-made DIO KH2002 Khaybar bullpup assault rifle to be better positioned to fire. Any movement, and that enemy would be his.

While moving with his SEAL platoon's alpha squad, Carter heard the distinct whine of a drone, which wasn't good. Whispering into his radio, he said, "To all on the net, we've been made. Platoon, prepare for contact. Air units, stand by for assist."

Both F-35s and the remaining Black Hawk acknowledged. The pilot of Stalker 12 wanted payback so badly he could taste it in his dry mouth.

A few seconds after Carter received the acknowledgments, he spotted someone at his nine o'clock, crouched low and running. He squeezed off several rounds from his M4 and saw the person take a tumble. The return fire was intense. Dirt and rocks began flying through the air as the Iranians' rounds hit close to home. In seconds, bullets and tracer rounds took over the night as the highly trained grunts tried to kill each other.

Seeing the muzzle flashes, Stalker 12's pilot lined up for an attack run. "Alpha 1," he said, "coming in hot. We have your IFF position."

When Carter acknowledged, both pilots could hear the gunfire over the comms. Flying low, the Black Hawk made its run.

"Engage targets," the pilot ordered.

Instantly, the miniguns came to life. Tracer rounds showed the stream of bullets heading to the IRGC position. On the ground, sparks and debris flew through the air as the rounds hit.

Suddenly, the radar warning receiver alarm sounded through the cockpit. The helicopter's computers responded immediately to the RWR by identifying an Iranian mobile missile carrier and letting loose with a salvo of Hydra 70 rockets. As the rockets stormed to their target, the Iranian armored vehicle let loose with one missile. The helo's advanced threat infrared countermeasure system activated, and the pilot made several high-G maneuvers, causing the missile's tracking system to fail. The missile ripped by within feet of them and blew a hole in the desert. Banking back toward its initial target, the Black Hawk again let loose with its miniguns. The muzzle flashes disappeared.

On the ground, Carter and his men flanked the enemy's position. After the helo pulled off, he ordered, "Alpha Squad move in." They secured the sector with little resistance and prepared to move onto the base.

Flying cover over Ahvaz Oil Field with things going sideways on the ground, Jessie knew Iran would be sending reinforcements of some kind. Since they had Russian-built Su-35s, the books said to avoid any engagements within visual range because of the Flanker-E's superior maneuverability, even though his Lightning II had the stealth advantage and sensors to detect the enemy first—an enormous benefit in aerial combat. Jedi flight personnel topped off their fuel tanks and quickly got back on station. It wasn't long before Jessie's radar picked up something.

"Jedi 12, Jedi 11. Two bogeys, ten o'clock, 130 miles out. Switch to combat mode and engage using stealth protocols."

"12, copy that, have them on radar, in stealth mode."

Both were armed with their newly installed AIM-260 Joint Advanced Tactical Missile, the highly sought-after replacements for the decades-old AIM-120. JATM had been around for several years but was just now getting into service thanks to a Department of Defense accelerated production program. As Jessie saw it, there was a problem because the evolving, uncrewed collaborative combat aircraft also used the JATM. But today it was no matter, because six of those puppies were tucked nicely in the belly of his F-35, thanks to the Sidekick adapter that upgraded the standard load of four missiles.

Jessie wanted to use the F-35's superior stealth capability to get closer and reduce the time the Iranian pilots would have to react. But he had to play it cool to stay beyond visual range. His aircraft's advantage was BVR combat.

Hampton got on the radio 100 miles out at 50,000 feet, knowing the higher altitude increased the JATM's range.

"Jedi 12, I have a lock on the port aircraft. You take the one on starboard. Fire two missiles ten seconds apart. On my mark, three—two—one—mark." As he fired his first AIM-260, Jessie yelled, "Fox three!" Ten seconds later, his wingman reported the same.

Both pilots made a high-G crank maneuver by flying perpendicular to their targets, the best strategy to minimize their exposure to enemy radar and missile threats. As they began their defensive maneuvers, both cockpits echoed with the sounds of warning beeps.

In the lead Su-35, Major Arash Zamani, call sign Simorgh 15, had heard of the attack on the oil field and had scrambled with his wingman to investigate and provide aid to the IRGC units fighting off a determined US attack. Nearing the oil field, the Su-35's powerful Irbis-E radar picked up faint signals of approaching threats.

"Unknown aircraft detected, bearing two-seven-zero," Major Zamani relayed to his wingman. "Engage and identify." Seconds later, he added, "Incoming missiles. Fire and take evasive actions now."

Each pilot let loose two Vympel R-27 long-range air-to-air missiles capable of speeds up to Mach 5. They were fire-and-forget missiles with combined inertial and active radar guidance.

Immediately, Zamani went into several high-G turns to break away from the lock of the probable AIM-260, just as his Russian instructors had taught him. He noticed that he had a death grip on the controls and told himself to stay loose. His fingers relaxed on the stick. Zamani didn't mind the adrenaline flowing through his body. He believed it would make him a better pilot during these next few live-or-die moments.

In the cockpit his warning light flashed red, signifying the missile had a lock on his aircraft. Zamani's eyes darted to his HUD, watching the trajectory of the missile closing in.

He instinctively pushed the throttle forward and was immediately rewarded with the feeling of being pushed back into his seat. Throwing the stick from side to side, he felt like the aircraft was on a rail as he made 7, 8, and 9-G turns, firing his countermeasures of chaff and flares as he made each one. He asked Allah to protect him and his aircraft as the turns got tighter and tighter.

Waiting until the last second, Zamani hit his thrust to perform Pugachev's Cobra maneuver, which was some crazy Russian term for a tactic he knew might work. His fighter pitched up sharply and rapidly decelerated, almost to a stall. One minute, he was pulling high-G turns, and the next, he was still and almost falling from the sky. The missile flew by him, and before it could turn to come back, it ran out of fuel and tumbled to the earth. A second missile struck his countermeasures and exploded.

As he searched the skies for his wingman, he saw a blinding flash and a massive ball of flames in the night sky. Pilots had strong bonds, and the sudden loss of a partner was a gut-wrenching feeling. However, as with all highly trained individuals, he remained focused and forced emotion from his mind.

As he made a 7-G turn to come under the protection of his missile defenses closer to his home base, he put out a call. "Command, Simorgh 15. Simorgh 16 is down. Repeat, Simorgh 16 is down, no survivors, returning to base." His eyes blurred with tears as he went to afterburner.

Meanwhile, in his F-35, Jessie thought he would never get used to the sound of another voice in his cockpit as his warning system announced, "Missile launch. R-27 inbound." It repeated the warning several times, and he turned it off when he saw the missile on his HUD. His instincts and training took over as if he were programmed.

He quickly analyzed the missile's speed and trajectory and understood the R-27 was a formidable threat. But his F-35 was equipped with advanced countermeasures to evade such attacks, so Jessie told himself to cut the bullshit and go into full defensive mode to shake this thing.

For a split second, his mind reached back five years ago to when he was in the same situation and was shot down by a Chinese fighter. He had failed then, but he wouldn't today. Jessie released a burst of chaff and flares. He slammed the control stick forward and to the left, forcing an abrupt 7-G turn down toward the desert floor. Out of the corner of his eye, he saw the flares surrounded by the reflective chaff strips to create—he hoped—multiple false targets.

At the peak of the turn, he grunted to force air through his lungs and keep from passing out. All the while, he watched his HUD and saw the missile path following his every move. "Go full throttle," he screamed into his oxygen mask. The F-35 roared as its Pratt & Whitney F135 engine surged with power and increased the aircraft's speed, making it much more difficult for the smart missile to maintain a lock. Jessie knew if he could keep pulling these maneuvers, the sooner the missile would run out of fuel.

While all this was happening, Jessie ensured his electronic warfare suite was initiated, emitting jamming signals to disrupt the missile's radar guidance. It was a lone missile computer versus an aircraft computer with a crafty pilot making it all work.

On his HUD, Jessie saw a break in the topography and a small valley just ahead. He headed for the valley at 1,200 miles per hour. In training, they called it terrain masking; but right then, he called it survival. As the missile proximity warning grew more urgent, Jessie performed a final series of radical turns and deployed another burst of chaff and flares as he flew into the small indent on the mostly flat desert floor.

It was working. The R-27 missile, confused by the combination of electronic jamming, decoys, and erratic maneuvers, struggled to maintain a lock on the slippery F-35. Suddenly, the missile veered off course and exploded in a huge fireball just behind him. The shock wave momentarily shook Jessie's F-35.

Darting up to 35,000 feet, Jessie scanned his HUD and found his wingman, who had also dodged his killer. No other threats were detected, and he got on the horn. "Nice to see you still kicking, Bulldog."

"I hear ya, Swagger. It was definitely pucker factor ten. But my countermeasures did the trick at the last second. I have a few holes in my plane, but it should be fine. We should head back to the boat. I'm almost bingo fuel."

"Roger that." Both F-35s headed to the USS *Ford* as the battle for Ahvaz Oil Field was about to enter a new phase.

Chapter 41

IRANIAN HQ, BATTLE FOR AHVAZ OIL FIELD
Khuzestan Province, Iran

Major Shadmani didn't like how things were going down. "HQ to R61, deploy along the perimeter. Enemy approaching." He had lost half his men and was now down to his Quick Reaction Force, his last line of defense. He would lose the entire oil field if he lost his current position. He also knew his IRGC men were warriors and wouldn't hesitate to lay down their lives for their country. But that wasn't part of the plan. He wanted the American infidels to die for *their* country.

"All units," he said, "motion in Sector 2 moving toward the east wall. Prepare for a breach attempt."

Several IRGC soldiers took positions near the east wall, taking cover and ready to assault any breach.

Suddenly, the loud crack of a powerful rifle came from Tower 2. Shadmani knew at least one of his snipers had taken a shot. Good, he thought as another shot sounded. That should slow them down. He hoped that men from the nearby town would come to assist them like they had agreed to. All he knew was that time was on his side.

Carter and his squad's SEALs used satellite imagery and their good old-fashioned compasses to find and approach the large wall around the main compound. Instinctively, they had found what little cover they could, and, using thermal scopes; they had noted two towers but no ground troops outside the wall.

Carter had ordered Charlie detail to move in, and a pair of SEALs designated as the breaching team had started to move toward the east wall when the sharp crack of a rifle echoed in the air.

"Fuck, I'm hit," one of the breaching men said over comms, then another loud report from a powerful rifle came from outside the wall.

"One Iranian shooter down," a calm voice said.

Unlike IRGC Major Shadmani, who had speculated about the second shot, Carter knew exactly who had fired and put out the call. It was Sierra 1, his sniper.

"Robert's hit," reported a breaching detail member. "He took one to his right foot and can't walk. Need a replacement now."

No sooner had the words left his mouth, one of the SEALs, who had once worked as a breacher, low-crawled forward with his partner, who dragged Robert back to cover. The rest of the team put down cover fire toward both towers as the new breaching team approached the east wall. There was little return fire, and the two men reached the base of the imposing stone wall.

Glancing up, the two men saw the top was lost in the gloom above. With their backs against the wall, they carefully unrolled putty-like explosive and molded it into place along the base of the wall. The rifle fire stopped, leaving it so quiet they could hear their own rapid breathing.

One of them whispered, "Charges set, moving back." They retreated to a safe distance, ducking behind what little cover was available. One of them pulled out the detonator, a small device with a single button. He glanced at his partner, who gave him a thumbs-up.

Over comms, he said, "Three—two—one—fire in the hole." He pressed the button to ignite the C-4. A deafening roar shattered the night for a second time, and a brilliant flash of light momentarily illuminated everything nearby. Both men felt the ground shake as chunks of stone flew through the air and pounded onto the sandy earth. Sneaking a glance, they saw the hole still taking shape as part of the wall continued to collapse. For a moment, there was just dust and the sound of rocks falling. Then heavy machine-gun fire came out of the hole like some fire-breathing dragon.

At that instant, another blast filled the air as the secondary breaching team blew a massive hole in the north wall of the compound. That seemed to distract the enemy troops on the east side, allowing the rest of the SEAL squad time to throw several M67 grenades and storm the opening while firing at anything that moved—or didn't.

Once inside, the SEAL squads split into smaller fire teams to cover more ground. Carter with one unit, Harris with the second. Carter headed for the main entrance to the only substantial building on site, which they had determined was the Iranian headquarters using satellite imagery during mission planning. The rest of the two squads were in firefights and attempting to establish control of the compound. The IRGC was putting up fierce resistance, but the superior training and tactics of the SEALs were shown by the increasing number of enemy bodies littering the ground.

At the front entrance to the HQ, Carter decided to try the easy way first. He got down as low as he could, then gently tested the doorknob. It turned, so he opened the door just enough to throw in a grenade. As the grenade rolled on the floor, a barrage of bullets greeted him, but he had gone prone, and the shots flew over his head. Milliseconds after his grenade exploded, Carter and one other SEAL entered, one going right and the other left, both spraying the area with gunfire. Any movement was greeted with several rounds as the SEALs kept moving. They cleared two rooms, and four more squad members announced on comms they were entering the HQ to provide support.

As they moved forward, they came to a room with dual glass doors, which appeared to be the command room. Carter gave a nod to his team, turned, and opened fire, spraying the area with bullets. There was no return fire. The SEALs entered the room. Scanning the area, their eyes rested on a major sitting in front of several monitors.

Shadmani slowly swung his chair to face the Americans. He felt great pride when he saw their eyes widen once they noticed he held a grenade with no pin. He still had one more play. "Praise be to Allah," he said as the charge went off.

The SEALs dove to the floor as the major said his last words. Although the concussion and noise were deafening, no one was hit. Carter looked at some of the other SEALs, shrugged, and went back to business.

"Command, Alpha 1," said Carter over comms. "Black Gold Phase 1 complete. Ahvaz Oil Field is secure. Send in support. Alpha 1 out."

Chapter 42

IRGC MISSILE BASE
Undisclosed location, Iran

It was time. All the meetings, all the strategy discussions, and all the planning now came down to this day, this hour, and soon, this minute. The Supreme Leader had ordered that Iran strike the United States before they could retaliate following the destruction of Independence Hall. It was a bold move, but one that Supreme Leader Amir Massad thought was in the best interest of Iran and their power projection in the Middle East. It was time to send a message to the world—especially the US and their surrogate, Israel—not to interfere in the affairs of his great nation.

Massad had prayed to Allah over the matter and saw in a vision that it was now time to act. The US had continuously violated Iran's sovereignty through sanctions, espionage, cyberattacks, and interference in their domestic affairs. There must be a war to liberate the region from US hegemony and imperialism. Massad had spoken many times about the concept of jihad and the duty of Muslims to resist oppression, and this war was a noble and just struggle.

General Jarari was the overall commander of the Islamic Revolutionary Guard Corps Aerospace Force. He took orders only from the Supreme Leader for anything dealing with missiles. Right this moment, he was preparing for actions that would define the rest of his life—the annihilation of the American infidels in the Middle East. Praise be to Allah. But first, he had to deliver a message to his missile legion. After picking up the mic that would broadcast his words throughout the missile base, Jarari spoke from his heart.

Ya Allah, grant us strength and courage. Bless our endeavors with Your divine support. Protect our soldiers and guide our actions to bring justice to our enemies. Let this be a reminder to the world that we are a nation of faith, resilience, and honor.

To our brave warriors, remember that you are the sword of justice in the hands of the Almighty. Every action you take today serves a greater cause, a cause blessed by Allah. Stay firm in your resolve, for paradise awaits those who sacrifice in the path of righteousness.

May Allah bless our mission, protect our people, and grant us victory over our oppressors.

Allahu Akbar!

Hidden in the desolate expanse of the Iranian desert, his base was known only to a select few within the highest echelons of power. Standing on an observation deck as if Allah had placed him there, the general scanned a large expanse of people, computers, and machines. Outside, the missiles stood like sentries, but that was about to change. It was 0300 hours, the zero-hour for General Jarari as he prepared to give the command to launch hundreds of missiles from here at this secret base and from others throughout his country.

He turned to his second in command. "Are we ready?"

"Yes, Sir. All systems are operational. The missiles are primed and ready to launch."

Jarari took a deep breath, knowing what wrath his missiles would deliver. He started the countdown.

"10—9—8—" He heard his voice echo through the room and beyond. Around the missile base, soldiers were busy entering launch commands to the missile computers.

"3—2—1—" LAUNCH!"

A deafening roar filled the room, enlightening his soul as the missiles ignited. Engines blazing with fiery intensity, they lifted off like a regiment of soldiers. The missiles boomed toward targets all over the Middle East. The massive rockets of destruction left behind thick trails of smoke that twisted and curled before they started to diminish.

Everywhere, the earth trembled as if in fear of what had just
been released, a reminder to all of the power of Iran.

Chapter 43

AL UDEID AIR BASE
Qatar

In the cool darkness at 0255 hours, well before the arrival of Big Red and the repressive heat of another day, Al Udeid Air Base was a beehive of activity. The wing commander had been informed base aircraft would participate in an attack on Iran at 0500 hours the following day—there were plenty of things to finalize. Brigadier General Farley "Tommy Gun" Tomason was making sure all his ducks were in a row. That began with enhanced surveillance and intel, and the unit was working around the clock analyzing satellite images and electronic communications for any sign of Iranian movements.

Most importantly, he had requested rigorous checks on the base's Patriot and THAAD missile defense systems. It didn't take a rocket scientist to appreciate the threat of missiles from Iran's stockpile. Tomason knew his base was squarely in the crosshairs of Iranian missiles.

He had his ground crews working tirelessly to maintain and prepare aircraft for rapid deployment. Each jet had a full tank of Jet A-1 fuel and was fully armed.

The next check box included something vital to him and many others on the base. He ordered all nonessential personnel to evacuate the base and find safer locations to hole up. When the word got out to the community, it was amazing how many Qatari citizens stepped up to take in the shaken military dependents, including his wife. If he were correct, this would be no place to be when everything went south.

Al Udeid Air Base

In the base's operations center, Major Amy Jenkins, a seasoned USAF officer with years of experience in intelligence and surveillance, was at her station. The large screens mounted in rows before her displayed a variety of data feeds that provided real-time updates on regional activities and the airspace surrounding the base and well beyond. The hypnotizing hum of computers and the low murmur of conversation filled the room.

Out of that trance-inducing white noise, someone yelled, "Incoming missiles."

Someone else yelled back, "Use your comms."

Jenkins looked at the info popping up on the screens and jumped into action. "Command, we have unidentified multiple launches from different areas of Iran. Scores of heat signatures detected."

In the background, she could hear multiple reports coming in from US missile defense agencies, an AWACS flying patrol, and others. She forced herself to concentrate on what her screens were telling her. Jenkins felt her heart beat faster as she leaned closer to her monitors. The trajectories were unmistakable. She skillfully confirmed the launch coordinates and estimated that fifty missiles would impact Al Udeid in fourteen minutes.

Jenkins took a deep breath and slowly let it out, just as she had practiced in yoga, to relax and focus. She said to her assistant, "Lieutenant, activate the base-wide alert. Get everyone to their designated positions. Prepare all missile defense systems—now!"

Over the noise in the room, she could hear the base-wide alert blaring its omnipresent warning, echoing across the sprawling complex. Quickly, military personnel went about their well-rehearsed duties as if the warning was just another training exercise. But this time, it was more than that; it was for life or death.

In the control room of the base's missile defense system, the colonel in charge ordered, "Prepare the Patriots and THADD systems." He issued the command knowing that all these things were already being done, but he didn't want to leave anything to chance—which in war could be deadly.

Inside their fortified Patriot missile defense control room, several of the seventy soldiers assigned to the battery were experiencing the most demanding day of their lives. They were the specialists who pushed the buttons to launch the Patriot missiles. Corporal Jesse Owens, named after the famous athlete, was about to make some history himself. He was the engagement control station operator who tracked and fired on targets. For reasons he couldn't explain, he was as calm as ever. Like a robot and without trepidation, he responded to orders and performed precise moves to make things happen.

As they should, the battery commander's directives came quickly. "Prepare the interceptors. We have 50 incomings. Prepare 100 to intercept." The operating procedure was to shoot two missiles at each incoming missile and use the "shoot-look-shoot" technique if additional Patriots needed to be fired.

Then he saw it. A sight he had hoped he never would see on his radar screen. "ECS, we have one confirmed Fattah-2 in the second stage of deployment. Program four missiles for this target, call sign Foxtrot."

Owens knew that this missile was a serious escalation by the Iranians. Simply put, US defensive systems were not designed for such an advanced missile that could maneuver at speeds reaching Mach 15. When he first heard that Iran had produced a hypersonic missile, Owens had been curious about what that meant. He looked it up and was shocked. It traveled at over 11,000 mph, roughly fifteen times the speed of sound. That was close to the speed of the International Space Station, which orbited at more than 17,000 mph. Hell, he thought, you could shoot a hundred missiles at it and would have little chance of killing the highly maneuverable missile.

Spread around the outside of the base, multiple M901 and M902 Patriot missile launchers rotated to face the direction of the incoming threats. Each truck-mounted launcher had four missiles. Since twenty inbound missiles were identified as less-maneuverable targets, those Patriot missiles were assigned as PAC-2 interceptors. The rest were assigned as PAC-3 with a hit-to-kill warhead, which destroys threats through kinetic energy. They also had active radar guidance, versus the semi-active on the PAC-2, which used only an explosive warhead.

With multiple launch commands issued, 100 Patriot missiles roared to life, their engines igniting in a blaze of smoke and fire as they shot skyward. The missiles arced through the atmosphere, leaving thick trails behind them as they raced toward their incoming targets, programmed with deadly precision to intercept the enemy warheads. Across the globe, everyone involved in US missile defense was on high alert. Soldiers in the control room at Al Udeid Air Base, sailors aboard Navy ships, aircraft crews, and military and civilian personnel at the White House and the Missile Defense Agency—each one was glued to their monitors. Since the crisis with China, the world hadn't witnessed anything on this scale.

Since the Patriots were propelled by their solid fuel rockets, they reached supersonic speeds quickly, entered the midcourse phase to continue climbing, and maneuvered toward the predicted interception points. Meanwhile, radar continuously tracked the missiles and the incoming threats, updating the missiles' flight paths via command guidance. Reaching their final phase, the missiles switched to terminal guidance. The PAC-3 variants used active radar homing so onboard radars would seek out and lock onto the targets. If need be, the Patriots would maneuver to align for direct hits.

In the final moment, the missiles' guidance systems made precise adjustments to ensure collision. Upon impact, the kinetic energy of the high-speed missiles got transferred to the targets, resulting in the spectacular destruction of both Patriot and enemy missiles.

Radar systems verified target hits by analyzing the debris and confirming the absence of radar signatures, which confirmed the kills. But in this case, the radar was also the bearer of bad news. Across all platforms, the missiles were monitored, and radar showed two enemy missiles getting through the US defenses.

One was an Emad missile with a more advanced guidance system that enhanced accuracy. It was programmed to strike the headquarters and command facilities used by senior US military leadership and staff.

Another missile that evaded all attempts to shoot it down was the one assigned targeting call sign Foxtrot. The Fattah-2 hypersonic missile carrying a massive two-thousand-pound warhead flew at Mach 15 and reached the base much sooner than the other incoming missiles.

As the warning sirens grew louder with each passing moment, personnel took cover in designated areas. But when a two-thousand-pound bomb hits, taking cover barely matters.

Near the parking apron that held twenty KC-135 refueling aircraft, Foxtrot hit with such force that it bored a thirty-foot crater into the tarmac and set off a massive firestorm when all twenty refuelers blew up. Several nearby hangers and three hardened aircraft shelters housing Boeing F-15E Strike Eagles were destroyed.

For the troops nearby, if they were not killed outright, they had severe injuries from the overpressure wave caused by the bomb, including pulmonary contusions, ruptured eardrums, abdominal bleeding, and traumatic brain injury.

Several minutes later, while base personnel were trying to fathom what had just happened, the Emad missile struck just outside the thick walls of the facility housing the base's operations center, the CENTCOM-Forward headquarters, and the SOCCENT headquarters. The resulting blast tore through the concrete walls, dispersing shrapnel and rubble. One of those killed by the explosion was Brigadier General Tomason, the commander of the Al Udeid Air Base. Another was Captain Jenkins, who was killed while giving updates on the incoming missiles.

The scene was too horrific for words to describe. An Associated Press reporter embedded with the Air Force was aware of that fact and took a wide-shot image showing the deep crater surrounded by piles of rubble and debris. Jetting out were tangles of metal, smashed furniture, and bodies that were specks in the pile of wreckage. He would later say he picked that photo to show the damage, not highlight the killing of so many military personnel. The photo encapsulated America's newest war and went viral across the free world. The destruction of the base, following the destruction of Independence Hall only a little over a week ago, caused anger in America to boil over into such a hatred for the Iranians that Muslims, no matter where they lived or where they were from, were persecuted like never before.

The tragedy struck a deep chord, uniting Americans in a way not seen since the harrowing days following 9/11. Across the country, an overwhelming sense of solidarity and determination emerged. Yet a somber realization loomed—this heartbreaking moment was merely the beginning of an uncertain and difficult journey ahead for the US and the world.

Chapter 44

TOWER 22

Rukban, Jordan

Private Adam Dankworth was in a perimeter bunker with his watch partner, Private Mitch Rawlins, at 0300 hours. As he took in the radiant night stars, he was half on the nod, thinking back to how fortunate he was to have had some judge stick up for him so he could get into the Army. Coming from a long list of foster homes, he couldn't remember the last time anyone took his side, especially a judge. In the Army, he had discovered that others cared about him and made him feel like part of a team. He was beginning to understand teams, and he liked how it felt. Having people accept him was something so new that he had to learn not to be so defensive and to listen to what people had to say. His mother might have been proud of him getting into the Army, if he had a real mother. Now he was part of something big, and he was digging it.

A loud whistling sound flew over their heads, followed by loud explosions toward the center of the base. Instantly, both men stiffened up. Dankworth positioned himself behind his M250 light machine gun. Rawlins did the same, saying, "No targets. You?"

"No, dude, nothing. Keep your head down."

More whistling sounds. A mortar round landed just outside their bunker, spraying them both with dirt, rocks, and the remains of an obliterated rat. Dankworth scanned his field of fire illuminated by outfacing lights. Explosions spread across the base, and his comms came alive with some people giving commands and others requesting medics. If this was war, Dankworth got it—it instantly seemed like a huge notch above all the street fights he had been in. He stayed calm, ready to lay down some fire. Rawlins was staying low.

Just as quickly as they materialized, the whistling sounds diminished, only to be replaced with a loud buzzing sound. The radio soon confirmed what Dankworth had thought—an Iranian drone strike.

Anticipating a drone strike to follow up on the mortar attack, base radar operators had detected fifteen inbound drones. Immediately, counter-drone units deployed several Raytheon Coyote Block 2 expendable drones, each designed with advanced sensors and an explosive warhead. They were hunting for Iranian Shahed-129 medium-altitude, long-endurance light attack drones, each armed with four deadly Sadid-1 missiles.

Using meticulously gathered intelligence, the Iranians had targeted the base's vital defensive structures. They knew the ensuing confusion would make follow-up attacks more successful.

As the ammo dump received a direct hit from one of the Shahed-129 drones, Dankworth figured a ground attack would soon commence. "Rawlins, stay on your 250. These assholes will be charging us directly" Looking over, he noticed Rawlins wasn't moving. "Rawlins, get your ass on that machine gun. NOW!"

As he yelled at Rawlins, all the overhead security lights were quickly shot out. Dankworth couldn't see shit. He quickly switched to his helmet-mounted night vision goggles.

As he did, he saw an Iranian infiltration team cutting their way through the perimeter wire. Dankworth swung his machine gun in that direction and fired. Using his tracer rounds, he walked the belt-fed bullets right into them. Return fire encircled him. He didn't flinch, and kept shooting until his M250 was empty.

"Reloading," he yelled and quickly threw in another belt of ammo. He heard Rawlins firing his machine gun. Good, he thought.

Makeshift command points were set up inside the wire, and a coordinated counterattack was organized. Over the din of the battle, Dankworth heard loud cracks from the base sharpshooters' rifles. They were doing their thing too.

Minutes later, Dankworth heard the distant roar of jet engines announcing the arrival of air support from Muwaffaq Salti Air Base. With the sky glowing red from all the fires, F-15Es could be seen streaking through it all, unleashing a torrent of precision munitions on enemy positions. Despite all the fire and smoke, Dankworth identified additional enemy troops and continued hammering them with machine-gun fire.

When the gunfire all but stopped and Dankworth's heartbeat slowed down, he felt something warm running down his left arm and a burning sensation coming from his upper arm near his shoulder. He ripped his shirt off and saw a bloody line in his skin where an Iranian round had just grazed him. Shit, that's nothing, he said to himself. He'd had worse wounds back in the 'hood, so he loaded another ammo belt into his machine gun and looked for additional targets.

Feeling like he had never felt before in his life, he yelled to no one in particular, "Come on, you Iranian bastards! The Bronx assassin is ready for your asses!"

This got the attention of Rawlins, who glanced over at his partner and smiled. Dankworth smiled back. A bond had begun, not just with Rawlins but with his new life in the United States Army. He felt alive, and the happiest he had ever been—even during a firefight.

Chapter 45

USS FORD

Persian Gulf

The United States military never slept. It was prepared to protect US interests wherever needed, 24/7, 365 days a year. Since TF-70 was preparing to launch a massive attack on Iran in less than twenty-four hours, more sailors were up at this absurd hour than were in their racks.

Working her usual midnight watch in the *Ford*'s CIC, Lieutenant Pavati Talas had recently defeated an Iranian cyberattack on her ship and was on the offensive this time. In cybersecurity, you defend against external attacks and then actively go after the adversaries attempting to infiltrate and exploit your networks.

First, you assault their command and control capabilities to inflict chaos in their chain of command. As she was using electronic warfare tactics and jamming Iran's radar and communications systems, she noticed a substantial increase in radio traffic. This was unusual and suspicious. She needed to alert her superiors, specifically the XO, who was also in the CIC at the TAO's station.

Using the secure communications everyone in the CIC monitored, she said, "Mustang, Guardian. I have a serious increase in radio comms mentioning the *Ford* and the task force. I can't say exactly what, but something is going down. Suggest informing Command."

The XO thought for a second, got on comms, and said, "Guardian, Mustang, what's your suggestion? Are we about to be attacked?"

"Mustang, I've never seen a jump in comms like this before. I would say yes. Recommend GQ."

There was no instant response. But seconds later, the announcement for general quarters went throughout the ship. Now everyone was up.

Also up was the crew of the ballistic missile submarine USS *Georgia*. For several days, the submarine had been shadowing an Iranian submarine, a contact tagged Sierra 1, as it worked its way inside the defensive perimeter encompassing the USS *Ford*.

The Iranian submarine *Fateh* was no outdated diesel-powered home-grown sub, but Iran's most advanced submarine. Its deadly abilities categorized it as a serious challenge to US forces. It had state-of-the-art technology, including high-grade sonar, an electric drive, and enhanced battle management systems. However, the most threatening aspect was its air-independent propulsion system. The AIP allowed the *Fateh* to extend the submarine's underwater endurance by replacing conventional batteries with the AIP plug, making it harder to detect. AIP enabled the *Fateh* to operate without access to atmospheric oxygen, so it didn't have to surface or snorkel to replenish. Being quieter than most nuclear American submarines gave the *Fateh* an increased advantage—not a good thing for the US.

A carrier's outer layer of air defense was like a dome, with a radius extending between 100 to 200 nautical miles from the center point of the carrier. This dome had a CAP that monitored the airspace using long-range radar, F-18s, and F-35s. Nothing came within that umbrella of protection.

The subsurface layer of defense was also critical to the carrier's survival. Equivalent to the air defense protection, it was like an inverted dome extended about 50 nautical miles underwater from the center point of the carrier, and submarines continuously monitored the sea for the enemy. Sierra 1 was crossing that red line into the carrier's safe space, and the captain of the USS *Georgia*, Mateo Navarro, didn't like it. He also knew the torpedoes it most likely carried ranged up to 30 nautical miles. That gave him a little leeway, but he had less tolerance than usual with hostilities already ramping up. He needed more information.

"Sonar, I want bearing and range to Sierra 1."

"Yes, Sir," said his most efficient and senior sonar operator, Petty Officer First Class Max Ripley, who had six years under his belt. "Sierra 1 bearing zero-niner-zero, range 6 miles."

So far, there was no indication that the sub knew it was being shadowed. But in this tactical dance, you always assumed they knew exactly where you were.

"Nav, plot course to position us 10 miles from Sierra 1. Maintain stealth profile. Stand by to launch a BWA."

The navigator got to work as the captain gave Comms the order to prepare the buoyant wire antenna.

"Course plotted, Captain," the navigator said after a few minutes.

"Helm," Navarro said, "make turns for 8 knots, depth 200 feet." Helm repeated the order and executed it.

After a bit, the captain said, "Helm, come right to new course one-two-two. Maintain depth and speed."

Sonar jumped back in. "Sierra 1 bearing zero-niner-zero, range 10 miles."

Navarro ordered, "Helm, come left to course zero-niner-zero, all stop."

Helm repeated the order and complied.

"Captain, Comms. All systems are operational, and the antenna compartment is clear. The BWA pre-deployment checklist is complete. Request permission to deploy."

"Deploy BWA" Navarro ordered.

"Deploying BWA now," replied Comms.

As the Buoyant Wire Antenna, a sleek tube-like device, floated to the surface, it extended its arm, which was activated by the communications team on the *Georgia*.

While submerged at two hundred feet, Navarro was shortly in contact with the outside world using very low frequencies and satellite signals.

"WEPS, I want a continual firing solution for Sierra 1."

"Copy continual firing solution, Captain," the weapons officer replied and, after a brief moment, said, "Ready when you need it."

"Captain, Comms. Flash message from the *Ford*."

"Let me see it."

A few moments later, the message was in Navarro's hands.

TO: COMMANDING OFFICER USS *GEORGIA*

FROM: COMMANDING OFFICER USS *FORD*

SUBJECT: GENERAL QUARTERS AND HOSTILITIES

DATE/TIME: 0700Z

MESSAGE:

USS *Ford* is currently at General Quarters. Possible attack imminent.

Hostilities against Iran are scheduled to commence at 0500 tomorrow.

END OF MESSAGE

Navarro handed the message back. "XO, sound silent battle stations."

"Yes, Sir," said the XO as he triggered the alarm. Immediately, the ship's lights flashed rhythmically, telling the sailors they were in GQ and to man their assigned battle stations. The vessel's hatches and compartments were carefully secured to ensure watertight integrity and isolate potential damage. At the same time, weapons were brought up to operational readiness. All stations reported their status by using the noise-isolated intercom systems. Navarro witnessed how training was paying off as the ship was prepared for battle—silently.

"Sonar, status of Sierra 1 and distance to the *Ford*," said Navarro

Ripley reported, "Sierra 1 bearing zero-eight-zero, range 12 miles, speed 8 knots, depth 300 feet, CPA 12 miles."

With that closest point of approach, it was decision time. Navarro silently calculated risk versus reward. Although his Mark 48 ADCAP torpedoes had a range of 27 nautical miles for strategic and tactical advantage, a distance between 5 to 10 would be ideal, giving his enemy less time to maneuver and counterattack. The counterpoint was the risk of detection and being shot at.

"Sonar, any deviation by Sierra 1?"

"No, Sir, no change."

"Nav, plot a course to bring us within 5 miles of the contact. Maintain silent running."

"Aye, Captain. Plotting course now." The navigator bent over his maps and got to work.

"Helm, make turns for 5 knots and 300 feet," Navarro ordered. "Come right to course zero-niner-five."

Navarro could feel the tension in the control room intensify as the USS *Georgia* maneuvered into position. He knew his advanced sonar systems gave him an edge. Noticing officers and sailors sneaking a look at him, he had no idea what they expected to see. His balancing act of getting close without being detected was working on all of them.

"Sonar, update on Sierra 1," Navarro requested.

"Sierra 1 bearing zero-eight-five. No change in speed or depth. Range is now 8 miles."

The distance was closing.

"Helm, come left to course zero-eight-five, maintain current speed and depth." Navarro kept them on the optimal intercept path. He barely heard the helmsman repeat his order as he concentrated on his next move.

"Nav, hold current position," Navarro ordered. "Helm, all stop."

"All stop, aye," replied Helm.

The submarine stopped silently, maintaining its stealthy presence in the Persian Gulf waters—the hunter was waiting for its prey.

Chapter 46

USS Ford

Persian Gulf

The sound of GQ echoed throughout the vast carrier as the *Ford* and all of TF-70 prepared for a possible Iranian attack. The wait was short-lived.

At 0300 hours in the darkened CIC of the *Ford*, Talas saw them, and radar operators reported that blips—perhaps hundreds of them—had suddenly appeared on their screens. Representing fast-moving objects coming from all over the Middle East, they were all headed for the position of TF-70.

"Multiple inbound contacts," said the XO over the task force net. "All stations prepare for action."

Missile batteries in Iran had launched volleys of Shahab-3, Khorramshahr, and Qader missiles. Many of these missiles were headed for the *Ford* and its safety net of support ships. Simultaneously, a swarm of small, fast-attack boats had launched from coves and sped toward the task force at speeds up to 75 knots. All the speedboats were armed with machine guns, and some had anti-ship missiles.

Flying CAP, flight leader Jessie "Swagger" Hampton ensured his five other F-35 pilots maintained sector awareness as they waited for their war to begin the following day. Suddenly, with its 360-degree situational awareness, his Distributed Aperture System started going nuts as if it were malfunctioning. Every warning voice and tone he had ever heard was going off—all at once. He had more blips than he had ever seen, even in training. Through all the noise, he heard a radio call from the *Ford*'s CAG, Mad Dog Johnson.

"CAP, Warrior. Multiple missiles inbound from the northeast. Intercept and neutralize. Engage at will. Good hunting."

Jessie called to his flight, "All Jedi, you heard the man and can see the inbound missiles. Use pre-briefed brevity and engagement procedures. Execute spread formation to cover a wide defensive perimeter."

As Jessie said this, he quickly toggled his systems to combat mode. The advanced sensors came to life with a flurry of information. The DAS identified the incoming threats—twelve high-speed missiles aimed at the *Ford*.

"Two," said Jessie to his wingman, Bulldog, on his flight's frequency, "you're with me, and we've got the first wave of six missiles. All others split and take out the other missiles." Five pilots acknowledged by repeating their flight numbers.

The F-35s split into three groups, weaving through the sky with high-speed precision and divvying up the other six missiles as the DAS fed real-time data into their HMDSs. Each group's targeted missiles were marked with bright red indicators, and each missile's trajectory, speed, and estimated time to impact was calculated and displayed.

"One has the three on the port side," Jessie told Bulldog. "Two, take the other three."

"Two has the other three," replied Bulldog.

Their radar and infrared tracking systems worked seamlessly to maintain precise locks. With a firm press on the trigger, Jessie launched the first JATM, Fox 3. He monitored his weapons display as the missile dropped from his plane and shot off, streaking through the sky. Its onboard guidance system homed in on its target. The missile's active radar seeker engaged, ensuring it stayed locked on even as it maneuvered through the sky. Its speed and agility were evident as it closed the distance in a heartbeat.

Jessie heard Bulldog announce his engagements and verified them on his HUD. Each watched as their missiles added to the digital chaos of the aerial battlefield. Both pilots executed their maneuvers with precision while deploying countermeasures. Chaff and flares lit up the sky, creating a dazzling display of defensive tactics.

The first JATM struck its target in a brilliant explosion that marked the end of one Iranian missile. The other Jedis reported several more kills. The F-35s' AN/ASQ-239 electronic warfare suites immediately recalculated and updated the statuses of the remaining threats.

The next missile approached. The Iranian forces had adjusted their tactics, launching from a slightly different angle. Hampton adapted quickly, his F-35 pivoting in the sky to maintain optimal engagement position. He fired.

"One," Jessie said, "second missile neutralized."

"Two copies," replied Bulldog, "ditto here. Going after missile three."

Both fired on their number three targets, the JATMs streaking away. The advanced radar seeker ensured a direct hit on Jessie's target, and another massive ball of fire illuminated the sky.

"Two has a miss," said Bulldog. Missile three has gotten through."

On the net, the CAG said, "Warrior copies all. We have the missile on radar. Jedi flight maintain CAP until relieved."

The *Ford*'s CIC and Aegis Combat System operators had monitored the air battle and marked that one Iranian missile had made it through and was headed for the carrier. Over the *Ford*'s 1MC came a warning. "Missile inbound. All hands brace for impact."

Chapter 47

USS Georgia

Persian Gulf

Lying in wait, Navarro weighed the decision to sink the Iranian *Fateh*. An intercom transmission broke the silence he had ordered.

"Captain, flash comms. The *Ford* is under missile attack."

Decision made. "WEPS, prepare torpedo tubes one and two for Sierra 1."

The crew worked with silent efficiency, loading the heavyweight Mark 48 ADCAP torpedoes into the tubes.

"Captain, tubes one and two are loaded, flooded, and ready," said WEPS.

"Sonar, update on Sierra 1."

"Captain, Sierra 1 bearing zero-eight-five, range 5 miles."

"All hands brace for potential counter-detection," said Navarro. "WEPS, fire tube one." After a slight pause, he said, "Fire tube two."

There was a barely perceptible recoil and a muted thud as two torpedoes left the *Georgia*, heading for Sierra 1. The tension in the control room was intense as the Mark 48, with its high-explosive warhead, ripped through the sea at 55 knots. The time to target was a bit less than five minutes.

Not long after, Sonar said, "Captain, incoming torpedo bearing zero-niner-zero, range 5 miles."

"Helm, execute evasive maneuvers," said Navarro in the calmest voice he could manage. "All ahead flank, come right to course one-eight-zero."

"Aye, Captain. All ahead flank, right to one-eight-zero."

"Launch countermeasures and deploy ADCs," ordered Navarro. He liked the acoustic device countermeasures because they emitted sounds similar to a submarine to confuse a torpedo's homing device.

A cold sweat began to bead on his forehead. Come on, he told himself, you've been through this drill hundreds of times. His other self told him he'd never had an enemy torpedo bearing down on him; those hundreds of times were just drills.

But he had another trick.

"Helm, take us down 600 feet, full dive on the planes."

Immediately, the crew felt the submarine go nose down. The noise from the sudden activation of the hydraulic systems that controlled the diving planes and rudder was noticeable, and some wondered if they would soon be dead. Every man and woman knew they were executing emergency maneuvers to avoid an incoming torpedo. But they remained focused on their jobs even as the hull creaked and groaned from the increased water pressure.

"Captain, Sonar. Torpedo still tracking. Impact in three minutes."

"Helm, make a sharp turn to port. Create a knuckle." As the captain's command was repeated, a freckled-faced twenty-year-old Petty Officer Third Class executed the command using his hand-controlled joystick, which looked exactly like a game controller.

In this cat-and-mouse game of undersea warfare, the mouse hopes the sharp turn creates enough turbulence to make a "knuckle" in the water. This chaotic, noisy water mass disrupts the ordinarily smooth water flow, generates an acoustic signature, and tricks the incoming warhead.

"Captain, Sonar. Two torpedoes hit Sierra 1, and sounds of breaking up."

"Launch countermeasures," Navarro ordered his crew. "Make a hard turn to port. Maintain flank speed."

His XO said, "Sir, torpedo tracking. One minute to impact."

As the final seconds ticked away, many counted the moments until their lives might end. Thoughts of loved ones filled their minds, and whispered prayers could be heard in the tense silence.

A massive explosion shook the *Georgia*, throwing some to the floor. A nineteen-year-old in engineering struck his head on some machinery. Blood gushed everywhere. Sailors near him looked around, expecting to be dead, but realized they were still with the living and ran to help their injured crewmate. Seconds passed, and the *Georgia* was still at speed—still in one piece. The countermeasures had worked, setting off the torpedo close in but not close on.

Good thing, thought Navarro, because we have a war to fight.

USS Truxtun

Persian Gulf

Unable to sleep after receiving notice from TF-70 about when combat operations would commence, Commander Anika Jones stood on the bridge of her command, the Arleigh Burke-class guided-missile destroyer USS *Truxtun*, taking it all in. A Massachusetts Institute of Technology graduate, she thought how strange it was to schedule a war. Like, do you put it on your calendar? Let's see, on Sunday at 0500 hours, War with Iran. Do I need a reminder? She chuckled to herself.

The daughter of a social worker and a jazz musician, she grew up with a blend of empathy, discipline, and creativity. During her rare off-hours, she would play the saxophone, her go-to means of stress reduction when it wasn't the wee hours of the morning. Throughout her career, she quickly gained a reputation for her technical acumen and was often called upon to troubleshoot complex mechanical issues.

Jones didn't like the Persian Gulf; she felt too confined. However, as one of the *Ford*'s guardians, liking her location didn't matter. Her responsibility was safeguarding the massive aircraft carrier, not unlike how the Secret Service protects the president.

At 0300 hours, she strolled into the CIC to see what was going on. It wasn't a formal visit but just something to do to wind down. She knew that if anything important happened, she would be contacted no matter where or what she was doing, even if she was playing the sax.

Heading over to radar, she knew they would be the first to know if anything bad was going to happen. When she got to the workstation, Petty Officer First Class Mark Thompson gave her a quick nod and returned to watching the radar while uttering, "Good morning, Ma'am." As the words escaped his lips, he almost jumped out of his chair.

"Captain, we have multiple bogeys inbound, bearing zero-seven-five, range 20 miles."

Jones didn't hesitate. "Sound general quarters. Prepare for possible engagement." All around her, sailors were rushing to their assigned positions.

"I want a visual on those contacts," ordered Jones.

What she saw nearly unnerved her—grainy images of numerous incoming missiles, many aimed at her ship. But being a professional, her training kicked in. "Deploy chaff and flares. Ready the CIWS and SM-2 missiles." The *Truxtun's* Phalanx Close-in Weapon System and missiles were the best defense systems in the world, and their crews sprang into action. Chaff and flares were launched.

"SM-2 missiles ready," WEPS reported.

Jones replied instantly, "Fire for effect."

"Captain, Comms. The *Ford* has numerous missiles inbound."

The ship's Vertical Launching System doors opened, and two SM-2 missiles rose 100 feet above the deck, ignited, and flew toward the first incoming missile. After ensuring that tracking and guidance were on target, the controller fired twelve additional missiles, assigning two SM-2s per incoming missile. Trails of smoke and fire crossed the dark sky as the SM-2s searched for their prey.

"Captain, four missiles down, two still inbound," reported Thompson.

Once within range, the Phalanx CIWS began tracking the two missiles that had managed to survive the SM-2s. The cannon's rapid-fire rate of 4,500 rounds per minute created bone-jarring noise.

One of the two missiles blew up close to the *Truxtun*, spraying the deck with shrapnel and killing numerous sailors left in the open due to their battle station assignments. As Jones walked out of the CIC, the second ballistic missile struck the bridge with tremendous force, killing her and almost everyone in the area, including those in the CIC. Quickly, the *Truxtun* was engulfed in a raging fire, with secondary explosions weakening the structural integrity of the ship.

Seeing there was no possibility of saving the ship, the XO gave the order to abandon the ship. But with no power on board, he could only yell the order. A few sailors heard him and managed to jump overboard, but most of the personnel aboard the ship were taken to the bottom of the Persian Gulf, making it their final resting place. Unseen by the world was a saxophone slowly floating down, landing in a sandy spot next to the *Truxtun*.

Chapter 49

CYBERSECURITY AND INFRASTRUCTURE SECURITY AGENCY (CISA) HEADQUARTERS
St. Elizabeth's West Campus, Washington, DC

Enjoying her new digs at the West Campus of St. Elizabeth's, Emily Hamal was at it again as a senior cybersecurity analyst for CISA. It was getting late, but there had been a priority notification stating that she needed to be fully staffed and prepared by tomorrow for a possible cyberattack initiated by Iran. Since they were the same bastards responsible for Independence Hall, she had no problem putting in the extra hours. Being prepared was in her DNA.

It began when Hamal grew up in Sugarcreek, Ohio, a place known as "The Little Switzerland of Ohio." Her dad, a small-town accountant, had been interested in computers when they first came out and never lost that curiosity. He had shared his love for technology with her ever since she could remember. Because of her dad's influence, she attended Carnegie Mellon University, which had the top cybersecurity program in the world. She earned a PhD.

Now, as a supervisor in CISA, she led a team of experts in identifying and mitigating cyber threats that could compromise national security. In a large auditorium, rows of high-tech workstations flickered with streams of data, and the screens displayed intricate patterns of network traffic and threat levels. The nation's first line of defense against cyber threats was maintained here using vigilant analysts and the maze of cutting-edge technology. No bullets were needed.

Her team analyzed intelligence reports, monitored network traffic, and developed strategies to defend against cyberattacks from power states. Iran led the list this week.

How interesting, she reasoned, that Americans had such short memories. When she was coming on the job in 2011, Iran had hacked into US banks. It used computer code to institute denial of service to fifty of the country's largest financial institutions, and the hackers shut down all of their targets. That incident should have been a wake-up call—but it wasn't, and soon, most of those banks went about their business like nothing had happened.

But Hamal wouldn't allow that on her watch.

As she was packing up to go home to her goldendoodle dog, Fred, alarms on countless computers in the auditorium sounded simultaneously. She looked at her four monitors and saw a notice on each.

ALERT: CRITICAL CYBER THREAT DETECTED

She glanced at the primary dashboard monitor high on the wall, which all twenty team members could see. It displayed a map of the United States with red markers highlighting critical infrastructure points—all under threat. There were so many. Scrolling across the top of the large monitor was the message:

THREAT IDENTIFIED—IMMEDIATE RESPONSE REQUIRED

Her threat intelligence specialist, Robert, used the primary room microphone at his desk and announced, "I have power outage reports coming in from several major cities. Comms with critical infrastructure operators are compromised."

Hamal yelled, "Turn off those alarms and report to the war room."

Quickly, the ear-piercing alarms stopped. She took a position at the front of a large room with another huge monitor overhead. Once everyone showed up, she spoke in a firm but reassuring voice. "Alright, team, this is what we've trained for. Listen up." She scanned each face to ensure she had everyone's attention. She certainly did, so she continued.

"As soon as I give you your assignment, go to your workstation and do your thing. Sophia, deploy our advanced intrusion detection systems. We need to isolate the breach points and contain the spread. Start with the most critical infrastructure targets first. Now go." Sophia took off like a cheetah chasing its prey.

"John, activate our incident response teams. Dispatch them to the highest priority sites—power grids and financial institutions. Make sure they have all the necessary tools and access permissions." He was gone with a whoosh.

"Lia, you're in charge of coordination. Contact DHS, FBI, NSA, and DOD. We need to synchronize our efforts and share intelligence. Set up a secure communication line with their response units."

"Yes, Ma'am," Lia said, and was gone.

"Emma, prepare a draft statement. We need to inform the public without causing panic. Emphasize that we're taking all necessary measures and provide clear instructions for any immediate actions they should take." Emma almost ran into the doorframe on her way out of the room.

"Jake, enhance our real-time monitoring. I want constant updates on any new developments. Set up a live feed to the main dashboard and flag any significant changes immediately." He drained his coffee cup before he left the room.

"Lucas, work on strengthening our defenses. Reinforce firewalls and ensure all backup systems are operational and secure. Prioritize the systems currently under attack." She paused as Lucas just stood there. "What are you waiting for?"

"Sorry, Emily, I'm on it." He stepped backward onto someone's foot, apologized, and exited the room.

"Rachel, start the forensic analysis. We need to trace the origins of this attack. Collect all relevant data and logs. Look for patterns that could help us identify the perpetrators. Start with the Iranians." Rachel nodded and headed out the door.

"Alex, initiate our backup protocols. Ensure that critical data is secure and backed up. Prepare for potential data recovery operations if needed." He had raised a finger for each assigned task and left the room with his hand still showing the number three.

"Everyone else, double-check our internal security protocols. We need to ensure there are no additional vulnerabilities within our systems, then work together on the attack on our power grid. I want specifics, understand?"

Everyone either nodded or said yes, then quickly went to their workstations. Hamal went to a secure terminal designated for interagency communication. Lia had initiated a secure video conference call with senior watch personnel from the Department of Homeland Security, the Federal Bureau of Investigation, the National Security Agency, and the Department of Defense. Emily started by briefing everyone that she didn't have any good news, then detailed her action plan.

She knew the nation's best minds were working on it and felt confident about this battle of ones and zeros.

Chapter 50

THE WHITE HOUSE
Washington, DC

The Associated Press reporter's photograph of Al Udeid's command facility, which quickly went viral, was the first to be released nationally but didn't suggest the full extent of the devastation. As more reports began to flood the news wires, it became evident that Iran had conducted a significant first strike against the United States and across the Middle East.

Besides Al Udeid Air Base in Qatar, Iran struck Al Dhafra Air Base in the United Arab Emirates and Naval Support Activity Bahrain, which was the home of the US Naval Forces Central Command and Fifth Fleet and housed 9,000 military and civilian personnel. In Kuwait, Camp Arifjan and Ali Al Salem Air Base were struck. Prince Sultan Air Base in Saudi Arabia, which supported air operations and provided a strategic location for the US in the Middle East, also got hit. In all, 40,000 military and civilian personnel throughout the Middle East were attacked by Iran's stockpile of advanced missiles and, in some locations, drones and ground troops.

President Mark Taylor addressed the nation from the White House after discussing the issue with his NSC.

My fellow Americans,

Earlier today, Iran launched an unprovoked attack against our forces and citizens in the Middle East, a clear act of aggression that has shocked the international community and demands an immediate and decisive response from our nation. This attack comes on the eve of our planned operation designed to address the unprovoked terrorist attack on Independence Hall and the threats posed by Iran's actions in the region.

The sinking of the USS Truxtun and the strikes against the USS Ford and all our bases in the Middle East are red lines Iran has decided to cross. Their unprovoked aggression has resulted in the tragic loss of American lives. It was a grave error on the part of Iran.

Let me be clear—the United States will not tolerate such hostile acts. We will respond with strength and resolve to protect our nation, our allies, and our interests. Our military is prepared to defend our people and ensure that those responsible for this attack are held accountable.

In this moment of challenge, I ask all Americans to stand united. Our strength lies in our unity and our shared commitment to the principles of freedom and justice. We are consulting with our allies and international partners to determine the best course of action in response to this aggression, and we will act in accordance with international law.

To the people of Iran, we do not seek conflict. However, your government's actions have forced us to respond to protect our citizens and our way of life.

May God bless our troops and keep our nation safe.

Thank you.

Chapter 51

*USS R*EAGAN
Arabian Sea

As she flew her E-2 Hawkeye, it seemed to Sarah "Danger" Freeman that the war with Iran was on, no matter what the brass said. Iran's preemptive attack on nearly every asset the US maintained in the Middle East had resulted in countless deaths and injuries. It was China all over again. She hated war, much like her hero, Ulysses S. Grant, but just as he had, she believed that if you fired on her, she would come after you with every ounce of her being.

Shortly after the *Reagan*, backed by its CSG, successfully intercepted and neutralized every missile targeting it, Sarah had taken to the skies to provide C2 from an altitude of 25,000 feet to the CAP, protecting the *Reagan*.

She had heard that the *Ford* and its CSG had been under heavy attack, which meant Jessie would have been right in the middle of things. There hadn't been time to find out how he was doing, but she knew he was a big boy and could take care of himself.

As she flew in her assigned zone, Sarah was mindful of her five-person crew and how well they were all bonding to become a solid team. This was important to her. She glanced over at her copilot, Lieutenant Jack "Eagle" Steller, who had a calm demeanor and sharp instincts. He was a steadying presence, balancing Sarah's daring nature with his calculated precision. Five years ago, it was a different copilot flying into war with her, a brave soul who gave his life to save hers after they crashed into the South China Sea. The thought of that still haunted her—and always would.

But it was inexplicable, she thought, that the only one who wasn't a team player was her CO, Commander Wagner. He was proving to be a real prick. In war or peace, you sure as hell didn't need that additional pressure.

Her radar operator, Petty Officer Third Class Mike "Tech" Collins, was absorbed by the streaming data and was scanning for anything in their area.

"L-T," he said, "we've got some chatter on comms about increased Iranian activity near the Strait of Hormuz. There's six fighters in the area monitoring."

Freeman nodded, her mind always a few steps ahead. "Keep your eyes on it, RO. Any sign of trouble, I want to know immediately."

Suddenly, a sharp alarm echoed throughout the aircraft. Freeman's eyes snapped to her radar screen, where a new contact had appeared, fast and low.

"Incoming missile bearing two-four-two, range 150 miles," Tech announced, his voice now full of urgency. "It's a Sayyad-4 and just locked on to us."

Perched on the edge of the carrier's air defense perimeter to maximize coverage, Sarah's E-2 was 150 nautical miles from the carrier and 200 nautical miles from any fighting. The reason was simple: to keep the crew out of harm's way. But right now, that formula wasn't working. The Sayyad-4 SAM was a formidable threat, capable of striking targets at high altitudes with deadly precision from extended distances. She quickly assessed her options. The E-2 Hawkeye wasn't built for combat maneuvers but had other defenses.

"Deploy chaff and flares now," Sarah ordered. Her hands held the controls with a white-knuckled grip. Take it easy and relax, she repeated to herself. Her grip loosened, as did her tense body.

The E-2's systems ejected a burst of flares. Simultaneously, a cloud of chaff was released, filling the air with a multitude of radar-reflective strips.

Freeman knew she would need more, given the missile's 6,000 mph speed when she could only do 300, tops. It was time to change the formula. "Strap it tight," she said, and then she skillfully threw the E-2 into a radical turn to port with a nosedive toward the sea. Anything the crew hadn't managed to tie down in a few seconds flew about the cabin. The crew could feel the G-forces pulling tight on their bodies. Buying some time, Freeman, grunting through the G-forces and exertion to control the aircraft, forced out, "CICO, get me a bearing on the closest friendly. We need support now."

With his fingers punching away at the keys, CICO reported back, "The closest fighters are Bonzo flight, two F-18s. They're vectoring in, ETA two minutes fifty seconds."

Sarah's mind raced. Almost three minutes was an eternity when facing certain death if you failed. She pushed the aircraft into another hard turn, feeling the strain in her muscles. The ocean surface was coming at her like a runaway freight train.

The missile, momentarily confused by the countermeasures and rapid altitude change, adjusted course and continued its pursuit. Sarah had a visual of a deadly streak against the early morning sky, growing larger by the second.

"Come on, baby, hold together," she muttered, coaxing the aircraft through another evasive maneuver just feet above the sea. "Eagle, ECM."

Her copilot activated the electronic countermeasures, sending out jamming signals in a last-ditch effort to break the missile's lock. There was nothing else to do.

At that moment, there was a tremendous fiery explosion as the Sayyad-4 surface-to-air missile was blown out of the sky, followed by the jet wash from two beautiful F-18s that screamed by while waving their wings in a friendly hello as if saying, *We just saved your ass.*

Sarah, with her composure still intact, toggled her radio. "Great work, Bonzo flight. You saved our butt on that one. See you back at the boat."

"Anytime, Danger. That's what we're here for."

Pulling the controls, Sarah headed back up to 25,000 feet. She couldn't help but feel a surge of pride for her crew and the pilots who had come to their rescue. They had faced the threat head-on and had emerged intact, a testament to their training and teamwork. And she hadn't made Jessie a widower.

"Alright, team," she said, her voice calm and steady. "Let's get back to work. Form a line for the head, for those that need it."

Chapter 52

USS Ford

Persian Gulf

As the Iranian missile evaded the aerial defenses of the CAP, the Aegis Combat System showed it was headed straight for the *Ford.*

"Captain, one incoming missile, bearing two-one-zero."

Captain Otis Albright replied, "Confirm the threat."

"Confirmed Shahab-3 targeting us. Estimated time to impact is three minutes."

"Captain, WEPS. ACS missile lock. Ready to fire."

"Fire three SM-3s. Launch countermeasures and commence electronic jamming," said Albright.

Despite the carrier's immense size, nearly everyone aboard felt the ship shudder as three SM-3 Block IIA ballistic missile interceptors launched from the VLS. The captain snuck a peek out the window and watched the smoke trails streak toward the incoming Iranian missile.

"Captain, WEPS. Phalanx set to auto and tracking."

From the bridge, Albright watched the battle unfold as blips on his radar screen converged. He saw two become one, indicating missiles collided, or so he thought. Seconds later, the Shahab-3's trajectory continued toward his ship.

"WEPS, fire two more SM-3s now," Albright said.

A second salvo made the ship shudder again. "Missiles away," replied WEPS. "Tracking target trajectory. Stand by for intercept confirmation."

"Captain, nine-zero seconds until impact," came a call from a radar operator.

As Albright watched what was his last and best chance at hitting the Iranian missile, the radar tracks were converging. He couldn't help himself as he muttered, "Come on, come on."

Again, there was another convergence on his screen. He blinked, hoping what he had just seen was real.

"Interception successful and target neutralized," said WEPS. One could almost hear a collective sigh of relief from everyone on the bridge as the *Ford* avoided a 2,600-pound warhead that would have been tough to survive.

"Captain, Radar. Multiple contacts detected, bearing one-four-five degrees, 8 miles out. It looks like a swarm of drones and a fleet of fast-attack craft heading directly toward us at high speed."

Albright's gaze narrowed, his mind swiftly processing the information about drones and FACs. "How many contacts?" he asked, his voice calm and steady in contrast to the growing tension around him.

"Dozens of drones, Sir, and at least ten FACs," the radar operator replied. "Estimated time to contact is ten minutes."

"Get me visuals."

"Aye, Captain," the Officer of the Deck responded, then relayed the command to the lookouts and surveillance teams. Within moments, the ship's high-powered cameras and binoculars were trained on the approaching threats, and the lookouts reported what they saw.

"Visual confirmed, Captain," the OOD said. "Drones are small, fast-moving, and traveling in a dispersed formation. FACs are heavily armed and moving in a spread formation."

"Assign the CAP and scramble our jets," Albright ordered. "We need to intercept before they get within range."

"Reserves are launching now, Sir," the Flight Operations Officer confirmed. "Aircraft will be in the air in two minutes. Our CAP is responding. ETA three minutes."

"Engage the drones with ACS," Albright said, "and launch SM-2 and SM-6 missiles. Set Phalanx systems to automatic. Prepare for close-range defense."

"Aye, Captain," WEPS replied, and after a brief pause, said, "missiles away. Phalanx systems online and ready."

"Deploy helicopters to engage FAC," Albright ordered. "Ready deck-mounted machine guns and small-caliber guns."

The OOD relayed, "Gunners, prepare to engage."

"Helicopters are launching now, Sir," the FOO reported.

As the combined air and surface attack rushed in, the *Ford* was doing what it did best—launching aircraft. Using the newly created Electromagnetic Aircraft Launch System instead of steam catapults, the *Ford* launched four jets every 45 seconds. First in line on the EMALS was Captain Mad Dog Johnson, and next up was Lieutenant Commander Jessie Hampton. There was no chance in hell that either would miss this battle.

While the aircraft launched, Lieutenant Pavati Talas did everything she could in the CIC to assist electronically. She broadcast a strong signal on the same frequencies as Iran's communication systems to drown out their signals. Knowing this would keep the enemy from sending and receiving messages, she hoped it would lead to a breakdown in coordination. Talas and her team also implemented high-powered interference signals over those same frequencies to further attack Iranian C2.

She decided to use another deception. "Initiate GPS jamming," she told the technician working with her. She knew this action would interfere with Iran's signals to the attacking swarm of drones and cause them to lose their course, effectively taking them out of the battle.

Outside the CIC and off the deck, the air battle took shape as F-35s and F-18s streaked across the sky. An E-2 helped identify and assign the numerous targets to those in the CAP and coming off the *Ford*. Mad Dog and Jessie, flying as a two-ship, had been assigned thirty drones.

"Jedi 11, Jedi Actual," said Mad Dog, "CAP aircraft still two minutes out. You take the east zone of bandits. I have the west. Start with the lead drones. Use brevity procedures."

"ONE, east bandits," replied Jessie to his CAG.

Both pilots marked their drones using their HUDs, advanced radar, and targeting systems. "ACTUAL switching to missiles," said Mad Dog, "lead drones are Karrars." Both pilots understood that the Karrar drones were jet-powered and capable of carrying bombs and missiles, so the switch to missiles was a good call.

"ONE, switching to missiles. I have Shahed-136s." Both pilots knew the Shahed-136 was a kamikaze drone used by Iran for precision strikes.

The highly maneuverable drones were spread out and skimming the sea swells. Using a swarm technique, the Iranians were employing a tactic to overwhelm the American defenses and deplete their missile inventory. The FACs would follow the drones, the small boats further pressuring the carrier's ability to protect itself.

The jets of the CAG's two-ship split out of formation, each diving toward the swarm and monitoring their HUDs carefully for other potential threats.

Since Mad Dog could see the drones, he armed his short-range heat-seeking AIM-9X Sidewinder, the perfect missile for WVR combat. The fire-and-forget missiles were also very maneuverable, with the agility to hit fast-moving targets. Using his F-35's advanced sensors, Mad Dog would know if any drones slipped through and could still keep an eye on Jessie's six.

"ACTUAL, Fox two," reported Mad Dog.

Not a second later, Jessie said, "ONE, Fox two."

The Sidewinders' advanced infrared seekers immediately locked onto the heat signatures of the drones' engines. Seconds later, the AIM-9Xs each hit a drone. The explosions took out several nearby drones, and cascades of explosions took out even more.

"ACTUAL, multiple kills," said Mad Dog.

"ONE, multiple kills," said Jessie.

"Jedi Actual, Jedi 21," said the CAP aircraft flight lead, who had finally reached the target area. "On station. Going after surviving drones."

"Jedi 21, roger. Actual flight has the FAC targets. Join us when you can. Good hunting."

Everyone used MADL and Link 16 to share real-time target data and imagery, so they were all on the same page.

Chapter 53

IRANIAN FAST-ATTACK STEALTH FRIGATE SHAHID SOLEMINANI
Persian Gulf

Standing on the bridge of Iran's newest frigate, Commander Hassan Rezaei of the IRGC navy relished the moment as he prepared for war with the United States of America. Rezaei had spent decades rising through the ranks in Iran's minuscule navy and was known as one of the most formidable strategists in the Iranian military. Today his mission was to test the power of a US carrier group stationed off the Iranian coast. It was an enormous undertaking, but he had a plan.

Rezaei knew that many pundits were calling his plan a suicide mission. He wasn't. The *Shahid Soleminani* was no ordinary ship of war. It was the lead frigate of the Iranian missile fleet. A catamaran with sharp angles to make it stealthy, its armament made it stand out. The ship was equipped with six anti-ship cruise missiles, of which four were long-range and two were short-range. The state-of-the-art vertical launchers that delivered those cruise missiles had space for up to sixteen surface-to-surface and surface-to-air missiles. Located around the ship were four 23mm Gatling guns and one 30mm autocannon. With additional mission capabilities, the *Shahid Soleminani* had the most advanced electronic warfare systems available. The frigate was powered by four locally produced diesel engines, enabling it to reach a top speed of 32 knots.

"Commander," Lieutenant Farhad said from behind him, "the American fleet is just beyond the horizon." His voice was steady despite the significance of the situation.

"Very well," Rezaei replied. "Initiate electronic countermeasures. I want their radar blinded."

As the *Shahid Soleminani* steamed ahead, its electronic warfare systems sprang to life and emitted powerful signals to jam the enemy's radar and communication systems.

"Captain, we're experiencing heavy jamming," reported Farhad. "We're losing contact with our outlying ships."

"Keep deploying countermeasures. Let's see if we can break through their jamming."

In the USS *Ford's* CIC, a small group focused on the non-kinetic battle that raged unseen to all but them.

"Mustang, Guardian," Talas said to the TAO. "We're experiencing another strong cyberattack directed at communications and radar. Some of our screens are going haywire."

"Guardian, stay with it," replied the TAO. "Deploy all electronic countermeasures. Let's see if we can overcome their jamming." The TAO relayed the situation to the bridge.

Talas didn't hesitate to tell her technician, "Activate our electronic countermeasures and initiate the cyber defense protocols."

The first step in her strategy was to isolate and identify the source of the jamming signals. Using the ship's advanced cyberwarfare suite, she identified the source as an Iranian ship and initiated a spectrum analysis to pinpoint the exact frequencies being targeted. When she found them, she sent them to her technician and said, "Deploy the adaptive frequency-hopping algorithm and reassign these frequencies. Let's disrupt their jamming pattern."

The adaptive frequency hopping would allow the *Ford*'s communication systems to switch frequencies rapidly, making it difficult for the enemy's jamming signals to keep up. As the algorithm was deployed, Talas focused on restoring the radar systems. She launched a diagnostic scan to check for anomalies or intrusions in the radar network. The scan revealed that the jamming was not just a brute-force attack, but synchronized with sophisticated malware designed to interfere with radar operations.

"Deploy the counter-malware protocols for radar systems," she said, directing her team to initiate a cleanse. The cyber defense suite began identifying and neutralizing the malicious code embedded in the radar network.

Meanwhile, Talas took a more proactive approach. She ordered the deployment of electronic decoys—drones and buoy-based emitters—designed to mimic the carrier group's electronic signature. The decoys would confuse the enemy's sensors and draw their jamming efforts away from actual ships.

"Ma'am, decoys deployed and active," an officer confirmed. "The Iranian source ship has been identified as the *Shahid Soleminani*, a missile frigate."

With the decoys in place and the frequency-hopping algorithm disrupting the jamming signals, *Ford*'s communication systems began to stabilize. Talas then took the offensive.

"Initiate a cyber intrusion into the enemy's electronic warfare systems," she directed. The goal was to breach the *Shahid Soleminani*'s network and disrupt their control over their jamming equipment.

Her team, more than happy to actively join the fight, launched a cyberattack aimed at the Iranian frigate using sophisticated cyber warfare tools. They targeted vulnerabilities in the enemy's electronic warfare suite, seeking to overload their systems with false data and commands. The intrusion team injected code that would create feedback loops to cause *Shahid Soleminani*'s jamming systems to malfunction, potentially damaging their equipment.

Quickly, good news started to filter in from the TAO. "Guardian, we're seeing a significant reduction in the jamming signals. Our radar and communications are coming back online."

Talas allowed herself a moment of satisfaction before turning her focus back to the ongoing battle. The defense against the cyberattack was a crucial victory, and she knew that her great-grandfather would have been proud of her.

Chapter 54

BATTLE FOR THE USS FORD
Persian Gulf

With his drones and attack boats providing a well-armed distraction, Commander Hassan Rezaei's ship was getting within an advantageous range. The American defenses had been struggling to adapt to so much input. "Prepare the missile batteries," he ordered.

In a synchronized ballet of precision, the *Shahid Soleminani*'s missile hatches opened to reveal an array of deadly weapons. Within moments, Rezaei gave the command to launch missiles, and the sky lit up with the fiery trails of multiple projectiles cutting through space like wrathful gods.

Explosions erupted in the sky as the American jets clashed with the Iranian drones. The ocean surface rippled from the force of the blasts. Plumes of smoke and pillars of fire rose into the air. Suddenly, the dawn transformed into a fiery morning that blended with the rising sun. Leaving the shield of the drones and FACs, the *Shahid Soleminani* headed at full power for the protection of Iran's missile defenses along the coast.

Well within the air defense umbrella of its strategically positioned array of support ships, the *Ford*'s ACS emitted a warning as it detected incoming missiles. At about the same time, the CIC received a missile warning from the E-2 covering the CAP.

Reacting faster than any human could, the carrier's automated response systems initiated, and the computers determined the optimal evasive maneuvers based on the missile threats.

The *Ford*'s helm automatically initiated rapid but smooth course changes, zigzagging the ship's heading erratically to throw off the targeting systems of the incoming missiles. Once again, Talas activated the ECM systems to jam the missiles' guidance systems.

While the entire carrier group was fending off the attacks, Iran launched another round of land-based ballistic missiles. Now, the *Ford* was on its own to defend itself because its supporting ships were fighting for their survival.

Capt. Otis Albright ordered, "WEPS, fire RIM-162s. Set Phalanx on automatic." It was up to technology to determine who would live or die.

In the air battling the drones and FACs, Lieutenant Jimmy "Jinx" Taylor was flying one of the *Ford*'s EA-18G Growlers. As he and his Electronic Warfare Officer, Lieutenant Commander Mike "Merlin" Davis, climbed to altitude, their task was to disrupt the enemy's ability to coordinate and strike effectively.

"Activating jamming systems," Davis said.

The Growler's powerful AN/ALQ-218 electronic warfare suite detected the Iranian drones' control frequencies, and the AN/ALQ-99 jamming pods began emitting signals to disrupt both the drones' control frequencies and the communication links of the FACs. The attacking force was now being jammed from the sea and the air. These jammers created false targets and ghost signals, which confused the Iranian operators and made it difficult for them to track and target the American forces accurately.

"Deploying radar decoys," Taylor said.

The Growler released chaff and flares. This confused the enemy's radar-guided weapons and helped protect the carrier group and the helicopters engaging the FACs.

As four Sikorsky MH-60 Seahawks sped just above the sea surface, flight leader Lieutenant Mark "Hawk" Hawkins was busy analyzing his digital displays and the horizon. His copilot, Lieutenant Junior Grade Martha "Sparrow" O'Neil, coordinated with the E-2, the other aircraft, and the carrier's CIC.

"Multiple FACs detected, bearing zero-four-five," O'Neil said. "Drones are approaching from zero-six-zero."

"All Seahawks, Seahawk 11," said Hawkins. "Split up to engage. Seahawk 12, you're with me, and we've got the FACs. Seahawk 13, take 14, and engage the drones."

All helos acknowledged. After quickly briefing Seahawk 12 about his plan of attack, Hawkins went tight right after the FACs, with Seahawk 12 on his flank. As they approached, Seahawk 11's radar lit up with multiple targets.

"Hellfires ready, Hawk," O'Neil said, locking onto the nearest boat.

"Light 'em up, Sparrow," Hawkins commanded.

The missiles streaked from the helicopter, trailing smoke as they zeroed in on the fast-attack craft. Explosions began to erupt on the water's surface as the missiles found their marks. Eruptions of fire and debris went in every direction.

The remaining boats used their speed and maneuverability to counter the attacking helicopters. As Hawkins adjusted his course for optimal missile targeting, one of the FACs let loose with its automatic 20mm cannons. A second FAC adjusted course and fired several SAMs.

Coming out of a turn, Seahawk 11 was hit by numerous 20mm rounds that penetrated the cockpit and killed Hawk and Sparrow instantly. Several rounds penetrated the fuel tank, and the helicopter blew into large chunks of twisted metal that crashed into the sea.

Seahawk 12's missile warning alarms went off. Just as the pilot commenced evasive maneuvers, it was struck by two Iranian SAMs. The MH-60 became a huge fireball.

The downed helos didn't go unnoticed by Capt. Mad Dog Johnson or his wingman, Jessie "Swagger" Hampton, had both been monitoring the battle on their HUDs.

"ONE, take the boat on the port side," said Mad Dog. "ACTUAL has the other."

"ONE, port side," Jessie said, acknowledging his assignment.

Both F-35 pilots pulled up their weapons menu to arm their Raytheon AGM-176 Griffin precision mini-missiles. They were the perfect choice because of their high accuracy against small, maneuverable targets. The aircraft computers calculated the optimal launch parameters, which included range, speed, and altitude, and both pilots maneuvered to those spots.

Mad Dog flipped the master arm switch to the "armed" position and was told he had a lock. He quickly squeezed the weapons release button on his control stick and felt the aircraft shimmy slightly as two AGM-176s flashed toward their target. He saw Jessie's Griffins launch also.

Both pilots watched on their HUDs as the two FACs were blown from the water into hundreds of burning fragments. "Fuck you, assholes," muttered Jessie to no one but for the souls of the American dead. "That's for my brothers and sisters."

Soon there were no more FACs left.

Overwhelming the defenses of the *Ford* with their sheer numbers, two of the Shahed-136 kamikaze drones made it through all attempts to shoot them down by hovering in the debris field of the two downed American helicopters. Consequently, the *Ford*'s radar failed to detect their slight silhouettes. Timing it perfectly, they roared past and maneuvered around the ship's defenses at water level, waiting until the last second to shoot into the air as they came alongside the *Ford*. Several Marines got a glimpse of them, but the drones were so fast that the defenders couldn't even swing their weapons around to get a shot.

Both Shahed-136 drones hovered above the ship. The first one maneuvered deftly to strike Catapult 1 with a 100-pound warhead. The explosion rocked the mammoth ship, creating a large fire. Fifteen sailors on the flight deck were killed, and numerous others wounded. Moments later, the second drone struck near Elevator 3, causing it to crash down one deck. Six sailors were killed, and ten others were injured.

A chaotic symphony of alarms blared across the *Ford* as the ship reeled from the two drones' devastating strikes. Smoke billowed from the flight deck and the acrid scent of burning fuel and scorched metal filled the air. The crew, trained for such crises, sprang into action with precision and urgency.

"All hands report to your damage control stations immediately!" the ship's Damage Control Officer, James Mitchell, said into his handheld radio. He ordered other response actions as he hurried to the scene.

Teams of sailors clad in firefighting gear rushed all over the flight deck and below, carrying hoses, extinguishers, and medical kits. The flight deck was a scene of devastation, with debris scattered from the explosions and fires raging near the aircraft elevator and starboard side.

Chief Petty Officer Tom Hernandez led the first team to the forward deck, where the fire burned hottest. "Get those hoses up here, now," he yelled over the roar of the flames. Sailors uncoiled hoses connected to the ship's firefighting system and directed powerful streams of water into the inferno. Other sailors used portable extinguishers to douse smaller blazes. They all worked in unison to prevent the fire from spreading.

Nearby, another team operated sprayers, coating the burning fuel with a thick layer of fire-suppressant foam. The combined efforts of water and foam began to take effect, reducing the flames and allowing the teams to advance closer to the fire sources.

Amid the firefighting efforts, medical teams navigated through the smoke and debris to search for wounded sailors and Marines. They didn't have to look far, as the dead and injured were scattered over the flight deck. Many screamed for help. One of the team members heard a faint voice cry, "Over here." They found six sailors trapped under a collapsed section of the flight deck.

A long line of sailors with stretchers quickly took the wounded to sick bay. Once there, it was chaos. The injured were spread out over limited space, and medics and doctors worked feverishly on those critical patients who needed care first. Others cried in agony while they waited.

Hours later, the fires were finally extinguished, and the ship was secured. Recovery operations began immediately for aircraft. The flight deck was scarred, and the starboard side bore the marks of the drone strike, but the crew had prevented a total catastrophe. As the last firefighter left the scene, the repair parties took over.

Admiral Holloway thought it essential to communicate with the crew. He addressed the *Ford*'s sailors who, for just a moment, stopped what they were doing. "Today, we faced a serious threat and met it with courage and determination. Damage control teams performed exceptionally under pressure, and thanks to their efforts, the *Ford* is still operational. We all lost brothers and sisters today, but we will continue the fight in their honor."

Chapter 55

IRANIAN FAST-ATTACK STEALTH FRIGATE SHAHID SOLEMINANI
Persian Gulf

As he sped towards the safety of the Iranian coastline and its protective shield of SAMs, Commander Rezaei thought he and his crew had stood up well against the world's largest and most modern aircraft carrier—the USS *Ford*. It appeared he'd had some hits, but he couldn't confirm it since he had to retreat from the area. He was proud and wanted to share his joy with his dedicated crew. After walking over to the ship's PA system, he thought for a moment, then addressed his crew of fifty-two.

Brave warriors of the Shahid Soleminani, today we stand together as a testament to our nation's strength and resilience. Our mission was clear, and our resolve was unwavering. In the face of a formidable adversary, the USS Gerald R. Ford, we have shown the world that we are not to be underestimated.

Each of you has played a crucial role in this achievement. Your dedication, skill, and bravery have brought us this far, and I am immensely proud to

After he finished, Rezaei turned to the crew on the bridge. "Radar, any contacts?" he asked, knowing the US Navy would be after him.

"No, Captain, nothing."

"Maintain zig-zag course at top speed."

Rezaei was correct. He was a target.

As captain of one of the six submarines protecting Task Force 70, Navarro had his crew on continued high alert since taking out an Iranian submarine, plus the land battery that sank a merchant ship. Monitoring all the action topside, he'd had a ringside seat but few targets. Now he had intelligence that the Iranian frigate *Shahid Soleminani* had used its stealth capabilities and diversions from drones and FACs to get some shots at the *Ford*. Those missile launches were just what Navarro needed to home in on the frigate.

"Captain, Sonar. I have a fast-moving contact on the edge of our range. Distinctive acoustic signature of the twin-hulled *Shahid Soleminani*," said PO1 Max Ripley.

Navarro knew he had been pushing Ripley, his most experienced and talented sonar operator, but felt the need outweighed all other choices.

"Bearing?" Navarro asked.

"Captain, bearing is zero-four-six, range 15,000 yards, speed 32 knots."

"Periscope depth," ordered Navarro.

As the periscope broke the service, Navarro used the electro-optical sensor, which enhanced imaging, to have a look-see. There it was, visible through the eyepiece and projected on monitors—the faint outline of a stealth-angled catamaran frigate.

Navarro's XO said, "Sir, computer verification that it's the *Shahid Soleminani*."

Georgia's Combat Control System took over. Collecting and analyzing data from all available sensors, the CCS built a detailed picture of the target type and the ship's current speed and course. Efficiently, the CCS also spit out an engagement plan, including the number of missiles required and the desired impact points on the target.

WEPS set the configuration for the Tomahawks, feeding the deadly missiles the flight path waypoints and target coordinates. After finishing, WEPS ran a final system check. "Captain, WEPS. Missiles ready."

"Fire missiles."

WEPS replied, "Missiles away, Sir."

The submarine vibrated slightly as the Tomahawks ejected from their vertical launch tubes. They streaked toward their target with deadly accuracy.

Just as the crew of the *Shahid Soleminani* started to quiet down from the deafening celebration following their captain's address, alarms began to blare, warning of incoming missiles.

Without a second thought, Rezaei ordered, "Take evasive action. Launch chaff and decoy systems. Fire anti-aircraft guns at targets."

As the frigate made radical evasive turns, the Tomahawks weren't fooled. Equipped with advanced guidance systems, they wove through the ship's defenses with unerring precision. The last things Rezaei ever saw were the streaking American missiles striking his ship. He sank with his crew in less than three minutes.

Chapter 56

*CYBERSECURITY AND INFRASTRUCTURE SECURITY AGENCY
(CISA) HEADQUARTERS*
St. Elizabeth's West Campus, Washington, DC

As the war in the Middle East was escalating, Emily Hamal was fighting a different kind of war, one that was attempting to shut down the infrastructure of the US completely. Over the years, Iran had quickly learned the art of cyber warfare. Hamal used to joke about Iran's cyber operatives being nothing more than the equivalent of high school bullies. But the bullies had grown up and were now very good at their trade. The Iranians were attacking on several fronts and gaining ground. She, her team, and the nation's cyber forces were fighting against multiple intrusions.

Already the attack had shut down much of the US power grid, causing huge chunks of the nation to go dark. The Iranians had accomplished this by infiltrating the networks of numerous independent utility companies and gaining control over their power distribution. Simultaneously, they manipulated Supervisory Control and Data Acquisition Systems, which caused power outages and fluctuations. This caused a cascading failure by activating critical nodes in the software, creating a domino effect that led to widespread blackouts.

As Americans went to bed, their homes already dark, they would next discover their drinking water had been sabotaged. Iranian cyber operators had hacked into water treatment facilities and, with a few keystrokes, had altered chemical dosing systems by raising the levels of chlorine and other chemicals used to treat drinking water. At the same time, the hackers had turned off sensors to prevent accurate monitoring of chemical levels.

They had also successfully penetrated banking networks and disabled ATMs and online banking services. Additionally, the assault included an attack on the nation's communication network by targeting internet service providers and cutting off internet access for large regions.

The Iranians had cut into television and radio broadcasts in some highly populated areas, including Los Angeles, Chicago, and New York. They had loaded prerecorded messages designed to spread misinformation. In one spot, the hackers had even cloned President Taylor's voice, and showed him in the Oval Office:

Fellow Americans,

It is with a heavy heart that I address you today. As you may be aware, our nation is under a severe cyberattack that has compromised many of our critical systems. I want to assure you that we are doing everything in our power to manage this situation. However, I have made a difficult decision after careful consideration and consultation with our security experts and allies.

Effective immediately, we must comply with whatever demands are made to prevent further harm to our nation. This is not a decision I take lightly, but the safety and security of our citizens is paramount. We must avoid any actions leading to further escalation and more severe consequences.

I have commanded all military and security forces to stand down and avoid retaliatory actions. Our priority is to stabilize the situation and protect our people. I also ask all citizens to remain calm and stay indoors. Please refrain from unnecessary travel and avoid crowded places.

Our financial system has been severely impacted, and we are working tirelessly to restore normalcy. In the meantime, I advise you to be cautious with your financial transactions and limit any large withdrawals or transfers.

For most people who heard the broadcast, their first thoughts were about their money. Even though the banks were closed, many citizens made runs on every ATM in the nation, but they got nothing since the Iranians had shut down most banking services, fueling the panic. Everything citizens had ever feared was coming true, and most had believed every word the "president" had just told them.

President Taylor ordered the immediate activation of the Emergency Alert System to counter the fake video. Within thirty minutes, a message went out over radio, television, and mobile devices, making it clear that the previous presidential broadcast was fake. The EAS message reassured those who were panicking.

Within an hour, the president had appeared live on every major network. Standing behind a podium displaying the presidential seal and with his most-trusted advisors behind him, he explained how the Iranians had done the voice clone. After this short speech, President Taylor asked reporters in the press room questions, proving to everyone watching that it was a live event. He also told the anxious public that, for the foreseeable future, all his broadcasts would be live in the same setting in the president's press room and would be daily—there would be no addresses to the nation with only him in the picture.

Initial feedback from the press was that the American public was very shaken. Some even doubted that the president's address to the nation was live.

Hamal and her team at CISA doubled their efforts to get ahead of this unprecedented attack on the nation's infrastructure. The public wanted results, and she would do her part to ensure they got them. Her team members all understood that their efforts would take some time. Still, with the best minds in cyberwarfare under her command, they were beginning to isolate and identify specific areas of the attack. They were going to counter the Iranians before it was too late.

Chapter 57

B-2 Spirit

Diego Garcia

Situated on a tiny atoll in the Indian Ocean was the strategic home for the US Navy, the US Air Force, and one oldtimer B-2 pilot, Lieutenant Colonel Dakota "Cowboy" Remy. After receiving his latest marching orders, Cowboy left Diego Garcia to conduct a strike on the Natanz Enrichment Complex. In his darling's bomb bay were two GBU-57 Massive Ordnance Penetrators. The MOPs were explicitly designed to target deeply buried and fortified structures. Cowboy wasn't told what specific target he was after at Natanz, but his intel briefer said an Iranian defector had provided exact coordinates for the bombs' guidance systems.

Each gigantic bunker-busting 30,000-pound bomb had a penetrating capability of up to sixty-five yards through concrete. The trouble was that the Iranians also knew that metric and had specifically designed Natanz with multiple layers of concrete that reportedly could absorb and dissipate the force of penetrative munitions. Cowboy reckoned it was time to see if the Iranian engineers were better than the engineers who designed his bombs. He loved his chances.

Flying at 50,000 feet, the two-person crew of the B-2 maintained radio silence and used the aircraft's advanced stealth capabilities to evade detection by enemy radar systems. The route had been meticulously planned to avoid known air defense networks, and the journey took them over thousands of miles of ocean and hostile airspace. But the B-2's stealth technology ensured it remained undetected.

"Cowboy," said the copilot, taking his turn at the controls, "contrail warning light just went off. Suggest descending to 42,000 feet."

"Thank you, George," said Cowboy. "I agree. Make it happen."

A few minutes later, George said, "Approaching Iran's coastline. Thirty minutes to target."

Ten minutes later, Cowboy said, "George, I have the controls. Descending to pre-programmed altitude for our run on Natanz."

Natanz was located 150 miles from Tehran in a mountainous region that, in most instances, provided natural cover. But nothing could hide from the B-2.

George studied the monitor before him, saying, "Spot-on coordinates. Aligned with proper flight plan."

"Perform final check on weapons and targeting information," said Cowboy, sounding as relaxed as he was.

"Roger," said George. "Confirm all green."

"Copy, all green. Ten seconds to release. Nine—eight—seven—"

The bomb bay doors opened with minimal noise.

"—three—two—one—release." Cowboy pressed a button, and the two MOPs were quickly deployed.

Cowboy immediately climbed and banked away from the target area. George monitored the bombs' trajectories using the onboard systems. "Ordnance on target."

Both MOPs penetrated deep into the earth, their hardened casings allowing them to smash through multiple layers of reinforced concrete. The delayed fuses did their job, detonating inside the mountain and causing a massive explosion.

After a short time, Cowboy said, "Take the controls, George, and don't disturb me unless we're being shot down. Got it?"

"Yes, Sir," said George.

Cowboy was asleep a minute later.

As Cowboy settled in for a snooze, the USS *Georgia* fired four Tomahawks, each with a unitary warhead designed to follow up on the MOPs. All four missiles penetrated Iranian defenses and struck hard, enlarging the growing hole in the side of the mountain.

Chapter 58

NATANZ ENRICHMENT COMPLEX
Isfahan Province, Iran

General Arman Shirvani was so close. In another twenty-four hours, he would have Iran's first nuclear bomb ready. He had overseen the use of his atomic enrichment centrifuges to enrich the device's uranium. It had been a complicated process, but he fully understood the utmost necessity of the enrichment process. He had repeatedly spun uranium hexafluoride gas within his centrifuges so that the lighter Uranium-235 isotopes would accumulate in the center for extraction and eventual emplacement in his weapon. He would soon create more.

The general knew the Natanz Enrichment Complex would be a prime target once the shooting started. That is why he, his centrifuges, and his initial bomb were 100 meters underground, as he had planned when the site was constructed. He knew that the Americans' biggest bunker-buster bombs could only go 60 meters deep.

All around him, his staff was working feverishly but delicately, guiding the fine dance of the centrifuges. Watching over all of it gave him a moment to reflect on the early success of Iran against the infidels. He had heard several US ships, including the mighty USS *Ford,* been sunk. He wanted to hurry and get his nuclear warhead completed so it could be delivered to the secret missile site, wherever that was, and add it to Iran's glory.

He was picturing himself being awarded a medal by the Supreme Leader when, suddenly, red lights flashed and alarms blared with an ear-piercing whine. A voice came over the speakers, "All personnel in lockdown mode—incoming bombs. Initiate safety protocols. Move unnecessary personnel to safe zones. Begin immediate shutdown of all sensitive equipment."

Shirvani hurriedly donned his safety helmet and put on his specially manufactured breathing device. He felt confident the valuable centrifuges would be safe since they were distributed throughout the complex in reinforced concrete bunkers he had designed to withstand anything up to a nuclear explosion. His centrifuge staff had already commenced emergency shutdown procedures.

In the middle of Shirvani calling out to one of his officers, the first MOP struck with such force that he was knocked to the ground. His ears ached from the force and pressure of the explosion. Even worse than the first, a second explosion knocked out the lights. It was pitch black. Seconds later, the generators kicked in, and as the room lit up, he saw destruction all around him. Some of his staff were crushed by debris, their blood oozing out from under the concrete as if the concrete itself was bleeding.

As he struggled to gather himself and rise, four more explosions erupted in rapid succession, shaking the ground beneath him. He was lying on the ground as shards of concrete and debris pelted his body. The air was thick with choking dust, making breathing difficult for those without a breathing apparatus. Anxiety surged through him. He prayed fervently to Allah, pleading for mercy—begging to be spared so he could fulfill his mission and strike back at the nonbelievers. Later, he recounted how he had heard Allah's voice urging him to continue his mission and felt the hand of Al-Malik, the King, lifting him from the ground and guiding him onward.

As he tried to comprehend the damage, he saw men in white coveralls with orange vests and helmets helping the injured evacuate. One such man grabbed him.

"What are you doing?" yelled Shirvani. "Don't you know who I am? I must attend to the centrifuges, you fool." Just as quickly as the medic had grabbed the general, he let go and went on to assist others.

Outside, miles up in the sky, an American satellite was sending a live feed of the secondary fires and plumes of smoke drifting over the mountain. There was no way to know of the strike's success or failure from the aerial view, but it was clear it was time to send in Special Ops to stop the nuke from being transported from the site. There could be no failure—the security of the world rested on what happened with Iran's first nuclear device.

Chapter 59

US CLANDESTINE OP

Natanz Enrichment Complex

He couldn't believe the scale of destruction. The Natanz Enrichment Complex was still smoldering as CIA operative Dallas Steele viewed the devastation through his night vision goggles. Watching his six was his driver, Ali Karimi, a former Iranian special forces soldier—former, because of the persecution he had received his entire life due to his mother being an American—even though she was married to his Iranian father. He'd had enough of the harassment, and when he had his head buried in a beer at a run-down Tehrani bar, Steele had taken notice of him. They hit it off from the start. Ali had a doctor friend write up some bogus papers, and he got a medical discharge. From that moment on, he'd been Steele's "driver."

Before the war started, Steele and Ali made it through a checkpoint into an area outside of Natanz by using Steele's diplomatic immunity and a cover story that Ali was a research scientist looking over the area for a study about rural development and infrastructure projects in Iran. The guards seemed distracted by the egghead, their preparations for war more important than stupid research papers. They let the two operatives pass.

Steele was on the most significant mission of his career. He was to assist a Green Beret team in stopping the delivery of a nuclear bomb from the Natanz Enrichment Complex to an unknown missile site for possible use against—well, the *who* didn't matter. Iran with a nuclear weapon just wasn't an option.

A transmission came over his SATCOM radio. "Lonestar, Campbell. Ten minutes out."

"Campbell, Lonestar. LZ coordinates are 34.1234 north and 52.5678 east. The LZ is a flat, clear area approximately 100 feet east of the tree line. Wind direction is from the northwest at 5 knots. No movement around target. Over."

Captain Roger Ashburger was the first one down the fast rope at the designated landing zone. When his feet hit the ground and he got clear of the rope, he scanned the area to set up a circle perimeter, kneeling where he thought the best initiating point would be. The other eleven Green Berets hit the ground and joined him to form the perimeter. The helos egressed the LZ, and without a word being spoken, the team moved out at a controlled pace in tactical intervals to minimize the risk of multiple casualties from a single attack.

Everyone maintained radio silence and monitored their GPS to stay on course. Communication was done with only hand signals, and they employed stop, look, listen, and smell tactics. The team approached the rendezvous point using all available concealment.

Ashburger found Steele and slid up next to him and an Iranian dude—definitely not someone he was expecting.

"Boykin," Ashburger said into his mic, "notify command we've joined up."

"Roger that," replied Boykin.

"Good to see you again, Steele," said Ashburger. "Who's your friend?"

"My assistant." Nothing more needed to be said.

After some fist bumps, Steele got down to business. "There's only one main road in and out of this place. Suggest we plant some concealed explosives on the route, just in case."

"Agreed," said Ashburger. "Let me get that going."

He signaled for his engineer, who quickly came over. "Demo, I want you plus one to set up C-4 charges with remote detonators along the road below us. Purpose of disabling large vehicles. Got it?"

"Confirm. On it now," said Demo, and he was off.

"Do you think launching a drone to recon the area is safe?" asked Ashburger.

"I like it," Steele said.

"Good, let me get my team set up."

Ashburger and his fellow Green Berets got ready. All they needed was for a nuclear bomb to roll.

Inside the smoldering Natanz complex, General Shirvani, although shaken, could still make his rounds to assess the damage. While extensive destruction and chaos surrounded him, the specially constructed centrifuge bunkers did their job. Not one centrifuge was damaged or taken out of commission—a testament to his design. He felt Allah was overseeing and blessing his every move.

Quickly, he ordered all production to continue and placed a twelve-hour time limit to complete operations. He notified command, promising them the nuclear warhead would be ready for transportation.

Chapter 60

Anti-aircraft Missile Platoon, Battalion Landing Team 2/6
Arabian Sea

There were so many rumors going around the USS *Bataan*. It reminded Gunnery Sergeant Harley "Snake Eyes" Jennings of the saying that a rumor goes in one ear and out many mouths. Such was the case for the 2,400 Marines of the 26th MEUSOC, who were awaiting orders to kick some Iranian ass. One rumor had the Iranians sinking the USS *Ford*—but Jennings knew there was no way that had happened.

Lined up neatly outside the ship's armory, his Marines got their weapons cleared, loaded them, and put them in "safe." The distinctive clicks, slides, and bumps echoed in the area. Jennings inspected each one to ensure their magazines were fully loaded. As he made his rounds, Jennings noticed a young private whose hands shook noticeably as he received his M4 carbine.

"How we doing, Marine?" asked Jennings.

The young man had a look on his face like it was his last day on Earth. "Ah . . . great, Gunny."

"Are you afraid?"

The young Marine hesitated. "No, Gunny," he said, trying to be believable but failing.

"Listen," said Jennings, "I've been in the Corps for twenty-plus years and have been to hell and back. Do you think I got scared? Hell yeah, I did. Still do, too. But I'll tell you something."

"What's that, Gunny?" He still didn't look confident.

"There's two things you must remember," said Jennings. "One, you've trained and prepared for this moment. The skills you've learned and the knowledge you've gained will guide you through any challenge." He stopped, letting his words sink in before continuing.

"But most importantly, you're not alone. Your team's with you. Together, we're stronger and can fight harder because we know we can rely on each other. Understanding that your brothers and sisters have your six is the best compliment you could ever give or receive. Son, I've got your six, so let's get out there and kill those bastards."

With that, Jennings slapped the young man on the back and moved out. He knew war scared even the enemy. Those who embraced their fear and adjusted first, lived.

Out on the open flight deck of the enormous ship, ol' Snake Eyes took it all in. Troop boots battered the deck, aircraft fired up their engines, leaders barked orders, and oorahs rang out—the noise of troops going to war. Jennings felt invigorated in a way he hadn't felt in years. God, how he loved this shit.

Jennings, along with Captain Ozzie Sullivan, organized to load a massive Sikorsky CH-53E Super Stallion. Including the two of them, there were fifty-five Marines with their gear waiting in line for the signal to load. As the helicopter's blades churned, it seemed the helicopter had a life of its own. The rotor wash and noise soothed Jennings. It was like the first hit in a football game. Once you took it, the butterflies were gone.

Jennings thought it was amazing how much gear each Marine carried, no matter their build, age, or strength—seventy to one hundred pounds, based on one's job. It included:

1. Primary weapon, an M16A4, with ten fully loaded magazines
2. Secondary weapon, an M18 Modular Handgun System, with three fully loaded magazines
3. Additional ammunition
4. Grenades, including fragmentation, smoke, and flashbangs
5. Body armor with ballistic plates and enhanced combat helmet with night vision device mount
6. Communication gear and GPS device
7. Load-bearing equipment such as a tactical vest with pouches for magazines, grenades, and other gear

8. First aid kit

9. Entrenching tool

10. Night vision devices and ballistic eyewear

11. Field rations

12. Water purification tablets

13. Personal hygiene items

14. Lightweight sleeping bag

15. Flashlight

16. Multi-tool and other specialty tools

17. Notepad and pen

18. Military ID, dog tags

19. Specialized equipment such as demolition kit, sniper equipment, advanced communication gear including encryption devices, and advanced medical supplies

20. KA-BAR knife

With 150 Marines loaded into two CH-53E helicopters and one MV-22B Osprey, the group took off and spread out in combat formation. Four Marine Corps F-35Bs, an EA-18G, and two Bell AH-1Z Viper helicopters provided cover for the mission. The Growler led the pack and laid down electronic countermeasures. Already airborne in the area and playing quarterback was one Navy E-2 piloted by Lieutenant Commander Sarah "Danger" Freeman.

The lead F-35 radioed, "All units, Raider 11. We have you on radar and are in escort formation. All Raiders spread out in tactical formation and engage any threats. Jammer 11, request status."

"Raider 11, we have begun electronic jamming. All units stay within the protected zone."

"Raider 11, Gunner 11. We're both on station and positioned to provide ground support."

"Raider 11, Hawker 11," came the voice of the Electronic Warfare Officer from the EA-18G. "We have four bogeys at 20 miles, bearing zero-four-five, altitude 15,000 feet, and closing fast. Radar indicates one MiG-29 and three F-4s. Engage and neutralize, over."

If there was any space left in their calculating brains, the Marine pilots knew they had the upper hand against the F-4s—from an era when people had black-and-white TVs—and the 1980s MiG. However, although the Iranian fighters were old, the pilots had a creed: Never underestimate the capabilities and strength of the old because they may surprise you.

"Hawker 11, Raider 11. Copy all. Raider flight, I have target acquired. Raider 12 and 13 break formation and join me to engage. Brevity comms and weapons tight."

All aircraft acknowledged, and targets were assigned in the appropriate HUDs.

Raider 11 got a visual on the MiG and said, "One's on the MiG." He fired an AIM-120D Advanced Medium-Range Air-to-Air Missile. "Fox three."

Just as quickly, Raider 12 and Raider 13 sequentially announced Fox three. Guided by the advanced electronics of the world's most advanced fighters, the AMRAAMs flashed toward their targets.

Immediately, two of the F-4s went down in spectacular balls of fire, but the other F-4 and the MiG somehow evaded the missiles and lined up for kills on the Americans. Now the adversaries were in an old-fashioned close-in dogfight.

"Three's on the MiG." Outmaneuvering the MiG, Raider 13 leveraged their superior agility, stealth, and situational awareness to get behind the fighter, then lined up their GAU-22/A Gatling gun. "Three, guns, guns, guns," Raider 13 called out. As the MiG attempted to dive, the computers on the F-35 adjusted, and lit up the outdated MiG, sending it and its Iranian pilot to their final resting place.

At the same time, the remaining F-4 got a missile lock on Raider 12 and fired an infrared-guided missile. Raider 12 immediately deployed flares and pulled high-G maneuvers to evade the incoming missile.

Raider 11, anticipating the F-4 pilot's moves, fired one AIM-9X missile, "One, Fox two." The Sidewinder's launch motor propelled it away from the aircraft, and after a safe distance, the main motor ignited and accelerated it to Mach

2. Its advanced imaging infrared seeker, directed by its onboard computer, predicted the F-4's course, made a few trajectory corrections and slammed into the fighter. The aircraft blew in two. Twisting in fiery circles, the sections of the antique fighter spun to the ground, smashing into several huts in a small Iranian village and starting secondary fires.

"Hawker 11, Raider 11. Four bandits down, no chutes. Area is clear."

"Raider flight, this is Hawker 11. Excellent work," Sarah said with joy in her voice. "Resume escort formation and continue to LZ Charlie. No additional threats detected."

On board the transport aircraft, the lead CH-53's back-end crew and Marines had no idea some Iranians were attempting to kill them. The pilot thought he should let them know. "Be advised that our escorts are engaging enemy aircraft. We're maintaining course to the LZ. Stay seated and secure your gear."

Sullivan yelled the message as best he could to Jennings. Two young Marines sitting near him looked startled. Jennings heard one holler to the other, "You hear that? They're in a fight up there."

The young soldier who'd had shaky hands glanced at Jennings and then turned to his buddy, answering with a steady voice and confident look, "Yeah, I heard. They're Marines, so they got our six." The kid turned to Snake Eyes and winked.

Jennings had heard everything and couldn't help but smile back at the smart-ass. He thought this new generation might make it after all. Oorah.

Chapter 61

USS FORD
Persian Gulf

On the bridge, Admiral Holloway and Captain Albright were observing the *Ford's* operations. Holloway had to admit that the Iranians had caught him with his pants down. Their surprise first strike was a ballsy move. Adding insult to injury was the drone strike on his flagship. It was the first US carrier to be struck by the enemy since World War II—and it had happened on his watch.

The admiral rationalized that even though Catapult 1 was temporarily out of service, the *Ford* still had three more from which to launch aircraft. Weapons Elevator 3 was partially demolished, meaning a longer transit for select munitions. More than anything else, he was sickened by the loss of life and worried for the wounded. But it was his job to encourage his team to press on and keep fighting to honor the sacrifice of those brave souls. As Plato notably said, "Only the dead have seen the end of war."

It was time for the United States of America to deliver retaliation for Independence Hall and all the lives lost, both then and now.

"Captain, launch your aircraft," Holloway ordered.

"Aye, Sir," said Albright, who said on comms, "CAG, launch aircraft."

The admiral's communications team transmitted his launch order to the two other carrier COs in the task force: the *Reagan* in the southern Persian Gulf and the *Nimitz* in the northern Arabian Sea. This was followed by official messages to all units in the task force to ensure everyone knew that combat operations had officially begun. Supporting commands across the Middle East also got messages, and every sailor, Marine, soldier, and airman began to fulfill their duties to demonstrate to the world that enemies should take heed of the might of the USA when they ruffled the feathers of the American eagle.

As the power of the US Navy waited in the queue to launch from three carriers, F-35 flight lead Jessie Hampton was first up on *Ford*'s Catapult 2. He got the go sign from the yellow-shirted shooter to launch. Jessie took an extra second to give her an impressive salute—then he was gone in the glow of his afterburner.

Chapter 62

St. Elizabeth's West Campus, Washington, DC

Across the globe at CISA Headquarters in Washington, DC, Emily Hamal was fighting her war with ones and zeros instead of missiles. As a team leader, she was amazed at how the normally bureaucracy-laden agencies of the US government had come together as one in the cyber fight with Iran. The DHS, FBI, NSA, and DOD were all on board with their cybersecurity units. Even the private sector, which overlapped in some areas with the nation's infrastructure, was assisting in any way possible.

She thought this collaboration enhanced everyone's effectiveness in cyberspace operations through shared intelligence and joint missions. While many of these interagency assets were battling Iran's effective cyberattack on US infrastructure, she was leading the cyberattack on Iran as a part of the US military operation that had just begun in the Middle East.

Fortunately, contingency plans were in place and constantly updated for such a situation, and she was putting them into action. Hamal's research identified and documented Iran's cyber vulnerabilities, which became attack points targeted by malware, ransomware, and cyber tools developed over the past year.

It was early in the morning in Tehran, Iran, when the restaurant cooks started making breakfast, and suddenly, their electricity went out. They had no idea why. Looking outdoors, they saw that the traffic lights were also out, causing massive traffic backups. Iranian engineers scrambled to identify the cause, unaware that their systems had been compromised months ago during a CISA reconnaissance. The planted malware, now active, initiated a series of cascading failures within the grid. Simultaneously, Iran's telecommunications infrastructure faced relentless attacks. CISA's team used distributed denial-of-service attacks to overwhelm key communication nodes, effectively severing lines of communication. Military and government officials were isolated and unable to coordinate a cohesive response.

With Iran's civilian infrastructure in disarray, the focus shifted to their military capabilities. Cyber units using intelligence gathered from months of espionage launched precision attacks on military command and control systems.

Iran's massive missile systems had been more challenging to penetrate. Hamal had noted those systems were heavily fortified with multiple layers of security, including air-gapped networks and advanced encryption protocols. In this attack, initial attempts to breach those defenses were met with failure.

In the rear conference room, with a clear view of a giant monitor constantly updating the cyber picture in both Iran and the US, Hamal met with her section chiefs to formulate a workable plan to overcome the formidable cyber defenses of Iran's missile systems.

"So Lia," Hamal said, "what about human intelligence sources? Did you get any info about the areas near Iran's largest missile bases?"

"In checking with the CIA," replied Lia, a sharp twenty-something, "they were hesitant to give many specifics, but they'll run our HUMINT request up the chain and get back to me. I think they have a couple of assets in place, but I'll let you know as soon as I hear back."

"I can't stress how important a wireless access point is," said Hamal. "Someone inside the facility must install a WAP to bridge the air-gapped network and allow us remote access. We have no other way in." Hamal understood that Lia knew this, but she wanted everyone to comprehend what the showstopper was. She moved on.

"Having a plan B is critical if plan A fails," she said straight-faced. "Jake, regarding their supply chain, what are the possibilities of going after the critical components used in the missile systems?"

"Ma'am, they're strong."

Every time she heard *Ma'am*, Hamal had to regroup as she pictured some old hag with her hair undone and looking like a scarecrow, but she told herself to get over it and focus.

Jake continued, "Two months ago, I oversaw the project to introduce malware into the hardware and software of missile components. To clarify for everyone, this malware will initiate a multistage attack, first disabling security protocols and then corrupting the guidance and control systems of the missiles. By inputting false data, the malware will cause malfunctions and render the missiles unreliable if all goes according to plan. It's in place and ready to go, Ma'am."

Ouch, Hamal thought before saying, "Activate it and keep me up to date either way." Just as Jake was about to answer, she held up her hand, saving herself another Ma'am. "Okay, let's put these into action, and the rest of you keep trying to penetrate Iran's missile system by any means possible. This is a war, and we must do our part. Got it?"

Heads nodded, and several "Yes Ma'am's" were uttered to the chagrin of Hamal, who felt like an old hag again.

Chapter 63

USS GEORGIA
Persian Gulf

Lying silently beneath the Persian Gulf's surface, the *Ohio*-class guided missile submarine's crew enjoyed a rare break from GQ. Some of *Georgia*'s sailors were getting fed, and others were catching up on their sleep, all in preparation for the start of hostilities against Iran.

Earlier, Navarro had received the orders he and his crew had been waiting for. He felt honored to be able to do his part for his country after the surprise terrorist attacks on Independence Hall and US forces in the Middle East.

In the submarine's control room, Navarro issued commands with calm authority. The target packages had been meticulously prepared, detailing the precise coordinates of multiple high-value Iranian locations. Among them were missile silos, radar installations, and Imam Ali Military Base. The objective was clear: to cripple Iran's missile capabilities and disrupt their command structure.

All was quiet at Imam Ali Military Base near Khorramshahr, Iran. Built in 2018, the base had only one commander—General Amir Nasserian of the IRGC Aerospace Force. Born into a family with strong military traditions, Nasserian had dedicated his life to defending his country. He was close to the Supreme Leader because of his commitment to Iran's sovereignty and ideological goals, and he was a man who could be counted on to get the job done. An IRGC Military Academy graduate specializing in missile expertise, Nasserian was promoted repeatedly due to his keen understanding of modern warfare and the use of technology such as missiles to control the battlefield.

Over the years, his base had been attacked so many times that he had lost track. Topping the list of enemies was the Israeli Air Force, which had attempted to bomb the base into the Stone Age. Not to miss out, the United States had bombed the base in 2021 for some made-up excuse, and later that year the infidels had come back to bomb his base again, killing a score of Iranian-backed Iraqi militia fighters—one a dear friend of his.

Yet, here he was, still in command of Iran's most strategically essential missile base. And it was protected as such. Imam Ali Military Base was surrounded by an intricate layer of SAMs, including his headliner, the S-300, supplied by his friends from Russia. It was capable of engaging multiple long-range aerial targets, including cruise missiles, aircraft, and ballistic missiles. The S-300 came with advanced radar, and complementing the SAM was the Iranian-developed Bavar-373. Like its Russian model, it was equipped with phased-array radar and could handle multiple targets simultaneously. Backing up these systems was the Russian-made mobile Tor-M1 using 9M331 surface-to-air missiles. Each mobile launcher had eight ready-to-fire missiles.

The air defense systems were integrated into a centralized command and control network, allowing Nasserian to share real-time data and coordinate defenses from his underground bunker.

Now that Iran was at war with the US, he expected Iman Ali Military Base to be number one on all the target lists. No problem—he'd been there before and had easily survived. He knew why. Because he believed with all his soul that Allah would bless and protect him against the nonbelievers of the US. He felt at peace with that, praise Allah.

Down on the USS *Georgia*, there was little time for praising anyone but the captain, not as a God but as their CO. His decisions could mean life or death for the crew on station and ready to fulfill his orders.

"Tomahawks ready in all tubes," reported WEPS.

"Commence launch sequence," ordered Navarro.

As the TLAMs were about to be fired, a quiet rumbling announced the missile canisters were prepared. Then, the hatches flew open.

"Fire one," Navarro said.

With a whoosh, the first missile shot out of its launch tube. After breaking the surface of the water, it roared toward its destiny—and someone else's. Many more followed.

After the last missile left from the depths, Navaro ordered, "Commence evasive maneuvers."

"Aye, Captain," said the officer of the deck. "Helm, execute evasive pattern Delta. Dive to 500 feet. Increase speed to 25 knots."

It was time to be a ghost again as the *Georgia* dove steeply through the dark sea.

Khorramshahr, Iran

In the fortified underground command center of Imam Ali Military Base, Nasserian's radar was screaming warnings, telling him of incoming missiles.

"This is General Nasserian," he said on the command net. "Activate early warning radar systems. I want a track on the trajectory and estimated impact points."

Knowing the tactical importance of the S-300s, Nasserian ordered their immediate activation. Operators in the missile defense units prepared to engage the incoming threats. The sophisticated radar of the S-300 systems promptly locked on to the Tomahawks, providing targeting data to the missile launchers.

"Activate electronic warfare jamming and spoofing immediately," Nasserian ordered. "Make sure they emit full signatures."

This was his ace in the hole. Around the critical components of the base, the general had built several mock structures using materials that mimicked the heat and radar signatures of actual buildings. They had electronic radio communications and decoy heat sources with moving parts that replicated the thermal and kinetic signatures of operational equipment.

Nasserian had also built redundant systems to ensure uninterrupted power supply, especially for maintaining the command and control systems. He had the Tor-M1 reserve missile batteries positioned at different locations around the base to provide overlapping fields of fire. His reasoning was simple: If one unit was destroyed or compromised, others could still engage incoming threats.

The first wave of Tomahawks reached the base's perimeter but were overwhelmed by a barrage of false signals as they locked onto decoy structures. One by one, the missiles struck the fakes, erupting into massive fireballs and scattering debris in every direction. Watching video feeds from his bunker, the general said, "Report the status of missile hits."

"Sir, decoys one through five have been hit with no significant damage to the main structures."

The sly general smiled. The actual radar installations, command bunkers, and missile launchers remained untouched, and they continued to operate under the protection of their hardened shelters. The decoys had served their purpose by absorbing the brunt of the attack and preserving the base's operational capability. Although Nasserian was cunning, he knew the Americans had deep pockets and a vast arsenal of weapons. This was just the first act in a play that he hoped had a happy ending—for him.

Chapter 64

US NAVY FIGHTER STRIKE FORCE
Northern Persian Gulf and Iran

Along with an E-2 from the *Ford*, Sarah Freeman flew over the northern Gulf to support the fighter aircraft assigned to attack Imam Ali Military Base. She was a bit edgy because something hadn't seemed right when she reviewed the intel and imagery after the post-mission brief on *Reagan*. Unable to shake her intuition, she felt some uneasiness that her copilot noticed but kept to himself.

Flying at 30,000 feet, there was a lot going on. The crew had witnessed the Tomahawk cruise missile attack on Imam Ali, which appeared to be successful—to all except for Sarah, who wasn't buying it. Monitoring the radar screen closely, she mentally reviewed the intel she had seen. The radar system could differentiate between various signatures, and she noticed they didn't match up.

Years ago, in advanced flight training, she recalled how her instructor made it clear not to make excuses for something you doubted on the battlefield, but to ask questions, be inquisitive, and not accept things at face value. If you have a suspicion, act on it—don't blow it off.

Running it by her co-pilot, "Eagle, there was something unusual about the emissions from those installations at Imam. To me, they didn't match the activity patterns we've observed in previous missions—you get what I'm saying?"

"Sorry, Danger, I had my hands full and didn't notice. Maybe run it by intel and see what they say."

"Good idea." Getting them on secure comms, Sarah asked the intel folks to cross-reference the radar data from her E-2 with recent satellite imagery. She heard back in minutes.

"Confirming visual anomalies. Satellite images show that several structures were constructed quickly, and their manufacturing doesn't align with typical military configurations. Additionally, the radar patterns don't match. We suggest that these are possible decoy facilities."

"I thought so, thanks," said Sarah. "I will get this out right away." Shit, she thought, the flight was headed straight into a trap, and one of the pilots was her husband.

She established a secure channel to the F-35, F/A-18E, and EA-18G strike forces en route to bomb Imam Ali Military Base. Glancing at the daily comm plan, she noticed that the strike force's flight leader was identified as Jedi 11, a callsign that sounded familiar to her."

"Jedi 11, Hawker 11."

"Hawker 11, Jedi 11," replied Lieutenant Commander Jessie Hampton. "What do you have?" As the words left his mouth, Jessie thought, That sounded like Sarah.

Sarah halted. Her crew noticed immediately that she had paused just a little too long. It was like she was speechless—and that never happened.

She couldn't believe Jedi 11 was her Jessie. She trembled for a brief second, telling herself to get it together. This was no time for a family reunion. She got control of herself. She had to—her husband was flying right into a trap!

Finally, she got the words out. "Jedi 11, be advised, we have identified potential decoys at Imam. Suggest you prioritize verification of targets before engaging. Maintain heightened vigilance for active installations that haven't been destroyed."

Well, shit, Jessie thought, that changed everything. Focusing on the mission and not the love of his life, who was always cool under fire, he recognized the entire strike force was in jeopardy from missile batteries that had not been destroyed.

"Roger that, Hawker 11. Thanks for the heads-up." He switched frequencies. "Strike Force, Jedi 11. Adjust to a new attack protocol. Verify all targets using FLIR and ISR before engagement. Maintain situational awareness and prepare for active defenses."

Immediately, the F-35 pilots, equipped with advanced forward-looking infrared systems, took the lead in target verification. The FLIR allowed the pilots to detect heat signatures and differentiate between active installations and decoys based on thermal emissions. The aviators began to scan each target area, looking for signs of genuine activity such as vehicle movement, active radar emissions, and heat patterns indicative of operational equipment.

Intelligence, surveillance, and reconnaissance drones deployed from the *Reagan* assisted the strike force by providing real-time high-resolution video and imagery of the target site. The aircraft computers were fed the ISR data, providing a comprehensive view of each target.

"Spooky 18, Jedi 11. You're up. Special attention to anomalies in radar signatures."

The two EA-18G Growlers ramped up their electronic warfare activities, jamming Iranian radar and communications while looking for decoy activity. As they approached the battlefield, the F-35 pilots used their advanced helmet-mounted displays to overlay FLIR and ISR data onto their visual field, allowing for precise identification and targeting.

"Toxic 11, Jedi 11," Jessie called to the F-18s flying with his F-35s, "confirm multiple targets. Marking high-value installations and missile batteries now."

The F-35s deployed laser designators and GPS coordinates to mark verified objectives. The advanced targeting pods on the F-35s ensured pinpoint accuracy. While the F-35s were selecting targets, careful not to sight the decoys, the F-18s remained out of range of Iranian defenses until making their target run.

Jessie assigned command centers, active radar sites, and missile locations as top priorities. He painted the targets using a designator that was invisible to the naked eye but easily detected by laser-guided munitions. He sent the coordinates via data link to the sixteen F-18 fighters. The weapon of choice for this mission was the Paveway with seeker heads that could detect the reflected laser energy.

"Toxic 11, Jedi 11. Prepare to engage on my mark."

The Toxic flight leader clicked his mic twice to acknowledge. Several miles from the base, the F-18s cruising at 30,000 feet saw their HUDs light up with each aircraft's target details.

"Toxic 11, targets designated," said Jessie. "It's all yours."

Plummeting to 15,000 feet for their attack run, the F-18s released their laser-guided munitions.

"Toxic 11, bombs away."

As the bombs silently dropped, they adjusted their fins to follow the laser path etched by the F-35s.

A warning suddenly came over the net. "Strike Force, Hawker 11. Incoming bandits, six Su-35s, bearing two-seven-zero." Sarah's voice was calm but urgent. At the same time, the E-2 sent the information over a data link, which was displayed on each pilot's HUD. Jessie noted the Su-35s were closing rapidly.

Major Arash Zamani, flying the lead Su-35, radioed to his flight, "Brothers, we have American F-18s on radar, approaching fast. F-35s are also reported in the area but not showing up on radar. Tighten formation. Stand by for target assignments."

Zamani wanted to increase their situational awareness by flying in a close formation. It also enabled his flight to execute coordinated missile volleys to saturate enemy defenses. "Assigned targets are on your HUDs. Fire—now." Not a half second after the words left his lips, warning alarms went off. "Missiles inbound. Take evasive maneuvers." Jessie quickly assigned targets to his flight of fourteen F-35s when he saw the Su-35s on radar.

"Spread formation," he ordered his flight, noting that the F-18s had just completed their bomb run, fired countermeasures, and gone to 40,000 feet as planned.

"Lock on your targets and fire one," said Jessie.

Rapidly, a mixture of fourteen AIM-120s and AIM-260s left their rails. The Fox three call filled the radio frequency.

Moments after each Su-35 launched two Russian-made Vympel R-77 fire-and-forget radar-guided missiles, similar to the US AMRAAMs, the onboard computers guided the missiles toward their designated targets. This freed the pilots to evade the incoming missiles. Using their RWR, the Iranian pilots calculated the approaching threats' direction, type, and range.

As their Russian instructors had trained them, several of the six advanced fighters went into break turns, a series of high-G maneuvers to rapidly change direction and put some space between themselves and the missiles trying to kill them.

Fully understanding the capabilities of the AIM-120 chasing him, Zamani utilized the S-turn. He threw his stick hard to the left, which created a substantial change in his trajectory. This initial turn forced the missiles to adjust accordingly, thus consuming more energy.

Just as he came out of the left turn, Azizi reversed his direction to the right, creating the first loop of the *S*. Again, the missile adjusted its course, challenging its ability to maintain a lock. Zamani continued to make drastic S-turns, forcing the AIM-120 to use its precious fuel. Finally, the highly maneuverable jet exceeded the missile's turning radius, causing it to overshoot and lose track of its intended victim.

Others in his strike force were less fortunate. The new JATM was blowing them out of the sky. While the Su-35s were more maneuverable than the F-35s, they couldn't out-maneuver the AIM-260s.

The JATMs flew by the Iranian electronic countermeasures as if they were an afterthought. They used their sophisticated algorithms to predict their targets' future positions based on current trajectories and behaviors. The missiles recognized S-turns and break turns like dragonflies anticipate their prey, killing them at nearly every attempt. Combined with thrust vectoring, which allowed the missiles to make extreme turns easily, the JATMs could keep up with their targets' high-G maneuvers. Even last-second evasive actions were futile as the missiles' proximity fuses ensured detonation close enough to cause significant damage—usually target destruction.

All four Su-35s targeted by the AIM-260s went down in fiery balls. With over half his flight destroyed, Zamani decided to save the remaining fighter and himself. He told the other pilot, "Disengage and fall back to base."

Using their afterburners for more speed, the two Su-35 pilots raced away, licking their wounds. Zamani muttered to himself, "We'll be back, and we'll be ready."

After chasing off the last two Su-35s, Jessie was saddened to learn that four F-18s had been lost to Iranian missiles. It was clear that the skies over Iran would now be a battlefield, with an unknown number of Russian-made Su-35s leading the charge. He returned to the *Ford,* troubled by the loss of great pilots but proud of working alongside his wife, who had saved his strike force from certain disaster.

Meanwhile, Sarah was headed to her home aboard the *Reagan,* pleased she had listened to her gut, pursued a hunch, and supplied critical information for the strike on Imam Ali Military Base. The fact that her husband was the mission lead added to her satisfaction. They both handled the situation like professionals, and hell, it would be a great story to tell their kids someday. She smiled broadly at that thought.

As the dust settled following the final wave of attacks back at Imam Ali Military Base, General Shirvani found himself facing a critical situation. Despite its elaborate defenses and decoy tactics, the base had suffered significant damage to its primary installations. High-value assets, including his command center, radar sites, and missile launchers, were largely neutralized.

Shirvani initiated emergency protocols to discover the extent of the damage. He ordered the remaining operational units to secure essential equipment and prepare for a tactical retreat. Communication lines to higher command were re-established, and immediate reinforcements and additional air defenses were requested.

In his report to senior Iranian military leadership, he advocated for more coordination with other military bases and units to bolster defenses and prepare for more retaliatory actions by the Americans. He shifted his focus to enhancing electronic warfare and improving his base's critical infrastructure reliability, and he ensured that Iman Ali remained a key component of Iran's military might.

Chapter 65

ANTI-AIRCRAFT MISSILE PLATOON, BATTALION LANDING TEAM 2/6
Ahvaz Oil Field, Iran

The sun had barely begun to rise over the horizon when the roar of rotor blades filled the air above the vast expanse of the Ahvaz Oil Field. Two CH-53E Super Stallions and one MV-22B Osprey, each bearing the United States Marine Corps insignia, sliced through the sky in a tight formation. Inside the aircraft, the Marines of Anti-Aircraft Missile Platoon, Battalion Landing Team 2/6 from the 26th MEUSOC, were preparing to relieve the platoon from SEAL Team 10.

In the lead CH-53E, Gunny Harley Jennings prepared to give a final brief to his Marines. Fifty-five pairs of eyes looked at him. Man, he thought, these guys are so young.

"Alright, listen up!" He had to work hard to yell over the rotor noise. "We're taking over from the SEALs. They've taken Ahvaz Oil Field, but now it's our turn to secure it. Our primary objectives are to establish a defensive perimeter, shut down the oil, and allow only people from the US of A to enter or exit. ROE is wide open. We're at war with these Iranian pricks, and they'll be wanting to take this huge oil facility back. That won't happen, will it, Marines?"

"No, Gunny. Oorah!"

"Let's go," yelled Snake Eyes.

The aircraft created a haboob as it touched down. After the rear ramps lowered, the Marines swiftly dismounted and efficiently spread out to secure the immediate area. Adding to the dust storm was the Osprey hovering nearby, its rotors tilting as it transitioned from flight mode to a landing configuration, more boots on the ground.

Once the dust settled, Jennings and Captain Ozzie Sullivan spotted Lieutenant Commander Ross Carter waiting for them. Everyone saluted as if they were on the parade ground at Annapolis. They warmly shook hands.

"Captain Sullivan, Gunny," said Carter, "it's good to see you guys. My men and I are ready for a break. The perimeter and facility are secure."

"Understood," said Sullivan, "we're happy to be here. We've got the oil field. Safe travels back, Sir." The men saluted again, and the SEALs loaded up in the Osprey, which quickly took off.

Sullivan turned to Jennings. "Gunny, secure the facility and call in the heavy stuff so we can get comfortable in our new digs." With that, he headed inside the main building to see where he would set up his HQ.

Jennings took it all in for a minute and briefly reflected on how different this was from China—from palm trees to desert. But it was war, and nothing about that changed except the scenery.

He noticed how the Ahvaz Oil Field stretched out in every direction, as far as the eye could see. It was a massive complex of pipes, storage tanks, and pumping stations. As he breathed in, the acrid scent of oil burned his nostrils. He could hear machines in the distance, and he needed to get busy and shut everything down. It was time to take some bills from the Supreme Leader's wallet.

Chapter 66

B-2 SPIRIT

Persian Gulf

Cruising over the Gulf as he flew his darling at 50,000 feet, Lieutenant Colonel Cowboy Remy had to admit his aircraft was getting old and would soon be replaced, exactly like him. Even though his B-2 was made of metal and electronics, the plane was like a living, breathing soul to him. He felt that both of them didn't regret growing older—hell, it was a privilege denied to many pilots and some B-2s. After all these years, he and his darling were still partners and still flying.

With a few minutes on his hands before he had to get working on the kill chain for today's mission, Cowboy checked his brain's filing cabinet and opened the file on the S-300 and S-400 Russian-designed SAMs. For good reason, these missiles were at the heart of Iran's air defenses.

The S-300 had a range of 120 miles and could engage multiple targets simultaneously to intercept various aerial threats, including advanced tactical and strategic aircraft. The S-400 was another story. It had a range of 300 miles and could engage a more comprehensive array of targets. He didn't want to think about it, but he had to admit that the S-

400 was the ideal weapon against stealth aircraft, even his darling.

Since their target for this mission was Eighth Shekari Air Base near Esfahan, he knew the SAMs would be a problem. They protected the target, which itself protected the Natanz nuclear site. As he and George went feet-dry on approaching the target, the two officers constantly checked their computers, updating the optimal course and adjusting it to minimize their radar signature.

"Target coordinates confirmed," said George from the right seat. There were no anomalies. Cowboy looked at his display, seeing a series of blinking markers, each representing a vital component of the Iranian air defense network.

"Initiate final approach sequence," ordered Cowboy. The flying-wing bomber adjusted course with the precision of years of development and testing. Both men were using every tactic at their disposal to avoid becoming a target of the missiles they were seeking to destroy. In the weapons bay was an array of precision-guided munitions best suited for the mission. Flying at a standoff distance, the AGM-158 Joint Air-to-Surface Standoff Missile was first up, which would attempt to demolish the central radar installations searching for them.

"Initiate JASSM launch sequence," said Cowboy. "Confirm target pre-loaded coordinates."

"Check," replied George. "Ready. Opening weapon bay doors."

Observing all the exacting details converging for a launch, Cowboy ordered, "Fire missiles."

The JASSMs dropped from the weapons bay, and just as they cleared the aircraft, their engines ignited.

"Weapons away," said George. "On course."

Using their internal navigation systems, including GPS and inertial guidance, the missiles adjusted course as they flew toward their destinies. Closing in, the missiles switched to terminal guidance mode and used their onboard infrared seekers to lock precisely onto the targets.

GHADIR RADAR SITE
Undisclosed location

Sergeant Amir Farzan was a top-notch radar operator for the Islamic Republic of Iran Air Defense Force. He grew up with a fascination for technology and a love for his country, which his father, a retired Air Force pilot, had instilled in him. He was noted as a radar specialist because of his uncanny ability to interpret radar signals and distinguish between genuine threats and false alarms. He consistently detected stealth aircraft and missiles. There was no one better at using the Iranian-built Ghadir radar system.

The phased-array Ghadir used a VHF band to detect low-observable targets that could outwit other radar systems. The Ghadirs were spread throughout Iran at fixed locations. Recently, they had been installed on mobile platforms and moved from place to place to better outwit their enemy's satellites and intelligence-gathering instruments. All sites were classified.

Farzan was on high alert since the Americans had launched attacks across his homeland. After being on duty for eight hours, he refused to let his weary body relax. He knew his job's importance and wouldn't disappoint anyone, including Allah.

Abruptly, a faint blip appeared on the radar screen. Most of Iran's radar operators would have missed it, but not Farzan. His eyes sharpened as he scrutinized the signal. It didn't match up with any known commercial or military aircraft signatures; he knew from experience that it was indicative of a stealth aircraft.

He quickly got on comms. "Captain, I have a possible stealth target detected near Eighth Shekari Air Base."

The command center sprang into action. Data was quickly relayed to the central defense headquarters, and additional tracking systems were brought online to validate Farzan's findings. He stayed with it, continuing to track the weak blip.

"Farzan, stay with your contact," said his captain. "Bogey identified as a B-2."

With the bomber now identified, the missile defense network went into action. Air defense operators coordinated with nearby S-300 and S-400 missile batteries to prepare them for an engagement. The target's coordinates were fed into the missile guidance systems, and the launch crews stood by.

"Target within engagement range," said the air defense coordinator. When the commander gave the order, the S-400 missile batteries thundered to life within two seconds. The missiles, designed to intercept high-speed and high-altitude targets, streaked into the sky, guided by the precise data from Farzan's Ghadir radar.

B-2 SPIRIT
Over Iran

As the first salvo of S-400 missiles launched, their exhaust trails brilliantly illuminated the desert. It might have been a pretty sight had the missiles not been aimed at Cowboy's B-2. Inside the bomber, Cowboy and George were at top speed after their bomb run, heading for the safety of the water. Suddenly, an ear-piercing warning alarm went off in the cockpit.

George yelled, "Multiple incoming missiles."

"Got it," said Cowboy. "Hang on, brother." He threw the jet into a hard turn, beginning a series of complex maneuvers designed to confuse an incoming missile. Immediately, the B-2's electronic warfare systems activated, attempting to jam the missile guidance systems and hopefully spoof the radar systems. At the same time, he deployed chaff and flares.

Cowboy kept maneuvering, trying to get over water and near the friendlies who would be there—if needed. Flying the B-2 like a fighter, he performed tight barrel rolls and evasive turns, each move like a silent prayer for survival. Little did he know that an Iranian sergeant named Farzan was able to keep his radar pointed right at the B-2 so that the incoming missiles could receive constant updates and adjust their trajectories in real-time to counter every move Cowboy made.

The first missile exploded nearby, and the shockwave rattled the B-2 but caused no significant damage. Cowboy's heart pounded as he fought to maintain control, aware that more missiles were closing in.

The second missile found its mark, ripping through the B-2's right wing. A bone-jarring explosion followed a blinding flash. The aircraft lurched uncontrollably. Alarms blared, and system failure lights added to the noises neither pilot had ever wanted to hear. Cowboy refused to give up.

He struggled to stabilize the spiraling aircraft, but the damage was catastrophic.

Realizing it was hopeless, Cowboy made a bleak decision. "Abandon aircraft!" he shouted, "Get to the escape hatch." George depressurized the cabin and manually jettisoned the hatch located in the lower part of the B-2's cockpit. As the two pilots strapped on their parachutes, both could feel the heat from the fire as Cowboy's darling was spinning towards her death. Cowboy ordered George through the opening, and then Cowboy jumped. The air was cold, and the rushing air tossed Cowboy around like a stuffed toy. His parachute deployed almost immediately, giving him some stability. Cowboy looked around and saw a demarcation between water and land; it looked like they would be drifting toward the water. He looked for Geroge but didn't see him. He pulled the "Shootdown" and "Evasion" files out of the very back of his brain's filing cabinet. As he drifted towards the sea, he had some time to review the files' contents and prepare for what could come next. And he kept looking for his co-pilot.

On the ground, Sergeant Farzan watched the distant fireball through binoculars, his face a mix of pride and purpose. He had been the key to neutralizing the B-2, but he also knew this was just one battle in a much larger war.

Chapter 67

USS CHIEF AND USS CANBERRA
Strait of Hormuz

After the attack on the USS *Ford* in the Persian Gulf, orders came down for the minesweepers *Chief* and *Canberra* to clear the Strait of Hormuz and create a safe zone in case the big carrier needed to traverse to the Gulf of Oman.

Lieutenant Brett Jansen had gotten the hang of clearing mines despite two significant attacks on his ship. He'd led his sailors through it all, and they were still floating and clearing. Despite this, he didn't like being in the Strait of Hormuz, where some areas were only 21 nautical miles wide. That wasn't much elbow room. Since the war with Iran was intensifying, he prepared his crew for any circumstance by being at abbreviated general quarters.

Hovering above the sea, Lieutenant Anne Hawthorne was at the controls of her MH-60R Seahawk helicopter, call sign Romeo 11. Three other helicopters now assisted the operation, which indicated command might be sending the *Ford* out of the Persian Gulf sooner rather than later. The minesweepers were, in essence, clearing the driveway. Missiles from destroyers had been flying overhead to pound radar and missile sites and hopefully keep the Iranians off their asses.

As Hawthorne's Seahawk descended closer to the water, its Airborne Laser Mine Detection System, mounted on the port side of her helo, was using its pulsed laser light to sweep the sea, searching for any mines lurking below the surface. The ASO watched the ALMDS display intently.

"L-T, contact bearing zero-three-zero, distance 1,600 feet," the Sensor Operator, Petty Officer Second Class Alfred Hamilton, announced.

"Roger that, deploy REMUS."

The Remote Environmental Monitoring UnitS, was one of Hawthorne's favorite tools of the trade. It used a high-definition camera to transmit real-time video and data back to a monitor.

Hamilton carefully watched his monitor as he maneuvered the camera to inspect and verify the target. He confirmed the mine and prepared the Remotely Operated Vehicle to glide into the target and detonate.

"Ready to deploy."

"Deploy when ready," came the reply from Hawthorne.

"Fire in the hole," warned Hamilton as he sent the ROV crashing into the mine. Seconds later, the explosion sent a plume of water into the air, making anyone who saw it thankful they weren't on the receiving end.

Moving on to the next target, the Seahawk continued its sweep while the crew repeated the process of detecting and neutralizing several more mines. Each successful operation was a significant accomplishment in clearing the driveway.

After an explosion of another Iranian mine, an E-2 Hawkeye transmitted, "To all on the MCM net, Hawker 31. *Chief* and *Canberra,* you have incoming drones from one-one-eight degrees above water height. Fifty bogeys identified. I say again, *Chief* and *Canberra* have fifty inbound drones."

On the *Chief,* Jansen took charge and announced to his crew, "CIC, activate electronic countermeasures. Crew, deploy for drone attack." This order put two sailors each on the pair of .50-caliber machine guns and several others on various stations across the vessel with rifles. Petty Officer 3 Jose Alvarez was the first on his M2, and he searched the skyline, daring any of the little pricks to get near him.

The captain of the *Canberra* quickly ordered the modern ship's defenses into action. "Activate SeaRAM and the MK 110. Deploy chaff and flares."

The Raytheon MK15 Mod32 SeaRAM close-in weapon system was modeled from the Phalanx system to target and auto-fire RIM-116s at incoming anti-ship missiles. Once activated, the guided missile weapon system's advanced radar and electro-optical sensors continuously scanned the surrounding airspace for potential threats. Immediately, the SeaRAM began tracking the drones.

Within two seconds, the computers prioritized the incoming drones based on their proximity, speed, and potential impact on the ship. The eleven-cell missile launchers spun toward the drones. Then the launch command computer took over—it could compute much faster than a human, no matter their rank—and sent a launch command. Using its solid-fuel rocket motor, a computer-selected RIM-116 missile was fired from the launcher.

The missile employed passive radio frequency homing to focus on the incoming drones' radar emissions and infrared signatures. During the initial phase of flight, the missile used data from the ship's sensors to guide itself toward the general vicinity. As the missile closed on the drones, it switched to active infrared homing to detect a target's heat signature and ensure precise engagement.

While the Iranian drones made several evasive maneuvers in quick succession, the RIM-116 mirrored them. It was also highly maneuverable, and capable of producing sharp turns. When the missile neared the drones, a proximity fuse detonated the warhead.

From the point of view of the *Chief* and *Canberra,* it was a beautiful sight. Spectacular little drone fireballs dotted the sky.

As pretty as it was, danger still lurked. Several drones leaked through, making things get ugly. With its ability to fire 220 rounds per minute, the BAE MK 110 Gun Mount provided a last line of defense, spitting a hail of bullets. Flashing red tracer lines flew from the ship to the drones. Electronic countermeasures were also working, taking several drones off their course.

Despite all these efforts, two drones made it through the defenses. One was a Shahed-129, which fired two Sadid-1 missiles, one striking *Canberra*'s bridge and one the ship's starboard side at water level. The other drone was a Shahed-136, a kamikaze drone that exploded near the MK 110, knocking the gun out of commission. Secondary fires ignited much of the ammunition, causing rounds to explode around the ship.

At the same time on the *Chief*, Jansen was continuing EW, but it wasn't working. Not even Alvarez's machine-gun fire was enough. A single kamikaze drone dove toward the ship. Using its advanced guidance system and high speed, it evaded defensive fire. With a loud explosion, the Shahed-136 slammed into the aft section of the USS *Chief*, just above the waterline. The impact caused a massive fireball, and the force of the explosion rocked the entire ship.

The blast threw Jansen to the deck, causing him to hit his head on the metal decking. Things first went blurry and then started to fade to black. He shook his head, trying to rid himself of the cobwebs that were trying to pull his eyes shut. He felt some hands under his arms and heard the voice of the OOD.

"We got this, Sir. Grab hold here."

Jansen managed to get up but felt very shaky. He knew he had to press on. Holding onto some equipment near comms, Jansen grabbed the mic and barked orders over the intercom. "Damage control teams to the aft section. Seal off compartments and assess the damage. All sections report damage. Corpsmen report aft and assist." He felt dizzy again and took a knee.

The Officer of the Deck took the mic from him. "This is the OOD. I need medical assistance on the bridge. The captain has been hurt."

Within minutes, a ship's corpsman appeared and set Jansen in a chair as he treated a large open wound on his forehead. Blood was gushing all over.

Jansen seemed to respond to this but had a one-track mind: "Look, Doc, patch me up so I can at least see and function."

"Easy, Captain," said the corpsman, "you probably have a concussion and definitely need some stitches, so sit still."

"Listen, our ship could be sinking. I'm not sitting here when I can help the crew save it." With that, he pressed a compress to his head and headed aft. He was so bloody that when the corpsman tried to stop him, the corpsman's hand slid off Jansen's arm, and Jansen was gone.

Arriving aft with an entourage after him, Jansen saw the damage control teams getting some mastery over the fire. He was told that the fire suppression systems were activated, and he watched as trained sailors with firefighting gear fought bravely to contain the blaze. Amid the chaos, the crew worked as one with practiced efficiency, sealing off flooded compartments and tending to the injured.

Although the *Chief* was considered a wooden ship designed to reduce the ship's magnetic signature so as not to get blown up by a mine, the ship wasn't made entirely of wood. The fiberglass coating and internal fireproofing on the ship were making a difference. The OOD appeared next to Jansen, and before he could say anything, Jansen spoke first.

"OOD, ensure all compartmentalization has been done and is sealed. Hurry, go now."

The OOD stared at him, saw the conviction in his eyes, and was off to do as he was ordered.

For the next hour, the crew battled the fire. Despite the intense heat and smoke, the well-trained crew, led by their bloody lieutenant, extinguished the flames using water and fire-retardant foam. Although still floating, the *Chief,* like her acting captain, had suffered severe damage and was out of the fight. Jansen went kicking and complaining as he was medevacked to a hospital in Bahrain.

Nearby, the *Canberra* was not so fortunate. It sank one hour after being struck. Most of the crew got off safely, but eighteen sailors lost their lives.

Surviving the blast, Lieutenant Hawthorne went from blowing up mines to rescue operations. Hovering over the sinking *Canberra*—which was listing heavily to starboard, its stern dipping dangerously close to the waves—she yelled to her Sensor Operator, "Go." Hamilton plunged down the winch line into the dark, fiery smoke. Hawthorne fought for control of the helicopter in the air turbulence caused by the burning ship.

"Two survivors hooked in," radioed Hamilton.

As the winch pulled the wounded sailors from the burning ship, she calculated her next move. Over the next six hours, Hawthorne and her crew would rescue fifteen wounded sailors by shuttling them to a nearby destroyer, refueling, and going back out.

Nearby friendly vessels picked up additional survivors and provided medical aid within hours. Word spread quickly about the brave crew who fought the fires and flooding to keep the ship afloat as long as possible, risking their own lives to save others.

The news of the sinking of the USS *Canberra* and the near destruction of the *Chief* spread quickly, as did the accounts of the crews' bravery and resilience in the face of overwhelming odds. Though *Canberra* was lost, its crew's actions ensured that those who lived could fight another day and carry forward the spirits of their fallen brothers and sisters.

Chapter 68

AN ORDINARY APARTMENT

Bahrain

The call came early and woke Aisha Bilal. "Yes?"

"Aisha, this is General Rostami."

"Yes, General," she mumbled, trying to force herself awake to handle this man who controlled her life.

"We can't wait any longer and are moving forward. Keep your scheduled rendezvous with Richards and ensure he suspects nothing. We will be logging into the device, so keep him occupied. You have done a superb job, Aisha, and you will be rewarded."

Aisha felt her cheeks grow warm. "Thank you, General. I am here to serve you and my country and will be able to do as you say. I have ways to keep him distracted."

The general smiled at this as he had firsthand knowledge about the pleasures her beautiful body could bring. "Thank you, Aisha."

There was a click, and he was gone.

Aisha knew that her culinary specialist, who worked in the admiral's mess on the USS *Ford,* had hidden the Raspberry Pi device in his locker. The device's remote-access software allowed the general's team to log in and interact with the ship's network in real-time. Secured by state-of-the-art encryption and authentication mechanisms, the Raspberry Pi could send commands and data.

The Iranians knew that if they wanted to destroy the *Ford*, they had to have constant updates on its exact GPS location. The *Ford* was fast, and the ship could be miles away in the time it took for missiles to reach it. With the Raspberry Pi active, the Iranians could program their ballistic missiles with the ship's precise location and get constant positional updates fed to the missiles while in flight. The massive carrier would have no hiding place if Aisha could keep her cook occupied. It could be the turning point in the war with the infidels.

USS FORD
Persian Gulf

With little sleep, Lieutenant Pavati Talas was still recovering from the missile attack on the *Ford*. But she was used to getting just five hours of shuteye, as she was getting caught up on her regular duties as a cryptologic warfare officer. One of those was monitoring the network for unusual activity, especially for unauthorized devices connected to the ship's network. Using IPS intrusion prevention and detection systems, her team would be alerted to suspicious behavior. While she usually assigned this task to others on her small team, she thought it essential as their commanding officer to do it herself sometimes.

Topside, the *Ford*'s crew was busy performing their duties. The hum of the ship's engines and the distant sounds of aircraft launching and landing created a familiar symphony. Talas was in the heart of the ship's Cyber Operations Center, surrounded by monitors displaying network traffic, security logs, and real-time alerts.

Leaning back in her chair to stretch her back and legs, Talas took another sip of her lifeblood, a hot mug of Navy coffee. Her eyes never rested, and she was scanning the traffic screen when something caught her attention. In the big picture, it was almost insignificant. Still, as she had been taught long ago, that was when you had to pay attention. The enemy knew most eyes would move on to something more interesting, allowing them to safely hide among the 1s and 0s.

She set her coffee down without taking her eyes off the screen. There was a small, intermittent data stream that didn't align with any known device or routine communication pattern. Although it was minor, she was nonetheless suspicious. Her fingers raced across the keyboard with practiced efficiency. She noted that the data packets were small, almost negligible, but persistent. They appeared to originate from a device within the ship—a device that should not have been there. Talas quickly initiated a deep network scan, deploying advanced intrusion detection tools to trace the source.

As the scan progressed, her screen highlighted a rogue device connected to the ship's internal network. She identified it as a Raspberry Pi, cleverly disguised and tucked away somewhere on the carrier. The device was transmitting encrypted packets to an unknown IP address, raising immediate red flags. Talas's heart raced as she realized the potential implications. She knew she had to act quickly and discreetly. She went to her superior, Commander Michael Harelson.

"Sir, we have a rogue device transmitting data to an unknown address," she reported with all the calmness she could muster. "I believe it's a Raspberry Pi, and it's sending encrypted packets. It's a serious security breach."

Commander Harelson, a seasoned officer with a stern demeanor, nodded. "Good work, Lieutenant. Isolate that device immediately and find out who's behind this." Talas assembled a small team.

ASALUYEH MISSILE BASE
Jask, Iran

General Rostami discussed the need to hurry things along with the commanding officer of Asaluyeh Missile Base.

"Commander, I have the exact coordinates of the USS *Ford*, its speed, and its course. We need to launch."

"General Rostami, while I respect your position with MOIS, this is a missile mission, and I do it my way."

"I see," said Rostami, "and do you have the cell phone number for our Supreme Leader? Because I do."

"Is that a threat, General?"

"Of course not, but Commander, I want this critical mission to begin while we have the advantage. This could change our position in the world."

"Then let me get back to work." With that, the commander turned his back on the politically connected general and walked off. The general followed.

In the mission control room, the commander fired out orders. "I want twelve Qader missiles uploaded with this coordinate." Turning to the Rostami, he said, "General?"

"25.5005 north, 56.5002 east." The general smirked.

"Captain," said the commander, "begin the countdown, set at three minutes."

USS Ford
Persian Gulf

Moving swiftly through the long corridors of the pride of the fleet, Talas used a handheld locating device that led her down to the galley's sleeping quarters. As she neared a locker, her device told her this was the spot, like a bird dog pointing at a pheasant. Opening the locker door, she quickly tore through the contents. Hidden in a boot was the Raspberry Pi, its LED lights blinking quietly. She suspected that it might be sending out information on the exact position of the *Ford*.

Just then, the 1MC came to life. "This is the Captain. General quarters. General quarters. All hands man your battle stations. Twelve inbound missiles."

Talas looked back from the speaker on the wall to the Raspberry Pi and carefully disabled it. She got on the radio to her CO.

The XO answered, "This better be important, Talas. As you heard, we've got incoming."

"Yes, Sir. I just found and disabled a device that's been transmitting encrypted data to an unknown address. I think the enemy knows right where we are."

She heard a click on the radio and then silence. Talas ran back to her workstation in the Cyber Operations Center.

ASALUYEH MISSILE BASE
Jask, Iran

After the missiles started their thirteen-minute attack run to the *Ford*, they were constantly updated as they sped toward the moving carrier. General Rostami could barely contain himself because his plan was working to perfection. Visions of the Supreme Leader praising him danced before his eyes.

"General," the missile base commander said, "updated coordinates, please."

Looking at his assistant, who was suddenly pounding on his computer keyboard, the general said, "Captain, give him the new coordinates."

After a few seconds, the captain looked up. "Ah . . . I'm sorry, General . . . I have lost contact with our device."

"What do you mean, Captain? We were connected just minutes ago. What's going on?"

"My guess is . . . the enemy discovered the device? And turned it off?"

"Keep trying to reconnect, dammit!"

The captain returned to pounding on his keyboard, knowing it was just for show.

USS FORD
Persian Gulf

Aware that their location was known to the enemy, Captain Otis Albright made an immediate radical course change. "Helm, course change to one-six-five, all ahead flank." He wanted distance from their current location and to make the *Ford* a difficult target to track. "Initiate zigzag pattern Charlie."

The ship began to veer to starboard, then quickly shifted back to port, repeating the actions for a rapid, zigzagging path. The deck tilted underfoot, a physical reminder of the ship's abrupt changes of direction.

"All stations, brace for evasive maneuvers," Albright announced over 1MC. "We're going to zigzag to evade incoming missiles. Keep your focus and stay sharp." He did the calculations and figured he could be seven miles away from where he had been when the missiles were detected.

The *Ford*'s escort ships tactically repositioned to gain an advantage in shooting down the incoming missiles. With the Iranians unable to pinpoint the *Ford's* precise location, the escorts efficiently shot down all twelve missiles. But there remained one small matter to take care of.

Seaman Albert Richards had spent most of yet another GQ in his berth, enjoying quality time with his girlfriend. After his screen suddenly went dark, he took a few minutes to compose himself before returning to the admiral's mess to do absolutely nothing during GQ but ensure that the coffee was hot.

Alone, as always during GQ and dutifully standing near the coffee pot, Richards saw two neatly dressed Marines with guns on their hips enter. He was about to remind them that only the admiral and his guests could enter when a Lieutenant wove between the Marines and walked up to him.

"Are you Culinary Specialist Seaman Albert Richards?" she said.

"Yes, Ma'am, I am."

The Marine closest to him said, "Richards, turn around and place your hands behind your back."

"What's going on?" Richards said to the Lieutenant.

"I'm Lieutenant Pavati Talas. Culinary Specialist Seaman Albert Richards, you are under arrest for espionage and the unauthorized use of a computer device."

"Espionage? I don't know what you're talking about."

"We have evidence that you planted a rogue computer device in your locker," said Talas. "It was transmitting sensitive data to a foreign entity. That's a serious breach of security."

Looking shaken to his core, Richards said, "It was just a Wi-Fi enhancement to talk to my girlfriend . . . she said everybody used it."

The Marines marched him off to the brig. Talas hoped this would be a warning to others and knew the kid would face a tough trial.

As Richards stepped into the brig, he wished he had his camera—what an excellent story for TopVid.

Chapter 69

NATANZ ENRICHMENT COMPLEX
Isfahan Province, Iran

Marveling at his achievement, General Shirvani stood before Iran's first nuclear bomb. The sight left him nearly breathless. The world remained unaware of his triumph, but his weapon would soon change history. Iran was on the brink of becoming a superpower. His country's nuclear capabilities would command the respect, fear, and capitulation of the international community. What a powerful tool to hold over their heads, he thought.

With a nuclear arsenal to ensure total American retreat, Iran was poised to dominate the Middle East. Using the right strategy, General Shirvani believed he could ensure that the Americans, who lacked a taste for prolonged conflict, would shudder at Iran's newfound power.

It was now time to complete the final test. His hands trembled slightly as he bent over the bomb. A series of clicks and beeps affirmed the bomb's readiness. Everything was spot-on and ready for deployment.

Watching the general off to the side, Major Farhad Daryani was hoping Shirvani was done slobbering over his bomb so he could hit the road. The fifty-one-year-old IRGC

Army officer was the man everyone wanted on their team. Standing a muscular six feet, two inches, and with two battle scars on his face that one could not help staring at, he was charismatic and authoritative.

"Good to go, General?" asked Daryani, with a hint of impatience despite the significant difference in rank. Daryani treated the general with the respect his position warranted. However, Shirvani wasn't the type he would share a beer with, not just because it was illegal for Muslim Iranian citizens to do so but also because Daryani didn't associate with intellectuals.

"Yes, Major," said Shirvani, "please load it up, and may Allah watch over your travels."

"Okay, you heard the general," Daryani said to his nearby men. "Let's get the package loaded."

Leading the convoy was a light-armored vehicle equipped with a mounted heavy machine gun. Behind the LAV followed the primary transport truck, which carried the nuclear bomb. The truck was armed with a machine gun featuring a reinforced cargo hold with lead shielding to protect the transporters against radiation. Equipped with a hydraulic lift system, the truck could efficiently, quickly, and safely load and unload the bomb. Additionally, the truck had a GPS and communication jamming system to prevent tracking and unauthorized communications.

Following the primary truck was an infantry fighting vehicle loaded with an autocannon, anti-tank guided missiles, and machine guns. The IFV held ten additional soldiers. Watching everyone's six was an MRAP with machine guns and grenade launchers.

Daryani had decided to forgo a helicopter escort because he didn't want to draw undue attention to the convoy. They would travel like so many others, just another bunch of trucks.

GREEN BERET AMBUSH SITE
Near Natanz Enrichment Complex

The Green Berets had adjusted their position to one mile west of the nuclear facility. They had eyes on the main road in and out, and a drone flying surveillance. They had chosen this part of the road because it narrowed slightly, funneling any convoy into a tighter, more vulnerable position.

Captain Roger Ashburger and CIA operative Dallas Steele divided the twelve Green Berets into three teams of four, with Steele and his Iranian driver, Karimi, making up a reserve team. Team Kilo was positioned on the high ground to the east to provide overwatch and sniper support. Team Lima was hidden on the western side and tasked with neutralizing the lead and rear vehicles. Team Mike was positioned near the road and ready to assault the transport truck and secure the bomb.

Rounding out the mission's force list was air support. Two Black Hawk helicopters escorted two Boeing CH-47 Chinooks assigned to transport the bomb. Four F-35s provided cover for everyone. All were standing by.

At precisely 0330 hours, Major Daryani launched a Shahed-129 for ISR. It was loaded with four guided missiles—just in case. The airborne US drone picked up the movement of the Iranian drone over Natanz, so the US drone operator notified Ashburger. It was the indication they'd all been waiting for that things were beginning to happen. Ashburger got on secure comms.

"Jedi 11, 18A Special, one Shahed-129 just launched from the site. I need you to take it out just before zero hour. I will advise."

"18A Special, Jedi 11," said Lieutenant Commander Jessie Hampton, "copy and awaiting your order."

At 0415 hours, Daryani gave a final briefing to his transport team and emphasized maintaining a steady pace and tightening the convoy to prevent gaps an enemy could exploit. Fifteen minutes later, the convoy's engines roared to life and the trucks left the protection of the Natanz Enrichment Complex. The heavily armored vehicles moved in a well-coordinated formation.

"Jedi 11, 18A Special, take out the drone when you hear the execute order."

"18A Special, roger. Jedi 11, wilco."

As the convoy approached the ambush site, the fourteen men were positioned and ready. The lead reconnaissance vehicle was the first to enter the kill zone.

Ashburger whispered in his radio, "Hold—hold—" After waiting for what seemed an eternity for the perfect tactical advantage, he said, "Execute!"

Team Kilo squeezed off the first shots. Two snipers armed with Barrett M82 .50-caliber rifles took out the gunners on the reconnaissance vehicle and the rear-guard MRAP. The other two members of Team Kilo used their M4s to provide covering fire.

Targeting the lead vehicle, Team Lima fired their Javelin anti-tank missiles. They streaked through the air and struck the LAV, causing a massive explosion that tossed the truck up and slammed it back to the ground. The convoy was dead in its tracks.

As the Iranian soldiers sought cover, all US teams laid down suppressive fire. The Iranian return fire was intense, and one soldier in Team Kilo was struck. His partner, seeing him hit, started to yell for a medic over the radio, but when he looked back, he realized his partner was dead. He returned to laying down fire.

Taking cover behind the transport truck, Major Daryani rallied his troops there, knowing the Americans weren't dumb enough to blow it up. As he searched for targets, smoke grenades began going off around him. Visibility went to near zero, but it didn't matter. Daryani just kept reloading and spraying the area in front of him.

Team Mike advanced in the smoke and surprised two Iranian soldiers. Everyone fired at point-blank range. One Team Mike member went down with a shot to his right shoulder, but he managed to return fire and kill his assailant while his partner shot the other guard.

Just then, Daryani came out of the smoke and shot one of the Green Berets in the head with his handgun. When Daryani tried to shoot the second Team Mike member, his gun clicked on an empty chamber. As he reached for his knife, the operator shot him in the forehead. After he fell, the soldier shot him four more times. Teams Lima and Mike converged on the area and quickly secured it. All the Iranians from the nuclear convoy were dead.

"18A Special, Jedi 11. You have movement coming from the complex—several large trucks. FLIR indicates the trucks are full of troops. My flight will engage."

"Jedi 11, 18A, roger. We're securing the merchandise. Break. 18A Special to Hawk 11, cover our six, and bring in one Chinook to our twenty, over."

Overhead, Jessie was giving orders. "Jedi 13 and 14 stay on station and watch our six. Jedi 11 and 12 have the Iranian response team. Engage EW. Use brevity calls."

Switching frequencies to his wingman, Jessie said, "One has the first three trucks. Two, take the rear vehicle. Use SDBs. The rear truck is a Bavar-373 missile truck. Two, go in first and get it. I'm right behind you. EW activated."

"Two going first, SDBs, rear vehicle," said Lockwood.

Jessie and Bulldog split off, descending to engage the convoy. Immediately, both aircraft RWRs went off. Bulldog came in hot and saw in his HUD the Iranian-developed Bavar-373 air and missile defense system, which was capable of taking out anything that flew at terminal altitudes.

"Two, target locked," he said after receiving a green light for weapons release from the onboard computer. "Two, weapons away," Bulldog yelled.

The Raytheon GBU-53 Stormbreaker small-diameter bomb was equipped with wings that deployed as soon as it was released, allowing it to glide toward the missile truck. The bomb's GPS and inertial guidance systems corrected its course in the last seconds. Although the sun was barely cresting the hills, giant fireballs and secondary explosions lit up the area like high noon.

A few seconds later, Jessie yelled, "One, weapons released," announcing the release of his SDBs—all were direct hits too. In just seconds, four heavily loaded Iranian trucks were gone with no survivors, and secondary fires burned throughout the area.

Working hurriedly but carefully, the A-Team's two demo experts declared the nuclear bomb safe. The device was loaded into the waiting Chinook's cargo bay using a winch system. With the atomic device secure and the Green Berets, Steele and his Iranian driver loaded, the helo was off to Ali Al Salem Air Base in Kuwait. For the moment, Iran had no nuclear bomb. And the US would continue to ensure they didn't construct another one.

Chapter 70

USS Reagan
Persian Gulf

Sarah Freeman walked briskly to the wardroom, partially to take the edge off her anger and partially to just get this shit over with. Why her boss, Commander Damien Wagner, was always on her case, she could not fathom. During her entire career, she had been promoted quickly and had received nothing but praise from all her previous supervisors and commanders. ALL, she screamed to herself, all of them except this prick.

Stomping into the wardroom, which was cleaned up from the last meal, she walked right up to Wagner, who was sitting down. She saluted him. "Lieutenant Commander Sarah Freeman reporting as ordered, Sir."

This time, Wagner wasn't doing paperwork but was snacking on a piece of pie. A cup of black coffee was next to the plate. He had a crumb stuck to his upper lip. Looking at her with a stern face as if he were getting ready to court-martial her, he returned her sharp salute with his normal sloppy one. Sarah had no idea how the guy had made it through Annapolis.

"Lieutenant Commander, it has come to my attention that on your last mission, you froze up while on comms—you failed to give any directives during the stress of battle."

Holy shit, she thought, what was he talking about? Was it about those brief seconds she was startled to hear that one of the pilots she was directing was Jessie?

She could feel her anger burning her cheeks. But she had to keep her cool because she knew he wanted her to lose it.

"Sir, I have no idea what you're talking about. At no time did I or any of my crew ever"—she held her fingers up to gesture quote marks—"freeze up."

"That's not what was reported to me. I have it under good authority that you were communicating with an F-35 pilot from the *Ford* who was, in fact, your husband, Lieutenant Commander Jessie Hampton."

There it was, she thought. Despite his allegations being a crock of shit, she replied, "Sir, you are correct about one thing, and that is I was surprised to hear my husband's voice since I never have any knowledge about what call sign he gets assigned for his missions. I only have the comm plan distributed to all aircrew before a mission, and as you know, those don't list names with call signs. I took an extra second to make sure what came out of my mouth was correct and appropriate for the situation. That wasn't freezing up, but being professional so that I could advise the pilot of the current situation in the airspace that my crew and I were overseeing."

"Does having your husband in the same war zone as you make it difficult for you to do your job, Freeman? Do you worry about him?"

Sarah couldn't believe it. "He's a grown fucking man, Sir," she said, making sure the "sir" was lightly laced with a sarcastic tone. "He's also one of the best fighter pilots in the Navy. So no, I don't worry that he could be shot down. We've both been there. We're combat veterans. We know the risks. And we both respect each other's skills and professionalism. We know that the mission comes first for each of us because we were Navy officers and naval aviators long before we became marital partners. So unless you ask your male pilots if they're worried about their wives and girlfriends while they're flying a mission, don't ever accuse me of not doing my job again, Commander, because that's not me. And everyone knows it except you."

She took one step back, snapped a salute, then made an about-face and walked out of the room, leaving her boss with his jaw on the table.

Sarah immediately requested a meeting with the XO to issue a complaint against Commander Wagner for his sexist remarks and constant harassment. With that done, she did some yoga to reduce the stress from the bullshit that was happening—during a damn war—so that she would be in the right mindset for her next mission.

Chapter 71

ANTI-AIRCRAFT MISSILE PLATOON, BATTALION LANDING TEAM 2/6
Ahvaz Oil Field, Iran

Within hours of taking over control of Ahvaz Oil Field, every available MV-22 and CH-53E was being used to transport the rest of the MEU's Marines. Even the KC-130J Super Hercules aircraft were flying overhead to a civilian airport located just miles from the oil field, which Special Forces had also taken during the raid on Ahvaz. The Chinooks were loaded with weapons so the Marines could consolidate the ground victory. The Naval Strike Missile Defense System was included in this logistics laydown to conduct anti-ship and coastal defense missions since the MEUSOC was only a few miles from the north end of the Persian Gulf. FIM-92 Stinger Man-Portable Air-Defense Systems were also coming in. The Marines would use the MANPADS to engage low-flying aircraft.

As part of the overall strategy, the US sought to control the three major oil fields in Iran. After that, the flow of oil would be shut off to deprive the Iranian government of money to fund the war.

During the SEAL platoon's raid to take Ahvaz, simultaneous raids were made on the Gachsaran and Marun oil fields by units of the 82nd Airborne Division. Although the raids were successful, counterattacks were expected. Harley "Snake Eyes" Jennings was busy securing his neck of the woods. He was tasked with setting up the NSMDS, a highly mobile system that consisted of the launcher, which in this case was on an Oshkosh Medium Tactical Vehicle Replacement, the command and control truck, and the radar truck. He also had two trucks hauling eight missiles each, and four Joint Light Tactical Vehicles armed with the Avenger missile system.

As they positioned everything, Jennings noticed the kid with the shaky hands standing by the MTVR. "Hey, Private, come here."

The kid came over at double time. Jennings looked at his name imprinted on his uniform. "Snyder, huh? What's your first name, Private?"

"It was Tommy, but since I enlisted in the Corps, I go by Thomas, Gunny. Tommy just didn't seem right."

"Bullshit. If you want to go by Tommy, then Tommy it is, and you come down hard on anyone who fucks with you. Be yourself, kid, and don't let others dictate who you are. I'm glad you're assigned to my team because you're going to do just fine. Now get your ass back to work and quit the bullshitting." Both laughed at that, and Tommy was off parking and aligning trucks, including the JLTVs.

Snake Eyes took it all in and thought, If you want some of this, you Iranian bastards, then give us a try.

Chapter 72

EAGLE 44

United Arab Emirates

Using satellite imagery and signals intel along with some HUMINT, the US was able to pinpoint the location of Iran's secret air base called Eagle 44. Intel verified that Iran's fourth-generation Su-35 fighters were hidden underground there.

Pilots in the 27th Fighter Squadron from Joint Base Langley-Eustis in Virginia gathered around a large table in a dimly lit briefing room. Satellite images of the target area were on a large-screen monitor. The mission commander, pointed to various points on the map as he explained the timing for the corridor that would be cleared for them by another squadron. Then he got down to their main event.

"Intelligence confirms the location of the underground base, here." He tapped the screen. "Our objective is to neutralize their air defense systems and infrastructure. Timing and precision are crucial. Tomahawks will be striking the base, so we don't have any room to dally. Snake, you'll lead the first strike with your flight. I've got the lead on the second."

A man of few words but all action in the cockpit, Captain John "Snake" Harrison nodded and uttered, "Got it."

Harrison had been given the call sign because of his agility and behavior in the air. He could snake his way into any situation and come out on top. The thirty-two-year-old was already a decorated pilot, logging over fifteen hundred hours in his F-22 Raptor.

After Kit reviewed objectives, routes, ROEs, SAR, and contingency plans, he turned the monitor off and said, "Let's get this done."

To a person, everyone was still pissed about the rocket strike on Independence Hall. That sentiment drove them all to achieve more—if possible with this group of overachievers.

In the squadron's life-support area, Snake stood next to his wingman, who was as much a snake as he was—Captain Bill "Gunner" DuBois. As they both adjusted their G-suits and strapped on their survival vests, he made sure to check his SIG Sauer M18 handgun. Snake liked guns and might even have chosen the weapon for his collection. The compact design was a nice blend of firepower and portability.

While some pilots liked to be transported to their aircraft, Snake and Gunner walked briskly to theirs. It got the juices flowing and their minds in the game. Once at their F-22s, they walked around the aircraft to check the airframe, wings, and control surfaces, then inspected the landing gear and tires. Lastly, they verified that the weapons and sensor systems were properly mounted and secured. And yes, they checked that the "Remove Before Flight" red warning ribbons weren't attached. They left nothing to chance since it was their asses in that cockpit.

Each pilot climbed into their jet. While Snake's crew chief assisted him with his harness and connections, he was already visualizing the target run.

As the canopy nestled into position, Snake ran through more of his pre-flight checklist.

Oxygen mask and flow—Check.
Comms tested and working—Check.
HUD and multi-function display operational—Check.
Navigation system verified and waypoints entered—Check.
Weapons system up and running—Check.
Switches and systems in the correct positions—Check.

His checklist continued for engine start-up procedures, and he ensured his crew chief had the auxiliary power unit connected. Snake started the engines sequentially, eyeing RPM, temperature, and other critical parameters to keep him in the air and not punching out at 20,000 feet. He radioed his flight to the tower and confirmed all was good to go. As Gunner taxied with him off the parking apron, Snake checked all flight control movements and armed his ejection seat.

During taxi, the flight received permission to take off. Once airborne, Snake went to Military Power, the highest thrust setting that could be used without engaging the afterburners, thus conserving the always-precious fuel. As he and his wingman gently rolled into the pre-briefed assembly point, Snake constantly communicated with the other two pilots in his flight, guiding them into position.

"Buster flight, line astern formation, 500 feet, on my mark—now." At Snake's directive, all four F-22s transitioned to flying nose-to-tail, presenting a narrow profile against enemy radar. The flight maintained radio silence as they approached Iranian airspace. Their radars were active, scanning for threats, but the corridor was clear.

"Execute combat spread, 2-mile spacing," ordered Snake.

The three other aircraft acknowledged using brevity calls. The formation spread out, each aircraft maintaining its position while covering a wider area. As they neared the underground base, the Iranian air defenses around it remained unaware of the approaching threat. The advanced stealth technology of the F-22s allowed them to slip through the radar coverage.

"Form line abreast with 1,500 feet of spacing. Engage designated targets on my command," Snake ordered.

The pilots flawlessly executed the plan they had meticulously crafted in the briefing room. Seconds later, Snake's voice crackled over the comms, 'Fox three!' His missiles blazed through the sky, locking onto the outdated Russian radar installation and obliterating it before the system even had a chance to detect their approach. Fox three calls echoed across the airwaves as the flight struck additional radar sites and a SAM installation. With no remaining radar emissions to engage, the SEAD mission was complete, and the F-22s turned back toward UAE.

Chapter 73

USS GEORGIA
Gulf of Oman

Having replenished missiles under cover of darkness at the Jebel Ali Port in the UAE, *Georgia* was back in the depths of the Gulf of Oman to join the *Ford*, which had used the path cleared by the minesweepers to head for the open space of the Arabian Sea. As *Georgia* headed out of the gulf, Commander Mateo Navarro received new orders to support an attack on Eagle 44, the top-secret underground facility housing Iran's Su-35s. The timing had to be precise since his part of the attack to deliver cruise missiles would follow the F-22s' SEAD and occur just before the F-35s came in for clean-up duty.

While navigating to the launch point, *Georgia*'s WEPS informed the captain of the correct launch time and programmed the precise coordinates of the underground base into the Tomahawks' guidance systems.

When the sub reached the launch point and the captain had confirmed the time, he ran through the launch procedures. "WEPS, status on missile readiness." Navarro requested.

"Missiles are ready, Captain, and all systems are green," came the reply from WEPS.

"Nav, confirm target coordinates," said Navarro.

"Coordinates confirmed. We're locked on."

"Prepare to launch Tomahawks," Navarro commanded, and watched the clock to ensure precise timing. "On my mark, three—two—one—launch."

Each TLAM flew low and fast, hugging the terrain to avoid radar detection. They followed their preprogrammed routes, making minor adjustments to stay on course. The first missile struck precisely, penetrating the surface and detonating deep underground. Secondary explosions followed as fuel and munitions stores ignited. The other missiles hit in quick succession, targeting aboveground hangars, command centers, and critical infrastructure buildings.

After the final Tomahawk missile had launched, *Georgia*'s control room was a flurry of activity as Navarro wasted no time for his next move. "Helm, take us down to 600 feet." The engines hummed softly as the submarine descended rapidly, slipping into the deeper, darker, and thus safer waters of the Arabian Sea.

"Sonar, keep an ear out for any active pings," said Navarro. "We're going to make ourselves as quiet as a shadow." He toggled the sub's intercom. "All hands, this is the Captain. Initiate silent running. Minimize all unnecessary noise."

As he looked around, Navarro reflected on how the crew was working remarkably well together and performing their jobs in an exemplary manner. That was good, he told himself, because in war, nothing was predictable except death for those who didn't adapt. And the crew of the USS *Georgia* was adapting very well.

EAGLE 44 UNDERGROUND AIRBASE
Iran

What bothered Jessie Hampton, who was leading a flight of eight F-35s, was the lack of secondary explosions at Eagle 44, which would have undoubtedly occurred if the concealed Su-35s had been hit. He queried intel and got an answer that needed to get to his flight.

"Jedi 11 to Jedi flight. Intel reports no significant secondary explosions. Be advised the Flankers might have been moved and could come calling."

After the other F-35s acknowledged, Jessie knew they needed good battle damage assessment. He adjusted the mission plan. "Jedi 11 to Jedi flight. Stand by for new mission plan. Jedi 13, get us a solid BDA. Jedi 15, begin your SEAD run. Jedi 16, fly CAP."

Flying over the smoldering target area, Jedis 13 and 14 used their electro-optical targeting system to get high-resolution imagery. The weapons storage area and some buildings were damaged, but that was it. No Su-35s were identified.

"Jedi 11, Jedi 13. We have some good hits but no evidence of aircraft destruction."

At *Ford*'s command center, intel analysts monitored the frequency and rapidly processed the incoming data from the F-35s to compare the high-resolution imagery and heat maps with pre-strike photos. They got back in minutes. "Jedi 11, Intel. It appears that the Su-35s were not parked at the base during the raid. Suggest they moved out ahead of the strike."

"Roger that," Jessie replied.

"Jedi 11, Jedi 15. One return on enemy radar taken care of with HARMs. No other radar activity."

Breaking into the reports came one from an E-2 off the *Ford*. "Jedi 11, Shepherd 21. Bandits inbound from the north. Eight Su-35s on intercept course. ETA two minutes."

"Jedi 11 to Jedi flight. Form up in defensive spread."

All the F-35s acknowledged the order with brevity calls and immediately fanned out into a wide formation, maximizing radar coverage and ensuring mutual support. Swagger and his wingman, Bulldog, led the formation, spaced two miles apart. Jedi 13 and 14 trailed two miles behind them, widening the sweep. Jedi 15 and 16 took up the

rear guard, completing the layered defense. "Fire at will,"
Jessie ordered.

SU-35 FLIGHT
Airborne over Iran

Major Arash Zamani, leading his squadron of eight Su-35s,
received the urgent directive: Intercept and neutralize the
American F-35s that had just destroyed their underground
air base. He barely needed the reminder—after all, it had
been his plan to relocate Iran's most advanced jets to a
secondary, inconspicuous base, knowing the Americans
would strike Eagle 44 soon enough. The bait had worked.
The Americans believed they had eliminated the Su-35s,
leading them to expect a feeble response from Iran's outdated
F-4 Phantoms. Now, with the element of surprise on his side,
Zamani would show them just how wrong they were.

"All elements spread out in a loose formation," Zamani
commanded. The Su-35s adopted a staggered approach,
aiming to confuse enemy radars and minimize detection.
"Once within range, we will use our IRST systems to locate
the F-35s. Prioritize stealth, maintain radio silence, and close
the distance for missile lock-on."

Zamani and his wingman were flying at the rear of his
squad of Su-35s. Both knew they had to fire first to spread

out the Americans and force them into a dogfight, where the Su-35 had an advantage due to its maneuverability.

When his Su-35's infrared search and track system picked up the faint heat signatures of eight F-35s, he said, "Targets detected at two o'clock, 48 kilometers out. Prepare for engagement. Fire missiles as you get a lock. Simorgh 16 and 17, flank left. Simorgh 18 and 19, maintain central position. Simorgh 20 and 21, flank right. Engage from multiple angles." Zamani had divided his forces to maximize their attack vectors.

As the Su-35s screamed toward their enemy for what seemed like an eternity, the fighters finally locked onto the F-35s and launched R-77 missiles. Fox three calls filled the airwaves, and the sky lit up with missile trails.

THE AIR BATTLE OVER EAGLE 44
Iran

For a split second, numerous R-77 missiles and AIM-120s, traveling at a closing rate of 6,000 mph, were streaking by each other. While their smoke trails converged, their sleek forms cut through the sky as they searched for their targets. How well each pilot responded to the onslaught of missiles would determine a victor—the last man still flying.

As the missile alert screamed in Jessie's cockpit, he felt a surge of adrenaline. An R-77 had locked onto his F-35, and he knew his survival depended on quick thinking and flawless execution.

"ONE, missile lock, evasive maneuvers," Jessie shouted over his flight's comms. He immediately banked hard to the right, pushing his F-35 to its limits. The G-forces pressed him into his seat as he fought blackout. He performed the anti-G straining maneuver by tensing his legs and abdominal muscles to squeeze blood vessels and maintain blood flow to his brain. He was grunting as he fought for a breath of air. Throwing his aircraft in the opposite direction gave him a split second to grab a breath before he went to a tight 6-G S-turn.

The alarm kept buzzing in what seemed a mocking tone, signaling the missile still had a lock on him. Releasing countermeasures again, Jessie spotted a nearby hilly area and headed for it, pushing his F-35 as hard as ever. It responded flawlessly. He darted through the valleys at treetop level, each maneuver having to be perfect and precise.

Jessie's heart pounded as he made one final, desperate move. He flew toward a rocky outcrop and pulled the stick back at the last second. Unable to make the sharp ascent, the missile exploded into the mountainside.

Major Zamani saw the F-35 avoid a missile, so he quickly maneuvered into position to finish the job.

As Jessie climbed almost vertically, his RWR blared a warning. A quick glance at his HUD confirmed he had company—a Su-35 was closing fast, trying to lock onto him. Swagger's instincts kicked in, adrenaline pounding through his body. Now within visual range, he spotted the enemy fighter, tightened his grip on the stick, and yanked it hard right. The Su-35 shot past, immediately losing its tactical advantage and putting Jessie back in control. Zamani silently cussed to himself as the American duped him. He had flown right past—precisely what he didn't want to do. Realizing his predicament, Zamani engaged afterburners and performed a series of aggressive maneuvers: barrel rolls, high-G turns, and rapid climbs. Constantly checking his HUDs, he couldn't believe the American was still on his ass, so he reversed his direction and dove for the ground.

Jessie was in a groove, anticipating every move made by the Iranian pilot, who he had to admit was pretty good. But being good wouldn't save your life when you had the best pilot in the Navy on your ass, thought Jessie. Although the Navy still taught the art of dogfighting, flight instructors mainly preached situational awareness and the use of missiles to avoid the unnecessary risks of a dogfight. As the Iranian pilot dove for the deck, Jessie got a missile-lock-acquired buzz in his helmet. An AIM-9X Sidewinder missile armed itself, its seeker head tracking the Su-35's heat signature with unerring precision.

"ONE, Fox two," Jessie called out as he squeezed the trigger. The missile tore from its rail, leaving a searing trail of smoke as it streaked toward the Su-35 with lethal precision.

Sensing an imminent threat, Zamani began a series of evasive maneuvers and deployed flares to confuse the missile.

Jessie adjusted his trajectory to keep the Su-35 within his sights. The Su-35 rolled and banked hard, trying to shake the Sidewinder.

The rocket, momentarily diverted by the flares, quickly reacquired the Su-35's heat signature. The Sidewinder closed the distance rapidly.

Despite Zamani's desperate maneuvers, the missile struck the Su-35's engine, blowing it up with a powerful explosion. The Su-35 shuddered and began to spiral out of control. Zamani tried everything to stop his Su-35's death spiral. Nothing worked.

What flight schools can't teach is the will to survive, and the major had it in spades. As the ground rushed up and he knew there was nothing else he could do, he yanked hard on the ejection handle. The canopy blew off in a loud whoosh, and he shot out of the aircraft at 250 mph.

As his parachute deployed and he drifted to the ground, his only thought was to find that American pilot and even the score.

Chapter 74

US Naval Branch Health Clinic
Bahrain

Lieutenant Brett Jansen found himself racing frantically around the deck of the USS *Chief*, disoriented and unsure of what to do. Sailors shouted his name, but their voices were drowned out by the chaos. Flames danced around him, and with growing panic, he wondered why no one was fighting the fires. Desperate to take action, he grabbed the first hose he could find—only to realize that it was just a plain garden hose. A feeble trickle of water sputtered out, utterly useless against the inferno raging around him. He started shaking with fear. "Lieutenant. Lieutenant, wake up. There's someone here to see you."

Jansen blinked his eyes, thankful he wasn't trying to put out his ship's fire with a garden hose. He sat up in bed and noticed a Navy captain sitting next to him. The captain introduced himself but Jessie missed his name. He tried to focus.

"Lieutenant Jansen, are you with me?"

"Yes, Sir, sorry. I was having a bad dream." At least he hoped it was a dream. Thoughts of a court martial flashed in front of him.

"After what you've been through, we're glad you're still with us. It was mighty brave of you to lead your command despite being seriously wounded. Many think your drive to fight the fire saved the old ship." The captain paused, making sure Jansen was grasping all of this.

"Thank you, sir. I only wish I could have done more."

"Jansen, you did all you could and then some. Listen, I'm here on behalf of Vice Admiral Sean McAdams of SURFPAC. He sends his greetings and good news for you. Since the *Chief* is too far gone to save, you're being assigned to the XO position on the USS *Sterett* and will be stepped up to lieutenant commander next command rotation. You've earned it."

Jansen had to ensure he wasn't dreaming again, so he pinched himself under the sheet and felt the pain. Damn, this is real, he told himself, then took a minute to process the fact that he was going to be the XO of an *Arleigh Burke*-class destroyer.

"Sir, I don't know what to say except thank you. I will do everything possible to be the best XO the *Sterett* has ever had. I mean that, Sir."

"I know you do, Jansen. You can expect your formal orders soon. In the meantime, get well and thank you for everything you've done for the United States Navy."

As the Captain stood, Jansen couldn't help himself and saluted even though he was still in bed. A big smile spread across the Captain's face as he briskly returned the salute. After the door closed, the kid from a small town in Michigan pumped his fists in the air.

"Yeah, I'm going to be the XO of the USS *Sterett*!" He had never felt better.

Chapter 75

AHVAZ OIL FIELD
Khuzestan Province, Iran

The early morning sun had barely begun to cast its light over the vast expanse of the Ahvaz Oil Field when, precisely at 0600 hours, Iranian missiles were launched toward their country's oil field. Their target was the 26th Marine Expeditionary Unit, which had little time to fully establish its missile defenses. Thankfully, Task Force 70 stood ready to lend a hand.

Sarah Freeman was flying her E-2 at 25,000 feet and was the first to detect launches from several Iranian missile bases.

"Hawker 11 to all units, multiple missiles launched from Iran. Target appears to be Ahvaz Oil Field. Transmitting information on Link 16. The *Churchill* and *Mahan* are in the most advantageous positions to respond."

Immediately, both ships used their onboard AN/SPY-1 multifunction 3D radar to detect the Iranian missiles' heat signatures and trajectories. The Aegis Combat System began to calculate targeting information and sent it to their SM-3s and SM-6s. The computer then assigned them to the warheads presenting the highest threats to the MEU at Ahvaz Oil Field.

The SM-3 and SM-6 missiles were fired from the VLSs in sequential launches. The ACS provided mid-course guidance to the interceptors, adjusting their flight paths to ensure they remained on collision courses with the incoming missiles. As the interceptors approached the target missiles, they switched to terminal guidance systems, using either infrared or radar homing to track and engage the targets. The missiles destroyed the incoming weapons either through direct kinetic hits or by detonating their warheads in close proximity to create fragmentation clouds that disabled the targets.

While the Iranian missiles received most of the attention, warnings went out about incoming drones headed for the oil field. Advanced radar systems picked up the drones as soon as they launched. The Marines had fortified their positions and were ready to defend the oil field with every weapon system available. This included a state-of-the-art directed-energy weapon called the High Energy Laser Mobile Demonstrator, affectionately dubbed "Thunderbolt" by its operators.

Corporal Britney Meyers stood by Thunderbolt's control station, her eyes locked on the screen that displayed data from integrated radar systems. A series of blips appeared, converging rapidly toward their position.

She reported over comms, "Incoming drone swarm, bearing two-eight-zero." The CO acknowledged her report and ordered, "All units, prepare for engagement. Arm Thunderbolt."

The HEL-MD's sensors locked onto the incoming drones, and the targeting system highlighted each one, providing real-time speed, altitude, and distance data. Orders came to engage as the first wave of drones came into range.

Meyers was a big fan of *Star Wars*, and nothing in the Corps's arsenal of weapons reminded her more of those movies than Thunderbolt. She activated the laser. A bright beam of focused light shot out from the HEL-MD, striking the lead drone. Within seconds, the drone's fuselage began to glow, bursting into flames, sending it out of control.

Barely getting out, "Target one neutralized," she shifted the beam to the next closest drone. The laser continued to fire, each shot precisely directed by the automated tracking system. Drone after drone fell from the sky, their circuits fried and their structures compromised by intense heat.

Meyers and her team were not alone in their battle against the pint-size killers. Across the oil field, another team of Marines was operating a Tactical High-power Operational Responder system developed by the Air Force Research Laboratory. The THOR was a microwave weapon designed to take down drone swarms by disrupting their electronics. As the drones approached, the THOR emitted bursts of electromagnetic energy, which caused several of the drones to veer off course and crash.

Nearby, Gunnery Sergeant "Snake Eyes" Jennings was getting his troops out of their bunks and into four JLTVs. Each vehicle had a .50-caliber machine gun and a turret with two missile pods containing four FIM-92 Stinger missiles. The turrets could be operated from inside the vehicles or remotely, allowing the crew to remain protected while engaging targets. While Snake Eyes could appreciate all the *Star Wars* crap, he was old-school, having been an Abrams tank commander before the Marines decided they didn't need them anymore . . . but that was another story.

"Rattler 1 to all Rattlers," Snake Eyes said over comms. "Spread out and follow me. Our primary targets will be the drones." Jennings had Private Tommy Snyder on the turret and Private First Class Manny Consuelos on the machine gun. The three trailing vehicles mirrored the setup, each crew ready to unleash their firepower.

The highly mobile vehicles thundered across the desert to an improved tactical position from which to engage. Meanwhile, Tommy swiveled the turret back and forth while checking the targeting system and searching for enemy drones. As they approached the oil field, the vehicles quickly dispersed to take strategic positions around the perimeter. Their goal was to create an overlapping field of fire and ensure that no drone could penetrate their defenses.

Snake Eyes positioned his vehicle on a slight rise, giving him a clear line of sight over the flat terrain. "Rattler 1 at position alpha," Gunny reported. "Setting up fire grid."

"Rattler 2 in position," came the voice from the second JLTV. "We're near the main access road."

"Rattler 3 in position," said Lance Corporal Jane "Pete" Peterson from the third vehicle, near a cluster of storage tanks. "Ready to engage."

"Rattler 4 just east of Rattler 3. Ready." Four was specially set up with Javelin ATGMs to support the others against heavy armor, such as tanks.

It didn't take long before Snake Eyes yelled out, "Contact! Multiple bogeys at my two o'clock, closing fast. Engage at will."

Tommy locked onto the first target and fired. The Stinger missile roared out of its launcher, streaking toward the incoming drone, finding its mark, and blowing the drone from the sky.

Both turrets quickly maneuvered and fired to intercept the incoming groups of drones. In support, the .50-caliber machine guns roared to life, shredding the smaller, closer drones with a hail of bullets.

A transmission came across the net. "All units, this is Javelin HQ. Enemy armor units converging from the north. Take up defensive positions now."

These strategic positions were built from the moment the Marines took over the oil field. Hastily constructed sandbags, barbed wire, and makeshift barricades had been laid. Engineers had worked tirelessly to place mines and set up explosive traps along likely enemy approach routes.

With HQ's call, heavy machine gun positions were manned at key points around the perimeter, and mortar teams set up sites to provide indirect fire support. Others, like Snake Eyes and his Marines, repositioned their combat assets.

"Rattler 1 to all Rattlers. Move to assigned sectors and prepare to fire." All four vehicles turned and sped off.

The ground began to tremble as the Iranian forces launched their attack. Tanks, armored personnel carriers, and infantry moved forward in a coordinated assault. Artillery shells began to rain down on the oil field, sending plumes of smoke and dust into the air.

The four JLTVs drove in a serpentine pattern, trying to avoid the artillery rounds landing all around them. Smoke made it tough going as they fought to get to their sectors and return fire. Abruptly, a massive storage tank blew up, throwing burning oil through the air and starting several secondary fires.

The Javelin teams took the brunt of the assault and headed for high ground. They took cover behind sandbags and barricades to minimize exposure and maximize their firing range. Taking up a position behind a brick wall surrounding some equipment, Corporal Jaime "Ghost" Martinez was positioning his vehicle to maximize his shots. He got his nickname because of his ability to move silently and strike without warning. A former high school baseball star, Martinez quickly rose through the ranks due to his focused tactical mind and exceptional marksmanship. His calm demeanor under pressure and ability to adapt quickly made him a natural choice for the Javelin team, where he thrived.

"Ghost, you ready?" asked Bullseye O'Neill, his assistant gunner. He had a reputation for hitting any target with his rifle, a skill that complemented Martinez's precision with the Javelin.

"Always," Ghost replied, his voice steady. "Keep an eye on our flanks. They'll try to overwhelm us with numbers."

As the rumble of Iranian armor grew louder, Ghost took a deep breath and focused on his training. "Target acquired," he whispered, locking onto the heat signature of the lead tank.

Employing the Command Launch Unit, Ghost used the daytime sight and put the crosshairs on the tank. He activated the seeker and squeezed the trigger. The Javelin missile launched with a soft whoosh before igniting its main engine. He tracked the rocket as it streaked toward the tank using a high-arc trajectory designed to strike the top of the turret where the armor was weakest. Moments later, an explosion lit up the battlefield, and the tank was reduced to a burning hulk. But there was no time to celebrate.

After launching the fire-and-forget missile, Ghost immediately loaded another, and he and O'Neill sprinted to a new position. As they ran, an Iranian APC spotted them and let loose with its machine guns, killing both Marines before they could reach new cover. The last thing Ghost saw was the burning hulk of a tank he had just killed. It gave him peace, fulfilling the proverb that courage is not the absence of fear, but the willingness to face it and pay the ultimate price.

Meanwhile, Snake Eyes' four vehicles arrived at their designated position and covered the terrain. They began to receive enemy fire almost immediately.

Snake Eyes yelled over comms, "Activate systems and get these bastards on the ground."

Tommy immediately took aim with his .50-cal, laying down fire on the fast-approaching infantry and light vehicles. Suddenly, their truck shook violently as a fast-approaching Iranian tank fired and barely missed them. As Snake Eyes attempted to relocate, a massive explosion destroyed the tank, sending burning shrapnel in every direction. He looked to his right and saw a Javelin team hauling ass to a new firing location—there was no time for a thank-you, but he acknowledged to himself that they had just saved his ass.

"All Rattlers, missile status," Snake Eyes said.

After each JLTV reported how many missiles they had remaining, Snake Eyes decided to send Rattler 2 and Rattler 4 back for a field reload. Once out of the line of fire, they unlocked the mechanisms holding the spent missile tubes and replaced them with new ones. The total time was six minutes. The other two Rattlers repeated the process.

Realizing the strength of the Marine defenses, the Iranian forces began to adapt, using speed and maneuverability to try to overwhelm them.

"Rattler 4, we've got movement on the east side," Snake Eyes warned over the radio. "Multiple technicals and APCs."

"Copy that," Rattler 4 replied. The gunner adjusted his aim and fired another Javelin, taking out an approaching APC. His assistant gunner provided covering fire with the .50-cal by targeting dismounted infantry.

Despite the Marines' best efforts, the Iranian forces continued to press the attack. The air was filled with explosions and gunfire, and the stench of burning fuel and cordite was thick in the air. The JLTV teams maintained a relentless barrage.

"Rattler 3's taking fire," came the call from Rattler 4. Seconds later, Rattler 4 saw Rattler 3 take a direct hit from an Iranian missile.

"Rattler 1, Rattler 4, just saw Rattler 3 take a hit. No survivors. Engaging."

The Iranian tank managed to close the distance, its main gun swinging towards Rattler 4's position.

"Tank at one o'clock. Fire!" Rattler 4 gunner let loose with a Javelin at point-blank range. The missile struck, detonating the tank's ammunition and sending a plume of fire into the sky.

A new voice echoed over the tactical radio. "All units, two F-35s inbound, call signs Raider 11 and 12. Prepare to mark targets and coordinate."

"Yes!" yelled Snake Eyes over comms. Shit, that was good news, he thought before saying, "All Rattlers, pull back and redeploy on my mark."

Forward air controllers on the ground used laser designators to mark the most critical targets for the Marine pilots. One controller said, "Raider 11, this is Lighter 1. Target marked. Tank column at grid reference one-four-one by seven-two-eight."

"Raider 11 on station. Ready to engage," the lead pilot radioed. The F-35's advanced sensors quickly identified multiple high-value targets, including enemy tanks and infantry formations. The advanced targeting system locked onto the laser designators, ensuring precision engagement.

"Raider 11 engaging," the pilot confirmed. The F-35 released a pair of GBU-12 Paveway IIs. The bombs streaked down, guided by laser designators. The first bomb hit the lead tank, resulting in a massive explosion that disabled several vehicles in the column. The second bomb struck an APC, shattering it and scattering the infantry nearby. The Marines on the ground fired on the exposed troops, putting that part of the battlefield in disarray.

"Raider 12 targeting secondary armor." The pilot released a mix of AGM-154 Joint Standoff Weapons and AGM-88E Advanced Anti-Radiation Guided Missiles to suppress enemy air defenses and destroy additional armored units.

The JSOWs glided toward their targets, each carrying a powerful warhead that obliterated multiple tanks and APCs. The AARGMs homed in on enemy radar and anti-aircraft positions, neutralizing threats to the F-35s and clearing the way for continued air support.

With the armored threats neutralized, the F-35s focused on enemy infantry formations. "Raider 11 shifting to infantry targets," the lead pilot reported. Using their 25mm GAU-22/A Gatling guns, the fighters strafed enemy positions. The high-explosive incendiary rounds ripped through infantry formations and lightly armored vehicles as if they were made of paper.

"Raider 12 engaging mortar position," the pilot announced, and an SDB struck an enemy mortar team, eliminating the threat and reducing incoming fire on Marine positions.

As the F-35s continued their devastating air strikes, Marine ground forces took advantage of the disruption in enemy lines. The order came out, "Javelin HQ to all units, advance and engage. Push them back!"

"Rattler 1 to all units," said Snake Eyes, "you heard the man, let's go, push forward now."

The F-35s maintained a presence over the battlefield, using their sensors to detect and intercept any reinforcements. "Raider 11, Lighter 1," called the forward air controller. We have incoming enemy vehicles northeast at 1.2 miles." The fighters responded by launching a series of AGM-114 Hellfire missiles, each finding its mark and destroying the incoming armor before they could reach the battlefield.

Parked on what might pass as a hill, Snake Eyes, Tommy, and Manny dismounted and stood side by side overlooking the battlefield. It was an amazing sight, and yet sad for the loss of US lives. As smoke and ash drifted through the battlefield, the three took in the wreckage of tanks and vehicles and the bodies of fallen warriors. They knew that Ahvaz Oil Field remained under the control of the US Marines, a testament to their resilience and combat prowess. It was one thing to casually mention in a White House meeting that taking control of the three largest Iranian oil fields was necessary, and it was another to make it happen. They did.

Snake Eyes glanced at the teenager, who now went by Tommy, and smiled. He knew that Tommy could do whatever he wanted in the Marine Corps after his brilliant performance in today's battle. In just days, the youngster had gone from a nervous, shaking-hands kid to a confident, self-assured young man. Such was the way of war, as was the inevitable changing of the guard; Snake Eyes could swear that Tommy now had his own snake-eyed stare.

Chapter 76

USS REAGAN
Persian Gulf

One day after contacting her XO, Lieutenant Commander Sarah Freeman was contacted by the ship's Equal Opportunity Advisor, Master Chief Petty Officer Jamison Yates, a seasoned and empathetic leader known for his integrity. They made an appointment to meet, squeezing it between Sarah's flight and crew rest schedules. And here she was. She had no second thoughts.

Sitting in a small, private room, Yates asked Sarah how she'd been doing given her combat missions and hectic schedule, which was pretty standard small talk these days. Glancing down, Sarah saw her personnel file in front of him, as well as that of her boss, Commander Damien Wagner.

"Thank you for coming forward, Commander Freeman," Yates said, to move on to the real purpose of the meeting. "I understand this isn't easy, but I want you to know that your complaint is being taken seriously, and we'll handle this with the utmost confidentiality and care."

Sarah nodded her head. "Thank you, Master Chief. As I'm sure you read in my package, I'm an exemplary officer and a skillful pilot. I'm currently second in command to

Commander Wagner, and I've never had any disciplinary cases against me or been written up for any reason." Looking into Yates's eyes, Sarah could tell he understood, and that made her comfortable to continue.

She went over every detail of Wagner's inappropriate and consistent harassment and abuse of power, his insistence that she get him coffee, his ridiculously short timelines to write reports, and his hints and accusations that she couldn't perform her job properly when her husband, Jessie, was involved in the same mission.

"If anyone is preventing me from adequately performing my assigned missions, it's him, my commander, who's badgering me about everything I do and treating me differently than my male counterparts. He has created a hostile working environment that isn't conducive to good order and discipline, especially in a combat setting. Something needs to be done. So how does this work?"

Yates nodded his head, showing he understood completely. "First, I'll notify the XO about your complaint, even though you've already gone to him as a part of your chain of command. Commander Wagner will issue a no-contact order to ensure he has no further interaction with you. We will then initiate a preliminary inquiry to gather facts. If the inquiry supports your allegations, then NCIS will conduct a formal investigation."

Sarah nodded, absorbing the information. "Just to be clear, I won't have to interact with Commander Wagner at all, correct?"

"Correct," Yates assured her. "You will also have access to counseling and legal support if needed. But let me ask: Since we're in the middle of a war with Iran and your duties are essential to the mission, can you continue your duties without impairment during the process I explained?"

Sarah thought for a second. "Thank you for asking. If I weren't flying missions, I would be devastated. Flying my E-2, leading people, and protecting my nation is my calling. But I will say, I can stay better focused on my missions if I don't have to see Wagner.

"Thank you for your honest appraisal. I anticipated that answer and have already cleared this aspect of the case with the XO and the CAG. From this point forward, you will receive your mission orders and briefs from the CAG. Does that work for you?"

Sarah couldn't help but smile as she answered, "It sure does. Flying for the Navy is my life."

"Alright then, Commander Freeman, go get 'em."

Sarah left the room feeling relieved as if the heavyweight she'd carried since arriving aboard the Reagan had finally been lifted. Eagerly, she looked ahead to her next mission.

Chapter 77

USS FORD
Arabian Sea

As part of the comprehensive US strategy, the decision to attack Iran included targeting the Iranian Navy and military infrastructure. This action, combined with the American seizure of the country's three major oil refineries and effectively disrupting the flow of funds to the Iranian government, would hinder their ability to continue the war and their global terrorist activities.

Keeping his operational strategy aligned with Washington's, the CENTCOM-Forward commander approved his J-5's mission analysis to eliminate any challenges from the Iranian Navy and the IRGC. Since then, Rear Admiral Marquis Holloway's planners had been working with CENTCOM-Forward's joint planning group on course-of-action development.

They began with extensive intelligence assessment of satellite imagery, electronic surveillance, cyber espionage, and HUMINT to identify and map out all Iranian naval assets, including ships, submarines, coastal batteries, naval bases, shipyards, and logistics facilities. In addition, they used real-time surveillance and reconnaissance by utilizing drones, maritime patrol aircraft, and reconnaissance satellites to verify the data. They also got the same level of detail about IRGC facilities and their affiliated militias in Iraq and Syria. Objectives, end states, constraints, restraints, assumptions, force lists, and ROEs were refined, and the time came when the course of action transitioned from planning to execution. The CENTCOM-Forward J-3 sent an Execute order to the TF-70 commander, who had been tasked as the lead for this vital aspect of the war with Iran. The TF-70 planners then led the task force's own planning efforts.

With many of his key personnel on the *Ford*, Holloway spoke to all essential ship captains and unit commanders via secure videoconference, a final brief prior to the launch of operations against the Iranian Navy and IRGC.

"Ladies and gentlemen, thank you for joining me today. We're on the cusp of a critical mission that will shape the region's strategic landscape and ensure the safety of international maritime routes. Our objectives are clear—to neutralize both the Iranian Navy and the IRGC, and render their supporting infrastructure ineffective. This will be a coordinated multiphase operation involving air, sea, and cyber components. I need each of you to understand this mission's gravity and your crucial role.

"We had just a short time to gather intelligence and conduct surveillance to pinpoint every significant Iranian naval and IRGC asset—but the data is accurate and current. Our reconnaissance efforts have given us a comprehensive picture of their capabilities and positions. Remember, intelligence is the backbone of this operation. Stay vigilant and report any anomalies immediately."

Holloway tried to read faces. Everyone seemed to be all in, so he continued.

"Our cyber units will execute targeted attacks on Iranian command and control networks. This will be followed by renewed electronic warfare strikes to disrupt radar and communications. Blinding and disorienting the enemy will give us an operational advantage.

"Then we will establish air superiority. With most, if not all, of their Russian-made Su-35s already destroyed, we will neutralize Iranian air defenses with fighter packages. Following up on this, a coordinated barrage of Tomahawk cruise missiles will target key naval bases, shipyards, and coastal defense installations. B-2 bombers will strike high-value targets. Precision and discipline are paramount, so execute your missions with the utmost accuracy.

"Now, for you strike groups, you'll play a pivotal role in supporting continuous carrier launches for sorties against Iranian naval vessels and coastal facilities, including IRGC facilities. Submarine commanders, you will hunt down and destroy any remaining enemy submarines and surface ships.

Surface warfare units must be prepared to engage with anti-ship missiles and naval gunfire to protect the carriers."

Holloway paused again, and everyone seemed ready to do their part. As he finished up, he addressed logistics.

"As you all know, logistics are the lifeline of all operations. Our supply ships and refueling tankers will ensure continuous support. Allied cooperation will be leveraged to enhance our operational capabilities. Stay coordinated and communicate effectively."

Holloway felt confident in the plan, which showed as he wrapped it up. "Ladies and gentlemen, this mission demands excellence, precision, and unwavering resolve. The eyes of the world will be upon us. We must conduct ourselves with honor and uphold the highest standards. Execute your duties knowing that you are contributing to a safer world and securing our nation's interests. Remember, success in this mission will rely on our ability to work as a cohesive unit. Trust in your training, trust in your teammates, trust in the mission—and by God, trust in the United States of America. Now let's get to work."

He pressed a button, and the TV monitor went black. Thousands of sailors and Marines began preparing for the most critical mission of their careers.

Chapter 78

USS FORD
Arabian Sea

In the ready room, Lieutenant Commander Jessie "Swagger" Hampton reviewed the details for the second time before giving his mission commander briefing to his strike force. He thought this was a big one, but they all were when it was war. He led sixteen F-35s, twelve F-18s, and four E/A-18G Growlers, with one E-2 assigned to provide C2. Their mission was to eliminate Mehrabad Air Base outside of Tehran.

"Okay, listen up," Jessie said. "I don't want to have to repeat myself because you dumbasses aren't listening. For everyone, launch time starts at 0600 hours. First up will be strike package one." He flashed a PowerPoint slide on a whiteboard and began reviewing its info.

MISSION: MEHRABAD AIR BASE: 33 A/C

- STRIKE PACKAGE ONE
- 8 F-35 - Yoda 21- Runways, Command Center
- 4 F-35 - Spooky 11 – SEAD
- 4 F-35 - Jedi 11 - CAP

- STRIKE PACKAGE TWO
- 8 F-18 – Toxic 11
- 4 EA-18G - Spooky 21 SEAD
- 4 F-18 - Venom 11 CAP
- Support E-2 – Hawker 31

"Eight F-35s, lead call sign Yoda 21, will be armed with JDAMs and SDBs to strike critical infrastructure such as runways, hangars, and command centers. Four F-35s, lead call sign Spooky 11, will perform SEAD and be armed with HARMs. Four F-35s, lead call sign Jedi 11, will fly CAP for the strike package and be armed with AMRAAMs and JATMs. I will be Jedi 11 and coordinating both packages from the CAP. Now for strike package two. Eight F/A-18Es, lead call sign Toxic 11, will have the same armament and complement the primary strike package by ensuring the destruction of high-value targets. Four EA-18Gs, lead call sign Spooky 21, will run SEAD for package two. Four F/A-18Es, lead call sign Venom 11, will provide CAP for the package's ingress and join the Jedis until I direct the CAP to egress. CAP aircraft will have the same armament. Finally, we'll be supported by an E-2, call sign Hawker 31. Maintain good situational awareness and use brevity calls when appropriate. Any questions?"

No one said anything, and they all got down to the business of war. After taking off the flight toped off fuel and assembled at 15,000 feet, with Jessie leading the strike force on its mission. Flying into Iranian air space, the SEAD aircraft were up first.

"Jedi 11, Spooky 11. Jamming initiated," said Lieutenant Emmerson "Notch" Smitson, his calm voice crackling through the comms. "Enemy radar is dark."

"Yoda 21, primary. Box formation."

Eight F-35s split into four flights to approach from different directions. They used stealth to their advantage while providing mutual support and overlapping fields of fire to enhance protection against SAMs. Using JDAMS and SDBs, they targeted runways, hangars, and communication centers. Meanwhile, Jessie was flying CAP and overseeing the entire operation.

As the first package's F-35s dropped munitions, the secondary package arrived to do clean-up, and their F-18s flying ingress CAP joined Jessie's CAP. Inside Jessie's cockpit, a warning sounded. His AESA radar had detected incoming missiles.

"Jedi 11 to Jedi 11, and Venom 11 CAP. Engage enemy missiles. Your HUDs have your assigned targets." The F-35 flight's computers had prioritized each missile according to threat level. Eight fighters maneuvered into firing positions and let loose with a group of AIM-120s and a few AIM-260s. The sky was dotted with fiery explosions as missiles hit home. But not all did.

Jessie heard Toxic 11 say he had a missile lock on him and was maneuvering. But it was too late, and the enemy missile struck the F-18 near the cockpit, instantly killing the pilot and sending the aircraft nose-diving into the desert.

Just then, the E-2 came on comms. "Jedi 11, Hawker 31. Fourteen bandits at 20,000 feet bearing one-four-six heading your direction at 300. Radar indicates one Su-35 and a mixture of F-14s, MiG-29s, and F-4s. They are in a spread formation."

"Hawker 31, Jedi 11 copies. Jedi 11 to all strike packages. ID types of aircraft in your current zone. Assess their capabilities, weaknesses, and threat level. Yoda and Toxic flights, continue strike. Spooky 21 flight, form up with the CAP to engage EW on incoming bandits. Spooky 22 flight, stay with Yoda and Toxic flights for strike."

As Jessie maneuvered to intercept the bandits, he said, "CAP, loose deuce formation." This formation split all aircraft into pairs, with one as the lead and the other as the wingman. Each covered the other, providing mutual support. This included lookout responsibilities, where each pilot scanned for threats and provided situational awareness to the other. In an engagement, one aircraft took an offensive role to attack the enemy while the other provided protection from potential threats.

"Sixteen bandits inbound, mostly older jets," Jessie announced. "Check your HUDs for specific aircraft for long-range and short-range missile engagements. Stand by for specific roles."

After checking his HUD and quickly assessing the situation, Jessie said, "Jedi 12, Jedi 11, and Jedi 12, you're with me for long-range strikes. Prepare JATMs for launch. Ensure radar locks and coordinate your launches with mine." He paused for a second before continuing.

"Venom flight, set your AMRAAMs for priority targets. Keep your radar active and follow my lead on launch timing. Use Sidewinders to engage any bandits that break through the JATMs."

As the Iranian flight of sixteen jets approached, Jessie was a bit surprised there was a Su-35 in the mix. He thought they'd all been destroyed. A part of him hoped the Flanker would break through the BVR laydown they were about to send. That Su-35 dogfight had been something. When the bandits got in range, his system notified him, and it was go time.

"Jedi 11, Fox three," Jessie called out as he fired his first JATM. The missile streaked ahead, guided by the F-35's advanced radar, and headed for the single Flanker. He announced Fox three again when he fired a second AIM-260.

The sky filled with the trails of multiple JATMs and AMRAAMs as both F-35s and F-18s engaged the incoming bandits. The missiles locked onto the Iranian jets using their active radar homing guidance.

Just then, RWR warning sounds went off in all aircraft. The Iranians had launched an assortment of missiles, including several R-77s and old AIM-54s.

Explosions lit up the sky as the JATMs and AMRAAMs found their targets, significantly reducing the number of incoming threats. However, a few Iranian jets managed to evade the first wave of missiles and continued their approach.

In his Su-35 Flanker, Major Zamani couldn't believe his luck. After being shot down just a day ago, he was now piloting the last Su-35 of the Iranian Air Force. With only some bumps and scratches from his ejection, he had been picked up and rushed back to the base. He was itching for the chance to even the score with that F-35 pilot, and he just knew that asshole would be in this large formation attacking his country. Warriors always found ways to get in the major battles.

That was why upon his return to the Su-35, Zamani had hurriedly formed a ragtag flight of working fighters to disrupt an attack on Mehrabad Air Base, an attack his gut had told him was imminent. He had hidden his flight away at a remote base and put everyone on alert, so when Iranian Integrated Air Defense Systems had picked up the approaching Americans, he had scrambled his flight along with his surprise, a flight of six Karrar high-speed, jet-powered unmanned aerial vehicles.

The Karrars could perform various combat roles, including acting as decoys. They were capable of high speeds, and Zamani was using them to mimic manned aircraft, hoping the drones would draw some of the American missiles.

As an AIM-260 approached, Zamani maneuvered his Su-35 so that two of the drones in front of him confused the rocket, causing it to explode on them. Unfortunately, the second missile took out his wingman in an F-14.

Zamani pressed on, noting which F-35 had fired on him. That had to be his nemesis warrior, he thought, and continued arming his short-range infrared-homing Vympel R-73 missile.

At the same time, Jessie saw the Su-35 had somehow managed to duck his two JATMs. As his eyes scanned his HUD, Jessie saw the fast-moving Flanker approaching him.

"Jedi 11, Flanker on my tail, bearing one-zero-five. Engaging."

Across the sky, Zamani received the alert that his sophisticated radar had locked onto the American stealth fighter.

The two veteran fighter pilots, seasoned and determined, knew this would be a fight in which one wouldn't enjoy the ending.

Jessie threw his F-35 into a tight turn and came out in a perfect launch position. He fired two Sidewinders at the Su-35 and let loose with chaff and flares.

At nearly the same instant, the Su-35 roared toward Jessie, its powerful engines pushing it to the limit. Zamani fired an R-77 missile, hoping to catch the American pilot off guard. The rocket streaked through the sky but exploded in Jessie's countermeasures.

Zamani rolled his fighter and deployed chaff and flares, which somehow confused the Sidewinder. With a quick flick of his wrist, he brought his aircraft around to face the American head-on.

The two jets closed the distance between them at supersonic speed, and the fight was now within visual range. Both Zamani and Jessie knew this was where skill and nerve would determine who lived or didn't. Both pilots thought of themselves as the most dominant pilots in their ranks.

Jessie used his helmet-mounted display to lock the AIM-9X onto the Su-35. Even though the Flanker was at an extreme angle, the missile's high off-boresight capability allowed it to lock onto the aircraft without having to line up directly—a significant advantage.

Zamani responded instantly by twisting in the air, pulling a Pugachev's Cobra move by using his thrust-vectoring nozzles. This allowed him to rapidly change his fighter's direction and speed, making it difficult for the Sidewinder to maintain a lock. It didn't, and Zamani immediately fired another R-73 toward his enemy.

Jessie now found himself on the defensive. He banked hard, deploying countermeasures and pushing his aircraft to the edge of the envelope. He skillfully looped around, coming at the Su-35 from below. With a quick lock-on, he fired another AIM-9X.

Zamani felt the impact, his aircraft shuddering as the explosion tore through its structure. The Su-35 spiraled downward, a trail of smoke marking its descent. Zamani fought for control as the aircraft quickly lost altitude, and he realized he was outside the ejection parameters. He rode his jet into the desert floor, his final mark in the world a fireball and scorched sand.

As Jessie maneuvered away from the incoming missile, his wingman got off a shot and took the R-73 out of the sky.

"You can thank me later, Swagger. Bulldog is out."

"Jedi 11, Yoda 21. Mission complete. All targets are dust."

"Jedi 11, Spooky21. Confirm dust."

"Jedi 11 to all flights. The skies in this area of Iran now belong to us. Great job, all. Form up on me at 30 angels in a spread formation. Spooky flights lead the way home."

The destruction of Mehrabad Air Base would mark a turning point in the war with Iran. Jessie was so proud. Not only had his flights beaten a worthy opponent, but he'd led the mission that made it such a success.

B-2 SPIRIT

Sepehr Radar Site

As he took off from Diego Garcia on another mission, Lieutenant Colonel "Cowboy" Remy could hardly believe he was alive and flying a B-2 again after being shot down just three days ago. His co-pilot, regrettably, didn't make it, having smashed his head on the aircraft as he ejected.

If there hadn't been a war going on, Cowboy thought, he probably would have hung it up after getting plucked out of the drink. But his country needed him, and like any good American, he cowboyed up so he could be counted on again. His new copilot was Captain Arnold Remington, a newly pinned captain who was an ROTC product from Harvard. Over Remington's objections, Cowboy called him Professor.

The early morning sun partially blinded Cowboy as his B-2 Spirit headed toward the Iranian coast. They were on a critical mission to strike the Sepehr Radar Site, an over-the-horizon installation able to detect targets at ranges up to 1,800 miles away. His B-2 bomber, the cutting-edge marvel of stealth technology, sliced through the air undetected—or at least he hoped so, because his last mission made his number of landings less than his number of take-offs. But his aircraft's radar-absorbent material and low-profile design rendered it nearly invisible to radar. To seal the deal on stealth, he and his copilot maintained radio silence.

At the Sepehr Radar Site, the operators diligently monitored the airspace. Radar screens displayed the usual air traffic—commercial flights, local patrols, and a few unidentified blips that were harmless anomalies. Suddenly, one of the operators noticed something unusual. "Commander, we have a faint signal at the edge of our detection range. It's barely registering."

Commander Farhad Shahin peered at the screen. "Increase the sensitivity and monitor closely. Alert the SAM batteries to be on standby."

As Cowboy flew nearer to the launching point, Professor armed the AGM-158 JASSMs. These long-range, precision-guided missiles were the key to striking the radar site without exposing the B-2 to immediate risk. "Target locked," Professor said, eyes glued to the display.

After Cowboy acknowledged him, Professor fired the missiles, and the JASSMs roared away from the B-2, streaking toward the Sepehr Radar Site. The rockets were designed to fly low to hug the terrain and evade detection.

Waiting impatiently, Cowboy finally saw the display showing breaches in the radar site's defenses and infrastructure. Without hesitation, he maneuvered the B-2 into the next phase of the attack.

"We're in range for the JDAMs," Professor reported. The Joint Direct Attack Munitions were GPS-guided bombs designed for precision strikes such as today's mission.

"Release on my mark," Cowboy commanded. "And—mark."

Instantly, the B-2's bomb bay doors opened, and the JDAMs fell silently into the sky. The bombs plunged toward the now-compromised radar site. Each one was programmed to hit specific structures and equipment. Moments later, there were massive explosions as the bombs found their targets.

"Maneuvering out of range," said Cowboy. "What do you have on the sensors, Professor?"

"Still emitting radar signals, Cowboy. Suggest we follow up with HARMs."

"Roger that. Coming around to 40 angels. Outside of missile launch sectors. Prepare to launch on my mark." When he reached the optimal parameters, he said, "Mark."

With that command, the AGM-88 HARM missiles were fired at the remaining radar emissions. Constantly scanning his instruments for any sign of trouble, Cowboy maintained course while the missiles found their targets. When he saw confirmed locks on the targets, Remy banked the flying wing to get to the preplanned egress route, which avoided known enemy defenses.

"Sensors confirm a direct hit, Cowboy. Nice job."

"Well, how could I fuck this up with a Professor sitting next to me guiding my every move? Nice job, kid. I think I'll keep you around—that is until I pull the pin, which I have a feeling will be very soon."

Chapter 80

Bandar Abbas Submarine Base
Bandar Abbas, Iran

Captain Reza Mahdavi hated this part of submarining—piloting his sub where the water was below, and his boat was on top. He was a fish out of water, and it wasn't ideal. A hunter like him wanted cover and concealment in the depths.

Leaving his submarine base at Bandar Abbas, Mahdavi was going hunting. War with the United States was going full tilt, and his country needed a noteworthy victory to rally the people behind the war effort. While there had been some successes, the military might of the infidels was powerful. The Islamic Republic of Iran needed a catalyst to ignite the spirit of unity and resilience that was suppressed in the hearts of its people.

The Supreme Leader had ordered that he, Captain Mahdavi, hunt down and sink the *Ohio*-class guided missile submarines that had been shooting Tomahawk missiles all over his country of eighty-four million souls. Mahdavi wasn't surprised. He knew precisely why he and his submarine had been picked for the mission: Both were the best at what they did, hunters who got results not by putting food on the table but by putting destroyed ships and bodies on the sea floor.

Mahdavi's journey to this point in his life started in Tehran. At a young age, he demonstrated a keen interest in mechanics and engineering by often dismantling and reassembling household appliances. This curiosity and skill led him to pursue a degree in mechanical engineering before attending the Iranian Naval Academy.

In the Navy, he had served on various classes of submarines and surface ships. He had earned a reputation for his pragmatic leadership and unflinching determination in the face of adversity. At forty-five, with gray just beginning to streak his temples, he was the perfect man for the hunt.

His weapon was the best in Iran's fleet of submarines. The *Tareq-901*, a *Kilo*-class submarine, had a reputation for being exceptionally quiet, making it difficult to sniff out. Its advanced sonar and sensors, long endurance, and ability to operate nearly 1,000 feet deep enabled its silent running. Plus, it was armed with a variety of torpedoes and anti-ship missiles. All that made it an apex predator in the deep ocean. But a good hunter knew he wasn't the only predator out there.

After traveling two miles on the surface, Mahdavi gave the order he had longed to give, "Helm, make your depth 90 meters, speed 5 knots, course one-eight-zero."

Chapter 81

USS GEORGIA
Gulf of Oman

While one predator took to the depths, another was already in the hunt. Captain Mateo Navarro attempted to locate *Tareq-901,* which was transiting from its home base and heading to the Gulf of Oman.

"Captain, Comms. SOSUS reports contact with one *Kilo*-class sub, classified as *Tareq-901,* at 26.2725 north by 56.1880 east. Heading one-eight-zero, depth 300 feet, speed 4 knots. Distance 35 miles. Classify target as Sierra 1."

Navarro was a big fan of the Sound Surveillance System, one aspect of the US's fixed underwater sensor network. This network consisted of arrays of hydrophones and acoustic sensors installed on the ocean floor. Underwater cables connected these sensors to shore-based processing facilities, where the data was analyzed and given to US submarines patrolling near grid reference points.

"Helm, set a new course to zero-two-five, speed 4 knots, maintain depth." Navarro wanted to get within 25 nautical miles, the optimal strike range for the MK 48 ADCAP. The advanced capability torpedo was ideal for the high-performance capabilities of a *Kilo*-class sub. He toggled the ship's intercom.

"Attention all hands, this is the Captain. Battle stations, battle stations. Man your battle stations. Set condition silent. Secure all nonessential systems. Minimize noise and maintain radio silence. Stealth mode engaged. Execute."

"Captain, Sonar. We have a fix on Sierra 1 at 26 miles, course our direction, speed 3 knots, and depth 300 feet."

A few moments later, Navarro said, "Nav, deploy an XBT and monitor CTD sensors. I need thermocline data ASAP. Ensure we're below the thermal layer and adjust depth to 725 feet."

Navarro deployed the expendable bathythermograph to measure conductivity, temperature, and depth, aiming to exploit the thermal layer—a zone where the water temperature shifts sharply with depth. He aimed to position the submarine just beneath this layer, where it would be more challenging to detect. By analyzing the XBT data, the crew could accurately identify the thermocline's depth and adjust the submarine's position accordingly. Operating below the thermal layer allowed *Georgia* to evade detection by surface and shallow-water sonar systems, significantly reducing the effectiveness of enemy sonar.

"Conn, set speed to creeping at 3 knots," Navarro ordered. "Maintain silent running procedures. All nonessential noise and communication are to be minimized. Sonar, distance to Sierra 1," Navarro queried.

"Sir, 22 miles."

As the Iranian submarine patrolled the strategic waters of the Sea of Oman, it received urgent communication from an Iranian maritime reconnaissance aircraft. The recon aircraft had detected unusual underwater acoustic activity indicative of a foreign submarine. Captain Mahdavi used this intelligence to focus his sonar sweeps on the suspected area.

"Bridge, Sonar. Sir, I have a very faint blip on the edge of my range. We need to close the distance for more accurate information."

"Helm, this is the captain. Increase speed to 12 knots."

Mahdavi did the math in his head. At this speed, it would take 20 minutes to close the distance by 4 nautical miles. That should be enough, he thought. He sensed an *Ohio*-class sub out there, no doubt looking for him.

Back in *Georgia*, the silence was broken by Petty Officer First Class Max Ripley. "Conn, Sonar. Sierra 1 is increasing speed. They're making a run for it."

"Any course change?" asked Navarro.

"No, sir, still navigating to our position."

Navarro pondered this information. Increasing speed made the *Tareq-901* more detectable, so the Iranian submarine's attempt to close might have been spurred by a realization that it was being hunted.

"WEPS, prepare to fire torpedoes."

The weapons officer and crew quickly inputted the data into the Mark 48 torpedoes.

"Conn, WEPS. Mark 48 torpedoes loaded and ready."

"Flood tubes one and two," said Navarro.

The torpedo room crew acknowledged and began the flooding procedure. Valves were opened, and seawater filled the torpedo tubes to equalize the pressure.

"Conn, WEPS. Tubes one and two flooded and equalized.."

"WEPS, fire one." Five seconds later, Navarro said, "Fire two."

The first torpedo shot out from tube one, slicing through the water. Just a few seconds later, the second torpedo followed from tube two. The torpedoes were fired in rapid succession to increase the probability of a hit and to complicate *Tareq-901*'s countermeasure deployment.

"Conn, Sonar. Time to target is 22 minutes."

Tareq-901

"Bridge," called the Iranian sub's sonarman, "doors flooding on unknown contact. Classify as Alpha 1."

"This is the captain," said Mahdavi. "Release decoys and ahead flank. Helm, sharp turns to course zero-one-nine."

"Bridge, Sonar. Torpedoes in the water. Two Mark 48s."

The *Tareq-901* deployed its decoys to create multiple false targets. Mahdavi ordered more erratic maneuvers and a dive to 900 feet. He aimed to evade the incoming torpedoes so they would get lost in the decoys.

Immediately after launch, the two Mark 48s followed their input coordinates based on where Sierra 1 was last seen. A fine wire between each torpedo and *Georgia* allowed a communication link so the torpedo could constantly update its targeting information based on changing conditions and new data.

Each torpedo's onboard sonar systems also provided feedback to *Georgia*, helping perfect the targeting data. So, while the *Tareq-901* zigged and zagged, the torpedoes accounted for those defensive moves.

Onboard the *Tareq-901*, those who could, stared at Mahdavi as if he were a sea god who could save all their lives. The captain kept releasing decoys and continued to change course.

"Bridge, Sonar," the *Tareq-901*'s sonarman called in a higher-pitched voice than usual. Two Mark 48 torpedoes have a lock and are tracking us. Five minutes until impact."

Not good, Mahdavi thought, but he was not a man to give up. He had an idea. "Helm, emergency dive to 400 meters. Execute."

Helm hesitated, knowing 1,300 feet was beyond the sub's safe diving depth.

"Helm, do it now," Mahdavi said sternly, and the helmsman complied.

Mahdavi had recalled from a class on the Mark 48 that it had an operational limit of 365 meters. From intelligence reports, he had heard that the 48s became compromised at that depth due to increased pressure and the limitations of their onboard systems. He also thought crossing through thermal layers might throw off the torpedoes' locks.

As the *Tareq-901* dove, the interior corridors of the sub seemed like steep downhill streets. Some crew members grabbed ahold of any fixed object to keep from falling. The intense pressure against the hull made haunting noises that got louder as they dove. It was nerve-wracking.

"Passing 335 meters," said the helmsman.

"Bridge, Sonar. Torpedoes have lost their lock and are circling to reacquire."

Just as Mahdavi was about to order Helm to level off, he heard a commotion, then loud screaming. A nineteen-year-old planesman jumped up and ran from his post, screaming, "I can't do this. We're going to die! Stop us, captain. Stop!"

As the young man started to run, the officer of the deck tackled him but struck his head on a pipe, knocking him out.

Blood flowed all over the kid, who now screamed even louder, making it difficult for anyone to think.

Mahdavi yelled, "Helm, level out now—now!"

With the planesman on the ground screaming and the OOD knocked out, the helmsman—another young, scared sailor—had a difficult time functioning. The captain yelled at him to change seats and stop the descent. But the kid hadn't done that job since he was in training a year ago and wasn't sure what to do. As Mahdavi rushed over to stop the dive, the submarine dove through 487 meters. It was too much.

The last thing Mahdavi saw was his hand touching the dive controls. It was devastating, with 48.35 atmospheres of pressure on the hull—the equivalent of having a 3,000-pound car balanced on every square inch of one's body. The implosion was instant and horrifying, and what had been a submarine was now just little shreds of metal, debris, and parts of what a second ago were living human beings. Fortunately, no one had to bear witness.

Only the sonarman on the *Georgia* could tell something was happening. "Conn, Sonar. The 48s have lost contact with Sierra 1. They are circling. I'm unable to communicate with them."

Moments later, Ripley said, "Conn, Sonar. I've got noises of Sierra 1 . . . exploding . . . wait, Sir—"

The sound wave from *Tareq-901* hit *Georgia*, an indescribable noise that was both terrifying and a relief. The crew cheered, slapped high fives, and fist-bumped throughout the submarine. Each of them fully understood that that could have been them under different circumstances—such are the horrors of war—it was time to rejoice.

Chapter 82

USS FORD
Arabian Sea

Rear Admiral Marquis Holloway had been in the CIC at 0500 hours when US Navy warships and submarines began a joint missile attack on Iran's military infrastructure to reduce its ability to sustain prolonged combat operations. It was a massive undertaking, but Holloway felt confident about the outcome. Aircraft launched from the three carriers were spreading out over Iran with a list of high-value targets. On the sea, he had all twelve guided missile destroyers and cruisers involved in the fight. The targets for Task Force 70 were numerous, but so was the stockpile of US missiles, especially Tomahawks.

The operation was a swift and decisive campaign conducted with surgical precision. Within hours, most of Iran's air defenses were neutralized, its missile capabilities crippled, and its nuclear ambitions thwarted. The coordinated strikes on command centers, naval assets, IRGC forces, and critical infrastructure left Iran in disarray, significantly weakening its military and economic power. The US was hoping that, faced with overwhelming losses,

Iranian discontent would result in a change in leadership. But all agreed it had to come from within.

Chapter 83

PARLIAMENT BUILDING
Tehran, Iran

Reeling from the last two days of attacks and the series of defeats, the Iranian military succumbed to the superior US military forces. Due to US control of Iran's most extensive oil fields, money to fund any retaliation effort was cut off. Key military leaders and many government officials stepped down from their positions. The Supreme Leader and other top generals either fled the country or went into hiding. The Iranian government was nonexistent, and the mood in the nation was for change, allowing many influential Iranians to come out of seclusion and advocate for a new governing body. One was Dr. Amir Mehrabi, a political science and international relations professor from the University of Tehran.

His time as a diplomat during the early 2000s gave him practical experience in understanding the complexities of international relations and negotiating with world powers. As the US military campaign against Iran reached its climax, Dr. Mehrabi emerged as a critical figure advocating for a peaceful transition to a new, democratic government. Recognized for his moderate views and ability to bridge divides, he was approached by various factions—including reformists, moderates, and even pragmatic elements within the military—to lead the national dialogue.

Dr. Mehrabi articulated a vision for Iran that respected its rich cultural heritage while embracing democratic reforms and human rights. His speeches resonated with a broad audience, from urban intellectuals to farmers. Leveraging his diplomatic skills in the weeks after the US stopped bombing Iranian military targets, he brought together representatives from the Assembly of Experts, Parliament, the military, and civilian society to form a transitional council. This council oversaw and organized a national referendum, and he was the spearhead of that council; therefore, he was effectively the temporary leader of Iran.

Under Dr. Mehrabi's leadership, Iran successfully began the first steps of the transition to a new era. The Assembly of Experts was reformed to include diverse voices, and a new Supreme Leader was selected; one who embodied the values of the revolution and the aspirations of the modern Iranian people.

Standing on the steps of the partially bombed-out Parliament building less than two months after the last bomb dropped on Iranian soil, Dr. Mehrabi addressed a peaceful crowd of thousands and promised a bright future for Iran.

Taking note was CIA operative Dallas Steele and his driver and trusted companion, Ali Karimi. Steele had received only a pat on the back for his part in capturing Iran's first nuclear bomb. That was fine with him because he knew all too well that the CIA's most significant successes were the ones no one ever heard about.

Chapter 84

USS Ford
Arabian Sea

Grabbing a bite in the wardroom, Captain Mad Dog Johnson felt like it had been days since his last meal. Combat operations had ceased weeks ago, yet their new mission of maintaining a robust presence in the Middle East was just as taxing. He was slumped over his chipped beef on toast, lost in his thoughts, when a pilot carrying his own SOS walked up with his signature swagger.

"Hey, Mad Dog, what's up?" said Jessie "Swagger" Hampton.

"You and the sun, I suppose. Take a seat, Swagger, before you spill your shit on the floor."

Sitting across from the CAG, Jessie dug into his breakfast. At first, there wasn't much talking. The two ate their food as if it were their last meal. When their plates were empty, they started swigging their second cups of coffee.

"So, how's the repairs going?" asked Jessie.

"When you get hit with three Iranian kamikaze drones, it's not a good thing, but it sure as hell could have been much worse. Thanks for joining me, as requested, because I need to run something by you. As you know, we're heading to the

UAE to lay up for a while since formal cessation of combat operations is forthcoming. We'll remain operational and respond when needed, but only as a last resort. With the Iran thing over, we may have some free time ."

"I hear that," said Jessie.

Both went quiet for a few minutes as they finished their coffees.

"So what's up, Mad Dog? You need me to do anything for you?" asked Jessie.

"I thought you'd never ask. Listen up because this is a biggie," the CAG said with a big shit-eating grin—and a tiny bit of food between his two front teeth.

"Shit, the tougher, the better. You know me."

"That I do." Mad Dog paused because even though he wanted to tell Jessie he would be getting his own command soon, the official orders hadn't come down yet. But he knew his hotshot, swaggering pilot would be just as happy to receive what he could offer for now. "The *Reagan* has requested a loan of one of our F-35s, and they need an errand boy."

"Are you shitting me?" said the pilot, who knew exactly who was on the *Reagan*. "Fuckin' A, I'm your man."

Mad Dog was enjoying every minute. He loved his pilots like they were his kids, especially this one, who reminded him of himself back in the day. "Okay, here are the ops. Tomorrow at 0530, you fire up your assigned F-35 and haul ass over to the *Reagan*. At 0600 hours, I'm told there will be one E-2 coming in from the CAP. I'm ordering you to personally extend my thanks to the pilot of that E-2 for what she did for us at Imam Ali Military Base by keeping my aviators from flying into an Iranian trap. Ask her if it's okay for you to give her a hug for me. Can you do that, Swagger?"

Jumping from his seat to attention, startling all those eating around them, Jessie snapped a textbook salute and said, "Yes, sir, I'm all over this one." With that, Jessie swaggered off like he was the happiest man in the world because, for that moment, he was.

Chapter 85

USS Reagan
Persian Gulf

Sarah "Danger" Freeman was a happy pilot. Before her flight, her Equal Opportunity Advisor had told her that the preliminary results of their initial investigation had come in and that she was not the only victim of Commander Damien Wagner. The other female E-2 pilot in the unit, Lieutenant Gail Osborne, reported that she had had very similar experiences with Wagner but kept it to herself because she thought such behavior was the norm and she should suck it up. After all, he was the commander in charge of all three E-2s on the *Reagan*.

The investigation also revealed other incidents that, when combined, showed a pattern of verbal assault against Wagner's female subordinates. There was no record of any men complaining or filing a grievance. In fact, all of his male subordinates received glowing FITREPs, while the same couldn't be said for any of his female subordinates. Consequently, while awaiting adjudication of the charges, Wagner was relieved of command and temporarily put on Non-Duty Status. He was ordered not to contact anyone from his previous command.

Upon hearing all that, Sarah thought it served the jerk right, and she wanted to get back to her job. She now flew her mission with a sense of freedom and happiness she hadn't felt since Wagner came aboard.

On the final approach to the *Reagan*, Sarah called out, "Reducing speed. 120 knots."

"Speed is good," Lieutenant Jack Steller said. "Altitude is good. LSO is giving us the go-ahead. Stay on the meatball."

Sarah adjusted the yoke slightly, fine-tuning their approach.

Steller called out, "Fifty feet—thirty feet—ten feet—touchdown."

The E-2's wheels hit the flight deck with a jolt, and the tailhook engaged the second arresting wire with a satisfying clunk. The aircraft decelerated rapidly, coming to a complete stop in mere seconds.

"Thanks, Danger, nice landing, as always," Steller said, a smile of relief spreading across his face. He's learning, thought Sarah.

Quickly, the yellow shirts disconnected the E-2, directed them to their assigned parking area, and cleared the landing area for the next plane. As her crew exited the aircraft, Sarah waited until last, as was her custom. Once off the aircraft, she noticed the deck around her was clearing out, giving her a brief moment to appreciate her job as an E-2

Hawkeye pilot for the United States Navy. It was her "me time."

As she was appreciating another safe mission, out of the corner of her eye, she saw a pilot running toward her. Before she could react, he yanked her off the ground and twirled her around. It was a WTF moment until she smelled her husband's scent and heard his voice.

"Sarah, God, I've missed you."

Sarah swiped at her cheek with the back of her hand and gave Jessie a kiss that showed exactly how much she had missed him. He kept spinning her, slowly coming to a stop before she broke away from their kiss.

"I've missed you, too, and I love you so much." Then, suddenly, she stopped hugging him and pushed him back a few feet. "Jessie, please tell me you're authorized to be here."

His grin was so wide that it almost split his face in two. "You won't believe this, but I'm hugging you under orders from my CAG, so please let me finish the job." He grabbed her tight and kissed her passionately. Stopping to take a breath, he said with his usual smirk, "CAG gave me two hours for this assignment, so how do you want to spend it?"

"Follow me," she said. "We're wasting time."

Chapter 86

THE WHITE HOUSE
Washington, DC

Five years ago, President Mark Taylor stood at this same podium, announcing China's defeat to the American people. Now, here he was again, standing before the nation to announce a new victory against another country that had believed its actions would solidify its position as a world leader. It had also been wrong. The weight of the president's decisions to engage in combat operations against those two countries was etched into his features so permanently that makeup could never cover it up. The red light illuminated atop a camera, indicating it was ready to record this event, which would be preserved for posterity. President Taylor began with a steady voice.

My fellow Americans,

Today, we stand at a pivotal moment in our nation's history. Over the past weeks, we've faced a grave threat from Iran and emerged victorious. This victory was not just a triumph of our military might but a testament to the unwavering spirit of our people.

He paused, letting the gravity of his words sink in.

Our brave men and women in uniform have shown extraordinary courage and dedication. They have fought not only for our security but for the values we hold dear. To the families of those who have served, and especially to those who have lost loved ones, we owe an immeasurable debt of gratitude. Your sacrifices will never be forgotten. This conflict has tested us in ways we could not have imagined. It has reminded us of the fragility of peace and the importance of vigilance. But it has also shown us the strength of unity and the power of resolve. As we celebrate this victory, I want to take a moment to recognize the exceptional leadership of Rear Admiral Marquis Holloway, who commanded Task Force 70 with remarkable skill and bravery. Admiral Holloway, would you please say a few words?

Instantly, the scene cut to a wide shot of the USS *Ford* and then to a medium shot of Admiral Holloway standing on the flight deck of the greatest warship in the world. As far as the camera lens could see, American firepower in the form of F-35s, F-18s, and E-2s was displayed behind him. He stood at attention in his khaki uniform, the short-sleeved shirt fitting neatly and his shoulder boards displaying the stars of his rank. The admiral looked directly into the camera lens.

Thank you, Mr. President. Serving as the commander of Task Force 70 has been the most incredible honor of my career. Our success in this conflict was not the result of any one individual but of everyone's collective effort. The courage of our men and women made this victory possible.

His expression turned somber, and the tone of his voice changed.

We have seen the cost of war up close, and we must never forget the sacrifices made by our service members and their families. As we move forward, let us honor their memory by striving for peace and stability at home and abroad.

The broadcast cut back to the president.

Thank you, Admiral Holloway. As we move forward, let us honor the memories of those we have lost by working toward a future where such conflicts are a thing of the past. Let us rebuild not only the damaged structures but also the bonds that hold us together as a nation.

The president paused for a moment longer than just a breath as if drawing the nation closer.

ABOUT THE AUTHOR

James Bultema is a military combat veteran and a retired LAPD officer with over twenty-five years of experience on the streets of Los Angeles. His debut novel, *Sea of Red*, became a bestseller, earning six prestigious awards and recognition as one of the top military thrillers of 2023. Drawing on his experiences from real-world conflict zones and urban policing, Bultema weaves authenticity into every battle scene. With a degree in history and a commitment to thorough research, he ensures his depictions of modern warfare are as accurate as they are compelling. Bultema's vivid, authentic portrayal of military life and his unforgettable characters ensure his thrillers resonate with you, the reader, long after the action has ended.

Look for *Invaders of the Heartland* in 2025 – a new series.

Welcome to Fairview, Oklahoma—a quiet little town on the brink of chaos.

In *Invaders of the Heartland*, the Chinese mafia makes a bold move into small-town America, establishing a massive marijuana grow operation under the guise of a legitimate business. But beneath the surface lies a dark world of manipulation, exploitation, sex trafficking, and murder.

Against this tense backdrop, Chief Jake Dalton—a former LAPD cop haunted by his past—fights against a web of corruption and deceit. His complicated relationship with his girlfriend, Samatha, only heightens the stakes. As secrets unravel, Jake must uphold the law and protect his town while navigating a community under siege.

Invaders of the Heartland is a gripping tale of crime, betrayal, and survival in a small town turned battleground. It's a story of power struggles and human resilience, where every character hides a secret, every choice has consequences, and no one is safe.